AN
AFFAIR
OF
STATE

ALSO BY PAT FRANK

AN
AFFAIR
OF
STATE

PAT FRANK

HARPER ● PERENNIAL

NEW YORK ● LONDON ● TORONTO ● SYDNEY ● NEW DELHI ● AUCKLAND

This book was originally published in 1948 by J. B. Lippincott Company.

HarperCollins books may be purchased for educational, business,
or sales promotional use. For information, please email the Special
Markets Department at SPsales@harpercollins.com.

First Harper Perennial paperback published 2017.

Library of Congress Cataloging-in-Publication Data has been applied for.

ISBN 978-0-06-242179-1 (pbk.)

17 18 19 20 21 LSC 10 9 8 7 6 5 4 3 2

For my wife, June

"*I am tired and sick of war. Its glory is all moon-shine. It is only those who have neither fired a shot nor heard the shrieks and groans of the wounded who cry aloud for blood, more vengeance, more desolation. War is hell.*"—WILLIAM TECUMSEH SHERMAN.

CHAPTER ONE

1

THE WAY JEFF BAKER got his name was like this.

His father, a State Department clerk, was called to George Washington Hospital at the lunch hour. He remained at the hospital all the rest of the day, and all that night, in the late September of 1919. Mabel Baker was thirty-seven, this was their first child, and it was a difficult labor. Through the whole night Nicholas Baker kept his miserable watch on the bench in the corridor, his hands locked across his sharp knees, and his unsubstantial frame braced against the muffled cries that issued from the delivery room, and rolled down upon him in ever-quickening rhythm like storm waves. Yet so unobtrusive was Nicholas Baker that when the baby was born neither the doctor nor the nurse remembered he was waiting. At eight in the morning he ventured into the hospital office and asked whether there was any news, and the startled telephone girl said the baby had been born an hour before, and it was a boy, and weighed five-and-a-half pounds, and where had Mr. Baker been all this time.

Mabel Baker was in a semi-private room, which was as much as they could afford. There were three other women in the room, and their unreserved inquisitiveness and rude staring made Nicholas Baker self-conscious as he took his wife's hand and bent to kiss her cheek. Her face was gray and showed all its lines. "Was it bad?" he whispered. "Was it bad, dear?"

"Not too bad," she said. "It's hard to remember. It was like a nightmare you didn't think would ever end, and now it has ended."

"It's wonderful—a boy."

"He's very small, the doctor said."

"He'll grow bigger. He'll grow big enough for the Foreign Service."

"He'll grow up to be Ambassador to London," Mabel said, because that was the grandest thing she could imagine.

"Won't he have to make a million first?" Nicholas laughed. Mabel was positive, but had never convinced her husband, that only his lack of money prevented him from crossing the invisible line separating the career diplomats from the clerks, the gentlemen from the shabbily respectable, in the Department. He knew, although he never mentioned it, that there were barriers more inflexible than penury. There was family, and school, and the clothes he wore and the way he wore them, and the people he knew, and the wife he had married.

They talked of the things to be done—the telegram to her family, the announcement cards, the eight dollars a week to the colored maid to clean the house and cook breakfast and dinner while she was in the hospital, and finally a name for the boy. "We'll name him Nicholas, junior," Mabel said, "and we'll give him Rowley for a middle name. That'll please my dad."

"All right," Nicholas agreed. It was certainly the conventional, the expected name. He took his watch from his trousers pocket.

"What time is it?" she asked.

"Eight-forty."

"Then you'd better get down to the Department," she suggested, accurately reading his thought. Nicholas had not been late to work in fourteen years. It was something of a record in the European Division. It was his only distinction, and it would distress him to see it shattered.

"You're sure you'll be all right? I'll stay if you want me to."

"Of course I'm all right. Anyway, the doctor is coming to look at me again at ten, and then you can come back at noon."

A nurse, gauze mask swinging below her chin, entered the semi-private room. "You want to see the baby, don't you, Mr. Baker?" she said.

"Oh, yes, of course I want to see the baby." He was surprised that he hadn't thought of this himself. One of the first things he should have done, he was sure, was to ask to see the baby. He hoped that Mabel hadn't noticed his lapse in protocol.

The baby was one of twelve babies, displayed like packaged dolls in a department store window, in a room shielded from the corridor by plate glass. "This is a new idea," the nurse explained. "Protects them from the flu germs." She pointed to one of the baskets. "That's yours."

Nicholas Baker saw a red face, wrinkled like a dried apple, but afterwards he was never absolutely certain he had looked at the right one. He wondered what custom required him to say, and how many minutes he should look at this wrinkled, red face. "Ah, fine, fine!" he said. After he was gone the nurse thought he behaved not at all like the father of a first-born son. It might have been his sixth, he seemed in such a hurry to get out of the hospital.

2

At the corner of Fourteenth and H Streets he detoured into a cigar store. "I want a box—no, twelve will be enough—twelve of your best cigars," he told the man behind the counter. "Coronas or Havanas or whatever is the best." He never smoked cigars himself so he wasn't sure of the brands.

"Fifty centers?"

"Well, I don't know. You've got good quarter ones, haven't you?"

"Sure."

"Well, quarter ones will do." It wasn't so much saving three dollars, Nicholas thought. It was simply that it would appear ostentatious for a man in his position to pass out fifty centers. Fifty centers were for Assistant Secretaries, and Chiefs of Division, and Consul Generals, and FSOs in Classes One and Two.

He ran up the steps of the State, War, and Navy Building at five to nine and when he reached his office on the third floor, West Executive Avenue side, he was gratified to find that as usual he was first. He went to the closet to change his coat and was astonished to see his blue serge on the hanger. If his blue serge was on the hanger then he must be wearing his alpaca office jacket. He looked down and saw that this was true. He had been wearing the black alpaca all along, since noon the day before. This was very disconcerting. He was glad he was alone in the office.

Miss Grimsby, the red-haired stenographer, came in a bit after nine, and the others in Eastern Mediterranean not long after that, and then at ten Horace Locke arrived.

Mr. Locke accepted a cigar and pumped his hand. "Nick," he said, "you did it. You produced a boy. I'm proud of you."

"Thanks, Mr. Locke." He was senior to Horace Locke by six years, both in age and in the Department, and had given him his elementary instruction in tariffs, visas, admiralty law, code, and cipher, and protocol. He had charted for him the often devious channels through which international gossip and information flowed into and through the Department. On both Horace Locke's tours of duty in Washington they had been in the same office, and shared the same work. Within this room they were friends. As men of comparable mentality and similar feelings they discussed the Department's policies and the great issues of the day—the peace treaties, the League, the Army's Siberian adventure, the disastrous strike of steel workers just begun and the threatened strike of coal miners within the next few weeks, the disquieting international organization called the Comintern formed in Russia, John Alcock's non-stop flight across the Atlantic, the new Volstead Act, and the HCL. But Horace Locke was a Foreign Service Officer, and Nicholas Baker was a clerk, and so it was always "Mr. Locke," and "Nick."

"What're you going to name him? Nicholas of course. He's your first."

"Well, my wife wants me to call him Nicholas." It seemed silly, to carry on a conversation like this. He couldn't imagine Horace Locke caring whether the boy was named Nicholas or Julius Caesar.

Nicholas Baker was wondering whether it would be proper, and politic, to ask for the afternoon off when Mr. Locke took him by the arm and led him to his desk, so that the others in the room were excluded from what next he had to say.

"Nick," he asked, his long, handsome face suddenly sober, "did you hear the news?"

"No. What news?"

"The President had a stroke yesterday. In Wichita. Apoplexy."

"No!"

"Yes. It isn't generally known yet. I heard it from the Undersecretary last night at dinner."

"Do you think it's serious?"

"Apoplexy is always serious."

"I wasn't thinking of that, exactly. I was thinking of the League." Nicholas Baker had a theory, which he discreetly pushed when the moment was right, that the League would fail unless it was led by the United States, and there would be another war. He had another theory. It was too radical to voice openly. He believed that all the countries in the world should be formed into one government, as all the states were bound together in the United States.

"The League is finished, I'm afraid," said Mr. Locke.

"It's certainly finished unless the President is able to continue his speaking tour."

Mr. Locke shook his head. "It seems that our people are aroused and united only when they are immediately threatened. You take away their food, or their jobs, or put fear of sudden death into them —then they are aroused. But this League seems to them a faraway thing. It's like joining a lodge in another city. They don't see any quick benefit. They don't see how it can help them personally."

"But certainly they must think of their children."

"They don't think of their children. Only one generation in ten considers its children, and we had that generation in the last half of the Eighteenth Century. Anyway, Wilson's speaking tour will have to be cancelled. He can't possibly go on."

"It's a shame."

Mr. Locke sat down in his swivel chair and looked out of the wide window, over the White House, and over the Capitol beyond, so that the warm autumn sun was full on his face. "Poor Wilson," he said. "Poor, idealistic Wilson. What was it Jefferson said? It went something like this, 'The tree of Liberty must be refreshed from time to time with the blood of patriots and tyrants. It is its natural manure.'"

"It's always the patriots' blood. The tyrants never seem to bleed," Nicholas said.

"Well, that may be because most of us are patriots, really. So there are more of us to get hurt."

"Do you think so, honestly?"

"Yes, I do. The world is getting better. It must."

"Perhaps. We're due, and overdue."

3

Nicholas Baker spent his lunch hour at the hospital, and washed down a cheese sandwich with a glass of milk at the drug store on the way back to the Department. Mabel had assured him that she was perfectly happy, and so he did not ask for the afternoon off. Just before he left the office at six he drew up a chair to Mr. Locke's desk and announced: "Well, I've decided on a name, Mr. Locke. Do you know what I'm going to name him? I'm going to name him Jefferson Wilson Baker."

"That's a very ambitious name," said Horace Locke.

"For my son," said Nicholas Baker, "I'm a very ambitious man."

As he left the Department he was already considering where little Jefferson should go to school, and what he should be taught at home.

CHAPTER TWO

1

WHEN JEFF BAKER got out of the Army he knew it was time for him to try to become a Foreign Service Officer. The War Manpower Act was a godsend. It saved him a written examination. Two years as a line private, and three as a company grade officer, and then two more on occupation duty didn't fit a man for passing written examinations.

He mailed his application after he returned from Vienna, and while still on terminal leave, and then tried to forget about it.

He was offered jobs by a New York import house anxious to start a flow of Florentine and Austrian hand-tooled leather goods into the United States; by an ambitious tourist bureau impressed with his service record and wartime travels; and by a brigadier general on whose staff he had once served, and who was now public relations vice president for a group of distillers.

He could have stalled them, on the grounds that he had to settle his father's estate, but he turned them all down. Ever since he could remember, he'd wanted only one job.

Early in 1949 the Department sent him a letter regretting the delay in passing on his application. There were thousands ahead of him. In addition, he must realize that delays and bottlenecks had developed in conducting the necessary investigations. That was easy to understand. With things as they were, practically everybody was being investigated.

He went to Canada and Mexico because he had never been to

Canada and Mexico. His friend, Stud Beecham, said the war had given him a chronic case of itchy foot. But he just felt restless. When his savings ran out he returned to Washington.

2

There was pitifully little to do about the estate. His father had died while Jeff was in Italy, about the time of the campaign on the Garigliano. (He hardly remembered his mother at all, for she was gone when he was six.) Nicholas Baker left the house in Georgetown, encumbered with a mortgage, and some victory bonds, and two thousand in cash after all debts were paid, and the deed to five building lots in Florida, at a town called Welaka Springs. The building lots had been purchased in 1927, and Jeff surmised, from his father's correspondence over twelve years, that they would still be under water.

The carefully kept private ledgers made Jeff realize how little he really knew about his father. Nicholas Baker had always seemed a man untouched by personal worries, but always ready to brood about the Manchuria affair, or the Bulgarian cabinet, or the war in Spain, or almost any Central American revolution. Yet in these ledgers he found proof that his father endured many financial indignities. There were Morris Plan loans, and furniture loans, and automobile loans, and the two years to pay for the refrigerator, and the dunning letters from grocers and department stores and the doctors and the Medical Credit Association, and even the undertaker. Sometimes the letters concluded: "If this account is not settled at once it will be brought to the attention of your employers." Always after that, payment was quick. In 1926 there was a bequest of $2500 from a cousin—that would account for the building lots in Florida. Once there was a notation—"Fifteenth wedding anniversary. Tickets to National Theater $6.60." It was the only one of its kind.

There were three puzzling loans, each for $500, from Horace Locke. This could only be the Horace Locke who for so many years had been a Chief of Division, and yet it seemed most unlikely that his father would know this Horace Locke well enough to borrow from him. The loans had been made in the years 1931, '32, and '33, always in September. What had happened in those years? Weren't they the lean years of government economy, and the fifteen per cent cut in his father's salary? Yes, of course they were. He also recalled them as three of the four years he'd gone to Lawrenceville. The notes, like all the notes and bills in the ledgers, were acknowledged, "paid in full."

The house on Q Street, its bricks crumbling under the porch and its bedroom wallpaper peeling, seemed dreary and aloof as a summer cottage in January. It held him a stranger, and hostile. When Jeff found he could sell it for twice the mortgage, and he might never get such a price again, and that he could move in with Stud Beecham, he sold it. They had grown up together in Georgetown, he and Stud, together fought the tough kids from Foggy Bottom, and double-dated to their first dances. Now Stud was a Field Inspector for Interior. He had a three-room apartment in Riggs Court, off Dupont Circle. It was ample for both of them, so long as they kept each other informed of their plans, and exercised consideration and discretion when returning home after midnight.

3

The letter from the Department reached him there. His application had been approved. He shortly would be asked to report for the oral examination. "Well," said Stud, who was watching him, "you're in! I can tell by your face. You'll have to do something about that. Diplomats have poker faces."

"Not yet," Jeff said. "Not hardly. Four out of five flunk the oral. It's supposed to be like the Spanish Inquisition in a one-hour capsule."

"You won't flunk it. You teethed on the stuff."

"Then there's the physical, and the final security check."

"Physically," Stud estimated, "you'll be the finest specimen in State. They'll keep you in Washington, and use you once a year to model striped trousers at the English garden party." He was okay physically, Jeff knew, so far as any Army medic could tell. Between the ages of eight and twelve his frame had sprouted out of his clothes every six months, to his father's astonishment and dismay, until in his junior year at Princeton he stretched to two and a half inches over six feet. His weight hadn't kept pace in school and college, but he had filled out in the Army so that now he was a fairly hard hundred and seventy pounds. But there was something about his physical condition—or maybe it was mental—that he never mentioned. It was a souvenir from September, 1944. It was very simple. Sudden, loud noises blacked out his mind and panicked his will and on occasion menaced his dignity as a human being.

"And as to security," Stud went on, "I guess you're secure enough. You don't know any Communists, do you?"

"Sure, I know some Communists," Jeff said, "but they're all Russians." He wasn't certain this was an accurate statement. He had met Russians in Bari and Trieste, and later in Vienna, but he wasn't sure all of them were Communists. Wasn't it said there were only three million in the party? And some of those he knew hadn't seemed particularly happy with the regime. "Stud," he said, "do you remember that girl at the Eaton party?"

"What girl? There were six or seven, or maybe ten or twelve. I don't remember so well."

"The one—you know, Susan something." He knew very well that her name was Susan Pickett, and she lived at the Bay State Apartments, 1701 Massachusetts, and her telephone number was Michigan 8218, and she worked in the office of the Secretary of State, and on the night of the Eaton party she'd come with Frederick Keller, who had some sort of a hush-hush job in the European Division. All this he'd managed to learn, although he'd been alone with her for only a minute or two.

"Oh, you mean Susie Pickett?" said Stud. "Is she a Commie? If she's a Commie I'll be a fellow traveler."

"That's the one." He realized, quite suddenly, that at least once each day since the Eaton party he'd thought of her. She'd said, "I

want you to call me," and it had seemed a definite invitation, and not
cocktail courtesy. He wondered why he hadn't called before, and decided he had been a little afraid. Of what? Well, he wasn't handsome. He had a half-inch more of nose and chin than is usually
allotted, and had always thought of himself as singularly gawky.
This hadn't seemed to matter to the girls in Milan or Vienna, or
Washington either since he'd been back. So he must have been
afraid because she worked in the Secretary's office, and therefore was
not common flesh, and approachable, until his application had been
approved. He knew this was silly. It was a reflex from his boyhood,
when he had been silently aware of the social barrier his father
could never pass.

"Well, what about her?" Stud said. "If you're going to celebrate
tonight, why experiment with new stuff?"

"She's pretty nice."

"Nice, hell, she's gorgeous. But how do you know she's not
shacked with Fred Keller?"

"I don't think so," said Jeff, but at the same time he suspected this
might be true. In a city where most of the women seemed as gray
and sexless as sheets of mimeograph paper, it wasn't likely Susan
Pickett would be unattached.

4

He called her apartment at six that evening, and she said of course
she remembered him, and wondered why he'd asked for her telephone number if he didn't intend using it. He asked whether she'd
like to go out that night, and told her of the letter from the Department. She said that was very exciting, and she would like to go out,
and should she wear a long dress. He said not to bother, and he'd
be around at eight.

The apartment was a Washington two-and-a-half, a bedroom, living room with alcove, and compact kitchen. She poked her head
out of the bedroom, and said she'd be a minute, and he prowled
around outside. It didn't look like a woman's apartment. There

were too many bookcases, and they were not lined with women's books. There were too many utilitarian ash trays. The bar in the alcove was solid masculine teak. There was a man's photograph on an end table. It was not Fred Keller, but a Marine Corps colonel in his forties, or older.

When she came out of the bedroom he wanted to put his hands on her, right then, and she instantly sensed this and seemed a bit amused and said, "Must be the perfume."

"It's something!" he said, alarmed that the girl could have such an immediate aphrodisiac effect on him. He thought, I've been too long without a woman, and then decided this couldn't be it, because he'd been longer, and he'd never felt quite like this before.

"It can't be the dress." She pivoted with a model's confident grace, and he saw that the dress was not daring, except for its color. Only a woman of her lustrous dark shading could wear such brilliant emerald. He guessed it was the way she moved, not deliberately sensuous, but with such constant, flowing vigor that you could not keep your eyes off her body.

"It could be the dress, or it could be the perfume, but it isn't. You know exactly what it is, and you ought to be ashamed."

"You're pretty direct, aren't you?" she said. "I'll be direct too. I'm hungry."

5

He took her to Hall's, down near the waterfront, and they ate lobster flown from Maine that morning. She knew how to eat lobster. She knew how to start at the tip of the tail, and draw all the meat from the shell in one skillful operation. She cracked the claws expertly, and neglected nothing, not even the succulent globules of flesh hidden under the base of the legs. "You must have eaten here before," he suggested.

"I ate here often until a few years ago. My husband used to bring me."

She would have been married, of course, but it didn't seem the proper time to ask about her husband. She would tell him of her

husband when she was ready. "Did you know this was General
Grant's favorite restaurant?" he asked.

"No, I didn't know."

"It was. He had a private dining room on the second floor, and
when he'd finished a couple of dozen chincoteagues and a three-
pound lobster he'd pace up and down on the balcony over the garden, smoking a cigar and shaking down his dinner."

"Tell me," she said, watching the thin spiral of smoke from the
clamshell ash tray, "what do you think of generals?"

"I think generals are fine for winning wars. Or used to be."

"Used to be?"

"Uh-huh. I think generals are archaic, like knights in armor."

"If you talk like that in the Department," she said, "you won't
be very popular. Generals are Chiefs of Mission in all the critical
areas, and more areas are getting critical all the time."

They talked of the successes and failures of ERP, the uranium
mines in Bohemia, British trade, Italian Communists, Chinese graft,
and the Japanese *Zaibatsu*. They leaped across the globe to The
Straits, and she asked him what he thought of the new Turkish
military loan. "It's ridiculous," he said. "There'll be big parties in
the Casino Taxim, and toasts to that noble ally and splendid democracy, Turkey. Then the pashas will take the hundred million bucks
and build more villas on the islands in the Marmara. The Turkish
Army doesn't need equipment. It needs education. It would take
one generation for the Turkish Army to learn to read, and another
to learn how to use radar and jets and rockets."

"Jeff," she asked, "do you always say what you think, like that?"
She asked this very quietly, and very seriously.

"Yes," he said, "I suppose I do."

"People don't like to hear that sort of talk. It isn't, you know, very
diplomatic. Particularly in the Department it isn't diplomatic. There
are men in the Department whose reputations suffer when any part
of our policy is questioned—even such a small part as the Turkish
loan. You could very well get your official throat cut, for a statement like that."

"Anyway, it's the truth."

"They'll ship you to Noumea, or Guayaquíl, or Addis Ababa," she predicted, naming some of the traditional Siberias of the Foreign Service. "I don't want that to happen to you." She seemed genuinely troubled. "I want you to go to some place where you are needed."

"Like where?"

"Like Budapest. Or Prague. Or Rome."

He realized for the first time that she had been dropping carefully chosen pebbles into the stream of his thought, and charting the spreading ripples of his reaction. He thought it wise to parry question with question. "Susan," he asked, "exactly what do you do in the Secretary's office?"

"I'm just the stenographer who takes the nine o'clock conference. I'm rated as a confidential secretary, and I'm an FSS, Class Eight, and make fifty-four hundred, but all I actually do is take the nine o'clock conference."

"That's pretty important, isn't it? Isn't that the Planning Conference? Don't you hear a lot?"

"I hear a lot, and I never talk about it. But sometimes I think."

He wondered how a girl with such irregular features could appear so beautiful. She had none of the vacant, antiseptic loveliness that the back pages of magazines made Americans in the middle of the century accept as beauty. But the eyes of the men at other tables were drawn away from their own women, and towards her. "How is it," he inquired, "that you were free tonight? I'm very happy that you are, but it doesn't seem logical."

"In the first place, don't you realize that there are a hundred thousand more women than men in Washington?"

"And in the second place?"

"In the second place, I don't sleep around, and I'm not getting married."

"You're human, aren't you?"

She didn't reply at once. She tapped her cigarette into the clamshell, and then cocked her head to one side in a way she had, as if this was a difficult and almost an unfair question. "There are two answers to that," she said finally. "The first is that I wish I could show you how human I am. The second is that I can't."

"That's no answer. That's a riddle."

"Wait. I'll unriddle it. I married when I was nineteen. My husband was much older. Not that he wasn't a good husband. He was. In every sense. He was also—I was going to say like a father but that's not what I mean. He was like a tutor—a wise friend. He was in the Public Health Service and when war came the Marines took him and shipped him out to the Pacific to clean up those islands. I'd see him every six months or so. He'd come back to get a plane-load of little fish to eat mosquito larvae—things like that. He was always fighting for supplies and medicines not only for the Marines but for the people in New Georgia, and the Marshallese, and the Gilbertese. He was that kind of man."

"And you lost him?"

"I lost him. I celebrated V-J day in a big way, because I knew he'd soon be back. I woke up with a hangover and a telegram beginning, 'The Secretary of the Navy regrets.' All I have to show for him is a Legion of Merit, posthumous."

"I'll admit that's tough. Okay. But other women lost their husbands and got over it."

"I know. I didn't. Other women don't have to take the State Department's nine o'clock conference."

"I don't understand."

"You don't? Put it this way. Lots of women won't have babies, nowadays, because they're afraid. They're afraid they'll lose them in another war. They're afraid babies will be killed in their cribs this year, or next year, or the year after. Right here, in Washington. In New York, and Pittsburgh, and Detroit and every other target city. Well, I don't want to have any more men, like other women don't want to have any more babies. I couldn't bear to lose another man."

Jeff Baker wondered whether it would be presumptuous for him to ask about Keller, and he decided it wouldn't be because she would understand it was necessary for him to know all he could know of her. "What about Fred Keller?" he said.

"I go out with him, very occasionally."

"That all?"

"That's all. He's a dear."

"You mean he doesn't make passes at you. That's what a woman means when she says a man's a dear."

"As a matter of fact, he doesn't. When he takes you out you feel that he's wearing you like a carnation in his buttonhole. He'd never do anything so crude as make a pass. Fred's a perfectionist. I don't know exactly how he'd go about having an affair with a girl, but I have a hunch the preliminaries would be sending orchids, and introducing you to his mother."

"He didn't look so damn safe to me," Jeff said. Keller was spare and tanned, still a bachelor at forty, and rich enough to have twelve acres in Berwyn, a shooting box on the Eastern Shore, and an oceanfront villa near Palm Beach. He had once been runner-up for the national squash title, and in 1947 had been picked as one of America's ten best-dressed men.

"Maybe you're right. Maybe he's not safe," said Susan Pickett, and Jeff knew she was not speaking of her relations with him, but of something else.

"Go on," he said.

"Nothing, except sometimes he gives me the shivers. He's so casual about war. When he talks about atomic bombs his mouth waters as if they were lemons."

"That's not unusual in these times. And after all, he's not so important. He's not Undersecretary of State, or Chief of a bureau or a division or even a section. He just has some sort of a control job on the European desk."

"He is important," she insisted. "He gets into everything. And he's going to Budapest."

Jeff recalled she had mentioned Budapest before. "Didn't you recommend Budapest for me?"

"I suppose so. It's been on my mind."

"What's cooking in Budapest?"

"Nothing that isn't cooking in Prague and Salonika and Trieste and Vienna and Berlin and Seoul and everywhere else where we're face to face with the Russians. Only in Budapest it's closer to burning." She was silent while the waiter laid the check on the table. "Jeff," she added when the waiter was gone, "sometimes I forget I'm not supposed to think. I'm just the girl who takes the nine o'clock conference, and I need my job, and if I do too much thinking and talking I'll lose it."

"What're you afraid of—thought control police?"

"Sure. We all are."

"Okay," he agreed, "we won't talk shop any more. Anyway I like Budapest. It lives."

"You've been there?"

"When I was a kid. In the summer after my sophomore year in college. The Department sent my father to help in an audit of the Balkan Missions, and we made a trip up the Danube. What a city!"

"If you're interested in what's going to happen to this world," she said quietly, "you should try to go there again."

He knew it was not necessary to talk any more of it. She was a puzzling girl, a skein of fear grown over her emotions, masking her desires, but he did not doubt her judgment. If she thought Budapest would be an interesting and instructive post, then he'd believe her.

It was something to remember, but not to count on.

Outside, in a taxi, he suggested the Footlight Club, but she said that while it was a nice idea, and she loved to dance, it was too late for her to go anywhere else. She had to be in the office, typing the agenda for the nine o'clock conference, at eight every morning. Therefore she didn't stay out late except Saturday nights.

6

He took her to her apartment door. She said, "I'd ask you in, but it wouldn't do either of us any good."

"I guess not." Still, he didn't want to leave. She seemed very small, standing close to him there in the doorway. When she was seated her straight shoulders and the way she held her head gave her an illusion of height, but when she stood up she really wasn't very tall.

"Well, goodbye," she said, her fingers poised to turn the key.

"Well, goodnight," he said, but he didn't go.

"You don't feel very platonic, do you?"

"Frankly, no."

"I'm not going to be coy, and tell you I never let a man make love to me the first time I'm out with him. I'm just going to say I'm sorry."

He cupped her shoulders in his hands. "Susan, this isn't the way I was hoping it would be. Look at me."

She kept her eyes on the key. "I didn't want it to be like this either. I wanted to go out with you and see if something wouldn't happen. It didn't."

"Suppose we *are* a pinch of ashes in the first day of World War number three? Why not have what we can now? I'm afraid I sound silly—like a kid quoting Omar."

"Oh, no, Jeff. You're not silly. You're perfectly logical."

"Well?"

She didn't attempt to move, or say anything more, until his fingers loosened. "I'm not afraid for myself," she said then. "If I thought the world would go up in one big bang I honestly wouldn't care much. I think I'd be sort of relieved. It's just that I'm afraid to have anyone else because I've got the damndest premonition I'd lose him."

"If you went to a psychiatrist," Jeff said, "which I think you ought to do, he'd tell you you were wrong."

"I'm sure of it. If I thought I could have a man without too many inner complications, well, we'd be in there, and not out here. Only I know I can't, Jeff. I've only had one man in my life. Well, not counting schoolgirl experiments. And if I had another I'd feel the same way towards him that I did towards my husband and then the war would come along and kill him."

"The trouble with you, Susan, is that you won't take a chance on the world."

"I don't see why I should take a chance when I know that the cards are stacked. Now go on home, Jeff. I'll stay as I am."

7

He walked up Massachusetts to Dupont Circle, feeling empty and frustrated and baffled. Stud was listening to the eleven o'clock news. "I see you didn't make the grade," Stud greeted him. "Not even lipstick. Is she tied up with Keller?"

"No, she's tied up with herself."

"There are two girls on the floor below," Stud said, "who have been running up here all evening to borrow ice cubes, glasses, bottle openers, and cigarettes. They work in Archives, and they're having a party for the Junior Archivists, Division of Useless Executive Papers. They want us to come down when the party is over."

"Not me," Jeff said.

"They're not bad," Stud said. "They develop a lot of compression, working down there three floors below the Archives Building. They claim all the men in Archives are unburied cadavers."

"I'll skip it."

"What's the matter with you? Sick?"

"Sort of." He didn't feel too good, he told himself. He took two aspirins, and chased them with bourbon, before he went to bed.

8

He spent the next week in the library of the Foreign Service Institute, studying the departmental regulations. Their complexities awed and alarmed him, but Mr. Dannenberg, the head of the training staff, assured him that the orals weren't necessarily based on knowledge of the regulations. "If they were," he said, "nobody would ever get in the Service. It used to be said that there were only three rules for making a good Foreign Service Officer—sit with your back to the light, listen to your superiors, and go to bed before you get drunk. Actually, you learn by osmosis. In the orals you'll be judged on poise and personality. We want our men to *look* like representatives of the United States. We want them to *look* American."

Dannenberg inspected Jeff, shrewdly as a horseman looks over a yearling at the Saratoga sales. "You do look American. You've got that gaunt, mussed-up Winant look."

"Thanks," Jeff said. "I'd like to be like Winant."

"But nobody can tell yet if you've got any brains."

"No," Jeff said. "That's the trouble."

Mr. Dannenberg himself didn't look like an FSO, or even particularly American. An expensive tailor could have given his stumpy figure and global belly some nobility, but Mr. Dannenberg obviously didn't have an expensive tailor. His trousers fell in double folds around his shoes, and the three lower buttons of his vest were usually open. His ties were cheap, and badly knotted. Jeff looked up Mr. Dannenberg's record, and discovered that while he was a Class I he had never held an important, or even an interesting post. Yet he liked Dannenberg, who always seemed eager to open for him the treasure chest of his experience.

9

One day Dannenberg called him and told him his oral was scheduled for Monday of the following week. "Dress carefully," he advised, "and better not drink Sunday night, and don't cut yourself shaving, and by all means be on time."

Jeff bought a new suit. It was a two-button blue pin stripe, a lounge that was being worn that year by all the successful young men, like Charles Luckman, Bob Considine, Richard Kollmar, and Fred Keller. He paid ninety-five dollars for it, which was more than he had ever paid for a suit before. He also bought black socks, and three white shirts with button-down collars—although his shirt drawer was full—and six handkerchiefs of the best linen that cost as much as shirts used to cost before the war, and a maroon tie that announced itself as at once restrained and expensive.

As an afterthought he bought a hat. He rebelled against hats. He had had to wear a cap as a freshman at Princeton, and he had been compelled to wear either a helmet or a go-to-hell cap during his years in the Army. Hats seemed to him a symbol of compulsion and conformity, and he had not worn one since he had been home. He selected a black homburg, size seven and a quarter. The clerk approved. As he wrote a check the clerk said, "You're in the State Department, aren't you, sir? When you outfit yourself for going abroad, we'll be glad to take care of you."

"Thanks," Jeff said. "Thanks very much." All day he wondered how the clerk could guess.

10

On Monday Jeff reported at Dannenberg's office at ten-thirty, although examination time was not until eleven. Dannenberg seemed excited and fluttery. "It's not going to be here," he said. "It's going to be in the other building. And we've had a surprise. The Secretary himself is going to sit in on the examining board. It's the first time he's ever done it. He's deeply interested in recruitment, you know."

"Will it make a difference?" Jeff asked. "I mean, what'll it do to my chances?"

"Now, don't worry," said Dannenberg, "and don't be nervous. Just sit down and read a magazine, and take it easy, and when the Secretary is ready they'll call and I'll take you over."

Jeff sat down, and picked up a copy of *Fortune,* and turned the pages. His eyes scanned sentences and paragraphs, and pretended to read, but his mind did not know what his eyes were seeing. It was stupid to be scared. The presence of the Secretary might even better his chances, for the others would not want the Secretary to waste his time on a failure. Yet he recalled all the gossip of the awful ordeal of the oral, how even graduates of the Georgetown University school came out of it shaken, inarticulate, and disapproved.

He tried to concentrate on Dannenberg's advice. You should appear confident, and yet respectful; listen carefully to the questions, and don't rush with the answers; don't smoke unless you are offered a cigarette; if you don't know an answer don't attempt to bluff; reply frankly to personal questions, for remember that the whole record of your life will be known to the board before you sit down; and above all don't give opinions, but stick to facts.

Dannenberg's phone rang, and he answered it and said, "We'll be right over." They walked out of the Institute building, and then across the street to the marble and limestone building known as New State, which had been New War but which the War Department had never occupied. Jeff remembered how in his boyhood State had shared offices with War and Navy in the rococo gray pile opposite the White House. Now State spread through twenty-six structures in Washington, and was still growing, and would continue to grow until its size and importance in the Capital was comparable to the power of the United States in the world.

They took an elevator to the fifth floor, passed through a double door over which was the Great Seal, through an anteroom with empty chairs lining its walls, through a secretarial office, and then through two more sets of double doors, and into a room deeply carpeted and utterly soundless, as if it were detached from the building, and from the city. Four men were seated at an oval conference table, with the Secretary at the end. The Secretary's head was down, exposing a bald spot in the gray, and he did not raise his eyes as they entered. He was reading a file of cables. He looked older than his pictures.

Dannenberg waited, standing, until the Secretary closed the file. Jeff was close at his side, trying not to stand to attention. "This is Mr. Baker," Dannenberg said, "who is to take the examination today."

The Secretary rose and put out his hand. "This will be a new experience for both of us," he said, "unless Dannenberg here has put in a ringer who knows all the answers."

"Oh, no sir!" said Dannenberg. "Mr. Baker's name just came up in the usual order." Dannenberg hadn't noticed that the Secretary was smiling. It was hard to tell when the Secretary smiled. Everything about the Secretary was contained—his strength, the quiet splendor of his bearing, his humor—as if he were conscious of his age and the necessity of conserving his emotions.

Dannenberg introduced the others. "Mr. Matson, Mr. Richards, Mr. Keller."

"We've met before, haven't we?" Jeff said to Keller.

"Oh, yes, of course," Keller said, but Jeff could see he didn't remember. He had heard of the others, but never seen them before. Matson was Chief of the Balkans Division. He had been Minister in Sofia and Bucharest. Richards was also of Career Minister rank, an expert on the Far East.

"All right, Mr. Baker, take this chair," Dannenberg said. Then Dannenberg seated himself at the opposite side of the table, and Jeff realized that Dannenberg would be the fifth man on the board, and that in the instant his manner had changed, and he was impersonal and distant, and seemingly increased in stature.

Dannenberg put his plump, white hands on the table, and said, "Would you care to start, Mr. Secretary?"

"No. You gentlemen follow your usual procedure. I may have a question or two later."

"Would you care to tell us about your schooling, Mr. Baker?" Dannenberg said.

Jeff told them of Lawrenceville and Princeton. He made it brief. He understood that a question like this was simply to put him at ease.

Keller seemed more interested than the others. "What class at Princeton?" he asked.

"Thirty-nine."

"I was twenty-nine myself. Any athletics?"

"No. I went out for freshmen football. Didn't make it. I was on the *Pricetonian* staff in my last two years."

"I didn't go in much for the literary side myself," Keller said, "but that sort of training is always useful."

Then the questions began, really. Richards wanted to know whether he could explain the functions of the Far Eastern Commission and the Allied Council for Japan. He could, in a general way. Did he know what parallel separated the American and Russian zones in Korea? Jeff recalled it was the thirty-eighth. What was the agrarian policy of the Kuomintang? He stumbled badly on that one.

The Secretary said, "This is like 'Information Please' in reverse. Five men ask one man questions."

Matson took over. What sixteen nations participated in the ERP conferences? Jeff thought he remembered them all. Outline the importance of the Danube to European economy. That was easy. He knew the Danube. He remembered watching the river in brown flood all one day in Vienna in '46, and seeing not one ship pass. He talked of the Danube as a vital artery now strangled by tourniquets of international red tape. He mentioned the Bulgarian fishing fleet, which for three years had been rotting up the Danube, seven hundred miles from its home ports. He noticed that he had captured the Secretary's attention, and that the Secretary made a note on the cover of his cable file.

Yet his answer did not seem to please Matson. "You understand, Mr. Baker," he said, "that if our people in Austria permitted those boats to go back to the Black Sea, then they'd only be used to catch fish for the other side. That's right, isn't it?"

He saw Dannenberg's eyes raise in mute warning. No opinions. He found himself saying nevertheless, "We cannot make an ally of hunger. That's a matter of national ethics. Furthermore, it's short-sighted to paralyze the Bulgar fishing fleet. It's just handing another propaganda weapon to the Communists in Bulgaria and Rumania."

"Very interesting viewpoint," said Matson. "Very interesting indeed. But obviously arrived at without benefit of complete information."

Matson's dark eyes, large and arresting in the pallor of his face, flicked once towards the Secretary. Otherwise he showed no change of expression, but Jeff knew he no longer would be friendly. Jeff's frankness was his affliction, and he was unable to control it, as some men cannot curb their temper.

Then the questions began to come in French, in Spanish, in Italian and German. He had been told that when they bothered to test your languages you had a chance.

"Now I'm going to ask you a question we ask all our candidates," Dannenberg said. "Why do you want to join the Foreign Service?"

Could he say that when you were a little boy you looked upon the Department couriers and messengers as most little boys regard firemen and policemen? And that when Tunney and Gehrig and Walter Johnson were the heroes of the other kids on Q Street, your heroes were Ben Franklin, and Silas Deane, and John Jay? Could you say that when you looked at a map, and uttered the names of cities, you heard the music of history? "I've always pointed for it, more or less," he said. "My father was in the Department."

This drew Keller's attention. "A legacy, eh?" he said. "I don't remember any Baker, but I suppose he was before my time."

"Baker? Baker?" murmured Matson. "I don't remember him either. Thought I knew everyone in the Department. But then, he probably was in London when I was in Sofia, and in Shanghai while I was back home. You know how it is."

"He was a clerk," Jeff said.

"Oh," said Keller, and the single syllable was toned with surprise and disappointment, as if he had been examining a handsome ring, and then been told the stone was imitation.

"There was another reason I wanted to get in the Foreign Service," Jeff said. He knew he had to get it out, because it was working inside him.

"Yes?" Dannenberg inquired.

"I don't want to see any more wars. I want to do what I can to prevent another war." He saw that they were all eyeing him now with fresh interest, as if he had told them some private thing about himself that was curious, such as his mother was an Indian, or that his heart was on his right side. "I suppose that's bombastic," he added, sensing the need of an explanation. "I suppose it's bombastic to think that I can do anything to help keep the peace, being just one little guy. But that's the way I feel, and I know that in the Foreign Service I'd have more opportunity to do what I want to do than anywhere else."

"Well, now, I think that's very commendable," said Matson. "Very commendable indeed."

"Oh, yes," said Richards. "That's a splendid aim." He glanced up at the wall clock, as if from then on they all would be wasting time.

The Secretary raised his head, and Jeff realized he had been watchful, though silent. "I take it you don't like war, Mr. Baker?"

"No sir, I don't."

"What outfit?"

"Eighty-fifth Division, 339th Regiment, sir."

"Coulter was a good general," the Secretary stated, in the professional way that one doctor speaks of another as "a good man." He ran a forefinger along the tabletop, and Jeff knew he was exercising his fabulous memory for the minutiae of battle. He knew something that in the room only he and the Secretary knew—that the Secretary was tracing Jeff's boot prints up the spiny back of the Italian peninsula. He was following Jeff's mad entry into Rome, through the ambuscades of the 88s on the road to Florence, edging with him across the minefields on the banks of the Arno. He was witnessing the heartbreaking attack on the Gothic Line, and suffering through the terrible winter in the Apennines, exulting a little in the last assault across the Po, and experiencing the sickening letdown and disillusion that followed victory. "I see," the Secretary said. "I think I see."

"If there are no more questions," Dannenberg said, "I suppose that will be all." They rose, and shook hands, and Dannenberg opened the door for him. "You can find your way out all right?" Dannenberg said. "You'll be informed by letter, in the usual way."

"Thanks very much," Jeff said. "You've been very considerate." He did not think he would see Dannenberg again. He feared he

had failed. As he walked back towards Dupont Circle he tried to
analyze his answers. He tried to remember what each one had said,
and how they had reacted to him, and how the Secretary had
looked when he left. He found he couldn't reconstruct the interview. He must have been very nervous. He looked at his watch.
The examination couldn't have lasted more than thirty minutes, yet
it seemed like the whole day. It was amazing that this was still
morning.

11

After Jeff was gone, Dannenberg took his seat again. Because of
the Secretary's presence there was not the usual relaxation after the
candidate left. "Well, Mr. Secretary," Dannenberg said, "what did
you think of him?"

"I'll wait to hear your reactions," the Secretary said.

"I think on the whole he's a very promising candidate," said
Dannenberg. "He has enthusiasm, background, and he knows Europe much better than most men his age."

"He doesn't know Asia," said Richards. "A man ought to be well
rounded, as the world is rounded."

Dannenberg tried to estimate the Secretary's opinion, and decided
to speak his mind. "On the other hand you can't expect him to have
encyclopedic knowledge at his age. What's your opinion, Fred?"

Keller lit a cigarette, tilted his head upward, and slowly blew out
the smoke, as if deliberating carefully on his reply. "He's a bit
visionary," he said, "but I think he has the makings of a first-class
man. I wouldn't mind having him work for me."

"When you said visionary you voiced my objection," said Matson.
"We need hard-headed, practical men in the Department today.
After all, we're engaged in a life-and-death struggle for our own
way of life with a merciless enemy. Why take a chance on a do-
gooder?"

"We took a chance on him before," the Secretary said under his
breath.

"What's that, Mr. Secretary?" Matson asked.

"Nothing. I'd surmise that he probably was a platoon leader, or company commander. He got hurt."

Dannenberg inspected the sheet of paper before him, headed RE-PORT ON FORM 57, BAKER, JEFFERSON WILSON. "There's no record of his having been wounded," he said.

"The way I look at it," said Matson, "is like this. We need real-ists—tough-minded realists—in the Department today as we never needed them before. Now I know from his spot check that this boy isn't a Communist, or a radical, or anything. But this is war. And the Foreign Service Officers we send abroad at this time are on the front line." Matson held out his hands, gripping an imaginary rifle at the port position. "We don't want woolly-headed dreamers out there. Not that I've got anything against ideals and ethics, you under-stand. They're all right, at the proper time and place. But the men we send out to defend our system of free enterprise and our demo-cratic way of life have got to be hard-headed realists."

"I think I'll take a chance on him," said the Secretary. "How do you gentlemen vote?"

"As I said before, on the whole I think he's a very promising can-didate," said Dannenberg.

"I'd like to have him," said Keller. "I think he could be shaped and molded."

"I've got reservations about giving him a post in the Orient at this time, but he might be all right for Europe," said Richards.

"He is a very personable young man," Matson said. "That I'll admit. And as he grows older he'll no doubt have some good, hard, common sense knocked into him. But right now he should be nursed along. There's a post open in Tananarive, Madagascar, that we always have trouble filling. I think he'd be a good man for there."

"No," said the Secretary. "If he asks for a Southern or Central European job I think he should get it. That's where he belongs."

So that settled it.

As he rose from the table the Secretary said, as if it were an after-thought and of little consequence, "Mr. Matson, would you mind sending me the cables on the Bulgarian fishing boats?"

CHAPTER THREE

1

FOR THE NEXT six weeks Jeff Baker became a blue peg that was moved across a board called "Orientation" in Mr. Dannenberg's office. He absorbed lectures on Atomic Energy and International Security, the Crisis in Britain, India at the Crossroads, The Petropolis Conference, Greece at the Crossroads, Political Problems in Southeast Asia, The Crisis in Germany, France at the Crossroads, The Arab Crisis, Italy at the Crossroads, Why The Straits Are Vital, The Austrian Crisis.

It was also a period of filling out papers and forms. One of these asked where he wanted to go—his "preference sheet." He was allowed four choices, and assured that only very bad luck could keep him from one of the four. He recalled that long ago his father had mentioned that the Department never, never, under any circumstances sent a man to the post of his first choice, probably under the assumption that he had a girl there. He doubted whether this custom had changed.

Originally he had wanted Rome, or Milan, or Trieste, for he knew the terrain of Italy better than he knew any state in his own country, and for the Italian people he felt warm sympathy and big-brotherly tolerance. He put down Shanghai, Trieste, Rome, and Budapest. He hoped it would be Budapest. This would interest and please Susan Pickett, but why it was important to please or interest Susan Pickett he didn't precisely know. He'd called her twice. The first time she'd been busy, and the second time she'd said, "Jeff, I'm thinking. You undertand, don't you?" He'd said sure, he understood, but he didn't understand at all.

Jeff's blue peg moved from the board called "Orientation" to the one called "Processing." He was briefed by the Department's travel experts, chivvied about his insurance and his will, given shots for typhoid, typhus, yellow fever, tetanus, and plague, and exposed to stern and somewhat melodramatic talks on personal security.

When he had been pumped so full of lectures and vaccines that it seemed both his brain and his body must burst, Dannenberg told him he had been assigned to Budapest, and would finish his training on the Balkans desk. "You'll get the big picture of what's going on in your area," he explained. "You'll report to Mr. Matson in Temporary Building P. You probably won't do much except read the dispatches, but that'll keep you busy."

"I want to thank you," Jeff said, "for all your help. That day I took the oral, I thought I'd never make it."

"Quite truthfully, I didn't either, for a while," said Dannenberg. "You know, Baker, sometimes agreeable silence is the best diplomacy. We all learn that. Some of us learn it too late."

"I see," Jeff said.

"I'd stick pretty close to Matson, if I were you. I'd try to understand his viewpoint. Since he'll be your Division Chief while you're at your first post, he'll have a good deal to do with the advancement of your career. He won't be so important as your Chief of Mission, and your senior colleagues, naturally, but it doesn't hurt to have friends in the Department."

"What's Matson's viewpoint?"

"Well, just between us, Matson is a war now man. I think he was a bit alarmed by what you said about war, and you'd do well to make your peace with him."

2

The next day Matson found a desk for Jeff in the Balkans Division. Over this desk began to pass carbons of the incoming file of cables. An American lieutenant had been beaten by the Jugoslavs; three conservative leaders in Rumania had disappeared and were presumed dead; the Cominform in Belgrade was sending propagandists into the Caribbean countries; a Viennese doctor, escaped from a Russian bacteriological warfare laboratory, reported the Russians had been extremely successful in their experiments with anthrax and bubonic plague. Prague was excited about the stepped-up production of the uranium mines in Bohemia, and was wondering what had become of some of our agents in the area. Four Soviet tank divisions were maneuvering in Lower Austria. Budapest said a Swiss traveler had talked to a German scientist who had helped perfect an atomic bomb, in one of the factories beyond the Urals, which would fit into a suitcase. A hand grenade had been thrown at the Legation in Tirana. The Consul in Salonika was sending his wife home.

The monotonous tidings of conflict, terror, and violence sucked at the reservoir of his hope. When he looked out on Constitution Avenue, clean and white in the late summer sun, on the cars shining like bright beetles, on the incessant antlike movement of people, grouping in little patterns, on the girls with hands linked to the arms of their men, it seemed unreal as musical comedy in technicolor. In this building was the real world. One day one of these cables would clatter out of the code machines, just like the others. Only this one would clothe half those puppets in uniform, send that man to Iraq, that woman to Alaska, bury the corner policeman in the rubble of his own home, or wipe them all out, entirely, as a bad production which had remained on stage beyond its time.

3

On the day that the Bulgarian Communists tried and executed Kenov for no greater reason than that he led the opposition, Matson called Jeff into his office. "Well, Baker," he asked, "what do you think of things? Still anxious for the Balkans?"

"Yes, I still want to go," Jeff said.

"You saw the dispatch about Kenov?"

"Yes, I saw it."

"He was a friend of mine," Matson said. "A good friend. Just as good a friend as any friend I have here in Washington. And he was a gentleman. He's been in my home a dozen times. Furthermore, he was a good public servant. He devoted his life to raising his people out of ignorance and poverty. He opposed the Nazi tyranny, and he opposed the Red tyranny, and now those damn beasts have killed him."

"They're bastards, all right. But do you think all of them are bastards?"

"Enough of them are bastards so sometimes I agree with those who say we can't be far wrong in wiping out the whole bunch, while there's time."

"You can't kill two hundred million people."

"Wouldn't have to. Just kill thirty or forty million, and hang the New York radicals from every lamppost on Fifth Avenue. That's what people are saying and perhaps that's the only answer."

"Isn't that genocide?" Jeff said. He knew he should be quiet. "Isn't that advocating the same thing for which we condemned the Nazis? Incidentally, for which we condemned some of them to death?"

Matson seemed whiter than ever, as if all the blood had fled from his face and hands to feed the hot ball of anger inside him. "I'll take my chances on being condemned," he said. "We are engaged in a struggle for survival—our world against theirs. You have been picked as one of the men to go out in the front line. You should have no doubts."

Jeff had to say it. "But I do have doubts. I'm confused. I feel like I'm wallowing around in a swamp and can't find my way out. I don't know what's right and what's wrong any more. Poor Winant must have felt like this, only worse, because he knew so much more than I know and I find that the more I know the more I'm confused."

He knew he had mentioned Winant because Dannenberg had said he looked something like Winant, and his subconscious had been considering Winant—and Winant's suicide—ever since. He knew now how dismayed he had been when Winant killed himself, and then Jan Masaryk killed himself. Their deaths had made him feel exactly as if he had lost an older friend out of his platoon. He knew neither of them, yet their deaths were personal.

Matson had been doodling a set of round noseless faces across his blotter. He punctuated them with grim little mouths before he spoke. "What you've just said proves I was right. I don't mind telling you that you're in my Division in spite of my protests. In times like these men of your temperament should be sent to Madagascar or New Zealand, whatever their experience. The Secretary insisted you go to Europe, and Dannenberg gave you to me."

"I didn't know that," Jeff said.

"I'm glad to have you, so long as you behave. You've been picked for Budapest, and you'll go to Budapest next week, and by God you'll go as a soldier. You'll take orders and carry them out."

"Yes, sir," Jeff said, because there wasn't anything else to say.

"I mean that literally," said Matson. "The Legation in Budapest is on a quasi-military footing. We now consider the Embassy in Moscow as nothing more than a garrison under siege, from which there can be few sorties for intelligence and information. But Budapest is a listening post and observation post deep inside the enemy lines. Exactly what you'll do there is up to Admiral Blankenhorn, as Chief of Mission. Maybe he'll let you work under Keller. Maybe he'll make you stable boy. I don't know."

Jeff knew from the cables that Fred Keller had arrived in Budapest a month before, and that his title was Special Assistant to the Minister. No reference to his work ever appeared in the cables. Matson guessed at Jeff's curiosity. "This is extremely confidential," he said. "It is probably the most confidential work going on in my area. You will have to know about it sometime, so I might as well tell you now. Mr. Keller is forming resistance groups inside Hungary. If it works out there we'll try it in other countries. We call this experiment the Atlantis Project. You know—Atlantis, the bridge between the continents. When war comes, we'll have an organization in Europe."

"When war comes?" Jeff said.

"Yes. War must come. I know it's not diplomatic to say it, but I'm a realist." He spoke with the finality of one who has stated the world is round. Jeff knew there was no use arguing, then or ever. Not with Matson.

4

Gerald Matson anticipated war with Russia with the mingled confidence and impatience of one waiting for the last act of a play in which it is certain the villain will get his just deserts, the hero will get the girl, and everyone will live happily ever after.

While others in the Department had blinded themselves to the Soviet menace, it had always been plain to him, and he had never dodged speaking his mind on it. Sometimes this had not made him popular in the Department. In the first two Roosevelt administrations, when the Reds and their allies—the C.I.O., the New Dealers, the radicals and social planners—had been running the country, he'd been buried in the Visa Division. He'd been able to perform useful services there, however. He'd guarded the dam of immigration quotas, restrictions, and regulations against the stream of refugees from Germany. It wasn't that he had anything against the Jews, although of course he was glad too many didn't get into the Department. It was simply that the National Socialists regarded Communists as their first enemy, and therefore it could be assumed that most of the people getting out of Germany were Communists.

He was in the Mediterranean area when the Spanish war flared, and he was able to use his influence to keep a steady stream of supplies going to Franco, and to discourage American enlistments and other help for the Reds.

When the Russians attacked Finland, and Molotov signed the pact with Hitler, he was rescued from the blind alley of the Visa Division, and once again sent abroad as a Minister.

His star dipped again when we entered the war, but once the war was over, and the intentions of the Soviet Union began to unfold, he became an important man in the Department who never failed to remind his colleagues that he had recommended the extinction of Bolshevism as far back as 1920, when we still had troops in Siberia.

He himself did not know at what precise point in his life he became aware of the Red menace. It may have started as far away as the dinner table in his boyhood, although it was not called a Red menace at the time, and indeed had no name. His father had his money in street railways in Pennsylvania, and was harassed by agitators, radicals, strikers, the damned Socialists who were advocating public ownership, and the damned laborers who didn't know what was good for them.

While he was at Harvard he became alarmed at the radical talk among some of the undergraduates and wrote a letter to the *Transcript*. The letter was printed, and there was a good deal of comment. His father commended him, praised his literary style, and said the family at last had produced a statesman.

In his second year in the Department he wrote an evaluation of the Lenin-Trotsky dogma of world revolution which was good enough to be used as source material for future studies.

In 1925, while he was in Bucharest, he met and married the lovely, sad-eyed Countess Anya Lewenska. This was before the Department tightened its regulations concerning marriage to foreigners. She was Russian, and the Bolsheviks had murdered her father and mother and confiscated their estates. He was never able to forget this, for in the years that followed their home became a port of call, refueling station, and sometimes a permanent harbor, for her brothers, uncles, aunts, nieces, nephews, and cousins twice removed.

Gerald Matson's brothers, who now ran the family utilities holdings, kept him informed of the close connections between the Reds in Russia and the Pennsylvania Reds whose unions each year became more powerful and demanding. All his life a Red conspiracy had been closing in around him, and he knew the only solution was war against Russia. As he constantly warned his colleagues, the United States was engaged in a battle for survival.

5

It was eight that night when Gerald Matson drove to his Alexandria home. For two weeks he had been working late in the Department, for Count Igor Lewenski, his wife's younger brother, was their house guest. The Count's dress shop had failed, and his perfume establishment had failed, and Matson knew he would be wanting capital to start another business. Matson was fending off the inevitable moment when money would be discussed. Whenever they discussed money, it ended with his having less, and the Count more, or at least some.

After coffee Matson remarked that it had been a long time since they had been to a movie, and Bob Hope was playing in Alexandria. He was aware that the Count professed to scorn American comedy, on the grounds that it was not understandable.

The Count, who had his sister's sad eyes, and who for twenty years had defended himself against the ways of this strange land by an air of bewilderment and surprise, as if he had just passed Ellis Island, saw his opportunity. "I hear there is much money in Hollywood—much."

"When did you learn that?" Matson said.

"I hear it. It is said that there is more money in Hollywood than there is in New York. I was told that if I had opened my salon in Hollywood I would have been a huge success. In Hollywood they have respect for blood and ancestry."

Matson made a rude noise with his thin lips.

"Gerald!" his wife said. "Let Iggy say what he has to say! I think he has a very good idea."

"Yes," the Count said. "It came to me last night when I heard the government has ordered there should be anti-Bolshevik pictures."

"The government didn't do any such thing," said Matson. "Some

Congressman merely suggested it. The government can't order movies made."

The Count shrugged. "When anti-Bolshevist pictures are made they will need technical advice. I will be there. It will be a great chance to make money and inform everyone about the Bolsheviks too."

"Meanwhile," said the Countess, "Iggy can open a dress shop. He will no doubt meet influential people. When they need technical advice he will be available. I think it's a remarkable idea."

"Yes," said the Count, "it will be a double opportunity."

"Iggy doesn't want another loan," said the Countess. "He just wants you to make an investment."

Matson knew he was trapped, yet he continued to struggle. "We'll discuss it tomorrow. I'm tired. They keep unloading pacifists on me. It's disheartening." He could always distract his wife with Department shop talk.

"Pacifists!" she exclaimed.

"Yes, pacifists." He told them about Jeff Baker, and how he had tried, unsuccessfully, to keep this dreamer out of the Department, and then out of Europe, and finally out of his own Division.

"Sometimes," said the Count, "it is apparent this government is crazy—insane. How this country ever became the leader among the nations is to me utterly incredible."

"And if he goes to Budapest he will work on the Atlantis Project?" said Anya.

"He might." Anya was still beautiful, and an imaginative and popular hostess, and she had been a great help to him in his career, but sometimes he wished she would not speak so carelessly of secret matters.

"What is this Atlantis Project?" asked Iggy.

"I don't think it should be discussed here, Anya," Matson said.

"Now, Gerald, don't be ridiculous. Iggy is one of the family, and anyway he'd be the last person in the world to mention it. I think it would be much safer to tell Iggy than have men like this Baker know about it, and perhaps even get into it."

"I don't want it discussed!" Matson said. He decanted a thimbleful of brandy into one of his King Alexander glasses.

"Don't you trust me?" the Count asked. "Me, your own brother-in-law—me, a man who is a victim of the Bolsheviks?"

"Gerald, you're so silly," Anya said. She talked on, and before Matson could stop her she had said, "I think it's the most wonderful idea, to build another underground."

"Shut up!" Matson yelled.

"Come, come," said the Count. "No quarreling. I don't wish to know your secrets, Gerald, if you do not trust me." He poured brandy to the rim of his glass. "I drink to the downfall of the Bolsheviks!"

"To their end," Matson said mechanically, and raised his own glass. It had to come sooner or later, and it was his judgment that the sooner it came the better. It should come before the Reds had atom bombs. To the war! The war would end this constant rasping of his nerves, his worry over money and his future in the Department. The war would eliminate the radicals and emasculate the unions and placate his brothers. The war would give jobs to his in-laws, and eventually send them back to their estates in Russia. For Matson, the war would mean peace.

CHAPTER FOUR

1

THE DAY BEFORE Jeff Baker was to leave for Budapest Matson summoned him to his office and said, "I had a call for you from Horace Locke. He wants to see you before you leave. Friend of yours?"

"Horace Locke? No, but I've heard my father speak of him. I haven't heard his name in years. I thought he was retired, or dead, or something."

"He isn't, but he should be."

"Yes?"

"He isn't very well liked in the Department. He's outlived his time, and should be out on pension. I wouldn't take anything he says too seriously. That's just a friendly hint."

"Thanks," Jeff said. He had tried to follow Dannenberg's advice, and understand Matson's viewpoint. He had been attentive, respectful, and had muffled his own opinions as much as he could. He tried to agree, at least outwardly, with whatever Matson had to say, as he did now.

"You're not to talk about anything that goes on in this Division."

"I won't, sir." He could not bring himself to like Matson. When he talked to Matson he felt that his distaste, no matter how carefully he censored it from his voice and masked it from his face, must somehow show, for he knew Matson could feel it. It was as if, like a dog, he exuded a hostile odor, for he could feel Matson bristle.

"If Locke has anything to say about this Division I want a complete report on it. He sometimes tries to start trouble."

"Yes, sir."

2

Jeff found Horace Locke on the second floor of Old State, across the street from the White House. The Department, in return for New War, had ceded Old State to the Presidential special agencies, so Horace Locke's office was like a forgotten island around which eddied and bubbled the activity of a foreign sea. On the office door hung a sign—"Adviser to the Diplomatic Monuments and Memorials Commission."

There was no anteroom, no secretary, no typists or messengers. There was only a thin, wispy, white-haired man, dressed in tweeds that were soft and silky with years, small in his loneliness. On his desk was the minimum issue, for one of Career Minister rank, of double pen set, water flask and glasses, metal calendar, two telephones, and in and out files, empty.

Jeff had expected he would be infirm, or dull-witted or cantankerous with age, but actually he didn't appear so old. He certainly wasn't any older than the Secretary of State, and he didn't seem much older than Dannenberg or Matson. His manner was composed and yet alert, his handshake quick and steady. "You're Baker, eh? Your father was Nicholas Baker, isn't that right?" he began.

"That's right, sir," Jeff said.

"I thought so. Didn't think there would be two Jefferson Wilson Bakers. Can you pull up one of those leather chairs? Don't know whether they're comfortable or not. Nobody ever sits in them." He waited until Jeff moved the chair, and then he said, "How proud your father would have been—how very proud! Guess I'll have to be proud for him. We were good friends, you know."

"I've heard him speak of you quite often."

"It was only luck that I knew you'd made the Foreign Service. Saw your name this morning in the Department bulletin. That's all that ever crosses my desk, now, the daily bulletin."

Jeff knew he should say something, but he was afraid that whatever he said would be wrong. Horace Locke was obviously in an uncomfortable position, and perhaps it would embarrass him to refer to it.

For a moment Horace Locke remained silent, too, although his clear gray eyes were inspecting Jeff, drinking in detail, analyzing, judging. "If I had known sooner," he said, "there are some things I could have—." He shook his head. "No, I couldn't have been of any help to you. Sometimes I forget I'm no longer a Division Chief. Anyway, you did all right for yourself. You're an FSO, Class V, and you're going to Budapest. That's good. What's your job going to be?"

"I don't know, exactly. I'll be one of the Third Secretaries."

They talked of Jeff's father. The way Horace Locke talked, Nicholas Baker had been much more influential, in the Department, than Jeff had ever guessed. Jeff remarked about this, and Locke said:

"Don't underestimate your own importance. Foreign policy is not made by speeches, or treaties, or directives, or proclamations. It is made by men, and what they do. That's why I stay in the Department. I've got too big a stake in the Twentieth Century to pick up my chips and get out. Some day I might be able to do something again."

Jeff said, "I did something once."

"What's that you said?"

"Oh, nothing," Jeff said.

3

He said, "Oh, nothing," but he knew now that it was something. It was something he couldn't speak of. He hadn't learned until much later what it meant. He hadn't known a military axiom—that the action of a junior officer can sometimes influence a skirmish, an engagement, a battle, a campaign, a war. History.

Nobody in the General's War Room back in Florence—a War Room in a tent, but commodious and comfortable nevertheless—

selected Jeff Baker to be the spearhead, the point, of the offensive against the Gothic Line in September of 1944. The General himself was not responsible for the offensive. It was ordered by the Combined Chiefs of Staff, who were worried. The Germans were planning to pull four divisions out of Italy and send them to the Western Front. If this happened the offensive in the West, already gasping for supplies, would certainly bog down. And if the logistics disease became worse, and the Germans counterattacked in the winter, those four extra divisions would become enormously important. So the General in Florence received a directive to attack the Apennines frontally from the south. If he pushed through to the plains of the Po beyond, that would be wonderful but most unlikely. In all history no army had ever successfully shoved upward through the shark jaws of the Apennines. That's exactly the way it was—like pushing one's naked hand through a shark's clenched jaws. If the four German divisions could not leave Italy—if they could be contained— that would be enough.

Back in Florence the General selected the 91st Division to assault Futa Pass, and fight its way up Route 65, the only hard-surfaced, all-weather road across the mountains. But before Futa Pass could be stormed and held, it was necessary to capture the high ground which commanded the pass. For this task the General selected the 85th Division, which was fresh and rested.

The general commanding the 85th looked over his maps, and saw that there were two mountains—Altuzzo and Traponi—that he must take. Between them rose a hill, unnamed and with its exact height not given, which could be useful if captured. He assigned the 339th Infantry Regiment to Altuzzo, the taller of the two peaks.

The colonel commanding the 339th, a West Pointer immensely proud of his regiment, planned to assault Altuzzo with one battalion during the night, and send in another battalion at daybreak, and keep his third in reserve. From his command post in an abandoned villa in Scarperia, curtained from German observation and fire only by a row of willows, the colonel looked up at Altuzzo and knew he would need all three.

It happened that Jeff's battalion was picked for the night attack, and his company was picked by the battalion commander as the spearhead, and his Old Man chose Baker's platoon as the point. So it was just accident that Jeff Baker led the attack on the Gothic Line.

It turned out that Jeff Baker's platoon did better than expected, and Futa Pass was stormed and held. They named a mountain after him. They called it Baker's Peak. People said we might never have got Futa Pass except for Baker's Peak. The four German divisions were contained according to plan, and final victory came in the spring.

Jeff never spoke of it, and indeed wished he could banish it entirely from his mind, for he felt more guilt than pride in his part in it. He had survived, but the crucible of fire had been too hot. It had altered the tensile strength of his inner metal.

4

Jeff said, "Mr. Locke, I'm sure with all your experience you'll be called on eventually. But why can't you do anything now?"

Horace Locke didn't seem to hear. He leaned back in his chair and half turned, so that he looked out over the White House, and The Hill beyond. "We were so proud of the Twentieth Century," he said softly. "Why, we even named a train after it."

"What happened to you? Why aren't you a Chief of Division any more?" Jeff hazarded.

"I'm going to answer you," Locke said, his voice still low. "Because I have dangerous and unfashionable thoughts. Because I won't go along with the 'you're another' school of diplomacy. Because I believe we can have another war, or we can have civilization. We cannot have them both."

Jeff said, "Maybe I've got dangerous and unfashionable thoughts too."

"Knowing your father, I thought you would have. But we are not alone. We are only two in a great majority. True, it is a majority inarticulate, confused, and almost ashamed of displaying its consum-

ing will for peace. We turned over our leadership to those who have
a vested interest in war, and we have had trouble getting it back. My
judgment tells me that we will never get it back, that the odds are
for another war, and the dissolving of all our rights and freedoms.
We will believe that thus we can beat the Russians, and survive. But
if we survive it will be only as blind ants underground, fearfully
guarding their eggs and breeding more soldier ants so they can continue to exist, always blind and underground."

"That's a pretty black picture."

"I know it. We have the choice of believing Patton, who said,
'Man is war,' or of believing Sherman. I'm afraid we'll believe
Patton."

Jeff thought of the *Nebelwürfe* coming in on the slopes of Mt.
Altuzzo, and the terrible winter of '44, when it was always cold and
always wet on Route 65, which the homesick doughs called Easy
Street. "When it comes," he laughed, "I want to be the guy who
hands out the doughnuts on the dock at Hoboken."

Horace Locke smiled, as though he had followed Jeff's chain of
thought perfectly. "I don't think that would help you much. There
was 'Remember the *Maine*,' and then there was 'Remember Pearl
Harbor,' and the next one will be 'Remember New York.' "

He paused, and the smile disappeared. "In every country are men
who want war for one reason or another. The military we can understand. They have been trained and educated for one purpose, and
when they pursue their *raison d'être* it is understandable. But there
are many others who want war, and their motives are not always so
clear as, say, the greed of our local Krupps, and the fear and suspi-
cion of the men in the Kremlin. All of them have some personal
reason—and to them a good reason—for bringing down the house of
man in atomic shambles."

"So what can we do?" said Jeff.

"We do what we can. It won't be much, but more than most.
Most people cannot make themselves heard above the din for war.
In the Foreign Service you can observe, you can report, you can
even act."

"I hope so. But I'm not sure how."

"I can't tell you. You'll know when the time comes."

"A Third Secretary can't do much."

"You'd be surprised what Third Secretaries have done. Of course they can bottle you up. They can stop all your reports. But there's even a way to get around that. It's been used many times."

"Yes?"

"When you have something to say, and you cannot say it officially, put it in a letter to some friend in the Department. A man you trust."

"Isn't there a regulation about that?"

"There is, but it's pretty elastic."

"I don't have any friends in the Department," Jeff said.

"You can have me."

Jeff wondered whether he was engaging in a conspiracy. He didn't feel as if it were a conspiracy. It seemed perfectly natural and normal. "I'll remember that," he said.

"I don't know whether I'll be able to do anything with what you write me, if you do write," Horace Locke said, "but I'll try." He put his hands on the arms of his chair, and Jeff knew their talk was over. "I have to keep trying," Locke said as he rose, "until they finally kick me out of here. But I'm afraid it is hopeless. If there is to be peace, it must be dictated from up there." He pointed his hand towards the old-fashioned, soaring ceiling, not self-consciously, but matter-of-fact as if of a certainty there were something up there.

Jeff could not help but look, and there was nothing up there except an embossed Great Seal, dirty and yellowing, and Jeff realized this once had been part of the suite of the Secretary of State.

CHAPTER FIVE

1

JEFF BAKER SPENT the rest of that day completing the list of purchases recommended by the travel experts in the processing section. He had been told that you could not be certain of buying anything in Budapest—a city where once you could buy everything—that the Mission maintained no commissary, and there was no PX closer than Vienna.

He bought vitamin pills, lighter flints, chocolate, sulfadiazine, a hundred razor blades and spare razor, a portable radio adjustable for all current frequencies, two dozen cakes of soap, and six tooth brushes.

2

He went back to the apartment and began to pack. As a Third Secretary and Vice-Consul he was entitled to a number of privileges, among them a five-gun salute when boarding a man-of-war, and an extra eighty-pound weight allowance on trans-ocean planes. So that gave him a hundred and thirty-five pounds in all. He found he could get almost everything he possessed, except his books, into the four-suiter, the two-suiter, and the pullman bag, all new and unscarred by travel.

He was even able to pack his maps. He collected maps as some men collect old theater stubs and programs, or first editions, or circus posters. He could look at a map with the rhapsody of a botanist examining a prize orchid. He knew maps. He loved maps. Everything on earth seemed to change except its contour, the depth of its oceans, the heights of its mountains. Maps were solid things. You could depend on a map.

He didn't pack the written and photographic memories of his father. He would ask Stud to put them in a safe deposit vault. He wasn't sure why he wanted to keep them, but he did want to keep them. He felt he could depend on them, too. Wasn't that a silly feeling?

He had also bought a diplomatic dispatch case, of handsome pigskin, tooled in London. It had cost him forty-five dollars, and this seemed a lot of money, especially when he had nothing to put in it except a handful of personal papers, and the parchment commission, carefully enclosed in cellophane, in which the President of the United States said he reposed "special trust and confidence in your Integrity, Prudence, and Fidelity." He was enamored of the dispatch case as a woman with her first mink wrap. It was the patent of his office, the insignia of his rank. Anthony Eden could possess no better. He was admiring its austere beauty, standing on the table with his black homburg beside it, when Susan Pickett called.

She said she'd just heard from a girl in Balkans that he was leaving soon, and she hoped he'd drop in and see her before he left.

"I'm flying at seven in the morning," he said.

"Oh! I didn't know it was that soon." She sounded upset. "I suppose you're awfully busy, packing and saying goodbye. I guess you won't have time."

"I'm all packed," Jeff said. "I've said all the goodbyes I have to say."

"Except me."

"Except you." He discovered that when he visualized her at the other end of the phone it stimulated and exhilarated him almost as if he could touch her. It was a phenomenon at once pleasant and improbable of fulfillment, like a schoolboy's desire for the prettiest girl in the senior class.

"Well?" she challenged.

"Can I see you?" Immediately her reply became important. If she already had a date, or she was tired, or busy, or he could come over but only for a few minutes, then it was going to mean much more to him than a barren final night in Washington. If she said no, he was going to be miserable for a long time. He had committed himself.

"I wish you would come over."

"I'll be over right away."

"Not too quickly. Give me an hour. I just got home."

"Okay. An hour."

He didn't need a shave, but he shaved anyway. He spent an unnecessary length of time changing his shirt, and he had trouble knotting his tie. He found he didn't have proper control over his fingers. They insisted on shaking. Maybe I'm in love with her, he told himself. Maybe this is the way love is, exicting and adventurous the way it was when I was sixteen. More of an adventure than flying to Europe in the morning. Much more.

He told himself he couldn't possibly be in love with Susan Pickett. He'd only been out with her once. Besides, he had always believed that when he fell in love with a girl he would think of marriage, and he wasn't thinking of marriage at all. He was just wondering what she'd do, if anything, this night. His mind was racing from one imaginary scene to another, savoring the possibilities. In a vague way he felt this was somewhat sinful, if he really was in love with her, and wondered whether the thoughts of other men were as gross as his own. He couldn't imagine his father ever thinking as he thought now. Others of his own generation, yes. His generation had attained a certain sophistication about sex. His generation had broken the puritan chains. His generation had traveled. His generation had been around.

3

He was at her apartment in an hour, exactly. She took his black homburg, smiled as she smoothed the new felt, and dropped it on a bookcase. Then she turned and raised her eyes to his, directly, as if to ask an important question, but all she said was, "Drink?"

"Please."

"Rye, right?"

"Right." She seemed different. It wasn't her dress alone. She wore a white blouse with a gold pin at her shoulder, and a black ballet skirt that seemed to possess rhythm of its own, and that eddied and swirled with her smallest movement. As she moved to the teak bar he noticed that her hair was different. It was loose and smooth like dark velvet brushing her shoulders.

Then he noticed that the room too was different. A room changes with the character of its owner, so slowly and subtly that it is always noticed first by the stranger, not by the one who lives there. Exactly how it had changed was difficult to say. Some pieces had been added, some subtracted. He believed the rattan occasional chair was new, but he could not be sure. The room seemed more colorful, yet it was bare of pictures. Even the photograph of the Marine Corps colonel was gone from the end table.

He sensed that this night would be different from the last time, and that there would be no need to persuade, flatter, cajole, or arouse her. He walked to her side at the bar. He took the just-made drinks from her hands and set them down on the dark wood. He put his arms around her, and he could feel her hands, wet and cold from the ice, at the back of his neck. She strained herself close, and he marveled that she could fit so perfectly and tightly against him. He held her like that until he had to catch his breath, and then he kissed her eyes and her mouth and her ears and the base of her throat and her breasts under the loose, silken blouse.

"You're ruining me," she said finally. "There isn't any hurry, Jeff."

"Yes there is," he said. "I'll be on an airplane in eleven hours."

"That's time enough."

"It's no time at all."

"At least we can have our drinks. I dressed very carefully for you, darling, and I'd like to keep my clothes on for another five minutes."

"Okay," he agreed. "Five minutes."

But it really wasn't that long.

Some time later—it must have been much later for the traffic noises were infrequent outside on the avenue—he awoke and started to rise. Her arm was across his shoulders, and the arm pressed him back. He lay still for a moment, reveling in the delicious relaxation, and her nearness, and his pride of mastery and possession. Then he said, "I'm hungry. I want a cigarette."

"Hush," she said. "In a while."

"What time is it?"

"About one."

"Six hours more. I don't want to go."

"Less than six. We'll have to leave here at five if you're going to make that plane."

"I'm hungry," he insisted. "I was planning to take you to Hall's again tonight."

"I made sandwiches," she said. "Wrapped them in wax paper so they'd be fresh."

"How did you know we weren't going to eat out?"

She put her head on his chest and laughed. "Do you want whiskey," she asked, "or milk?"

"Both."

Then for a time it was Susan who slept while he remained awake. He propped his head on one hand, and smoked, and looked down on her, breathing slowly and quietly, her skin pale ivory in the reflected light of stars and street lamps.

At four he woke her with his lips, and she responded to him, her eyes still closed.

"One for the road?" she whispered.

"One for the road."

4

They left her apartment at five, at an hour when all else in the city was still, and even the drying August leaves slept silent, waiting for the morning breeze from the river to shake them into life. They walked together without speaking, their footsteps strangely distinct on the empty pavement, her hand under his elbow, her shoulder pressed close to his arm. Jeff's legs felt hollow and numb. They didn't feel like part of him. They moved of themselves.

He thought, this is a dream. I'm going to wake up in a minute and find I've got what's left of the night to toss and want her, and try to bring back this dream. She didn't call me. I didn't possess her all the night. Girls like her don't do things like that for guys like me.

He saw a bus stop ahead, on Dupont Circle, and heard the squeal of its brakes. This was real, all right, but it didn't seem credible that she should be walking at his side now, and in twenty-four hours he would be in Budapest. It was unreal and frightening that he might never have her again. He would not come home for three years, and in that time anything could happen, and something was almost sure to happen. Now that she had overcome her fear, conquered her phobia, she might find someone else. Probably would. Almost certainly would.

"What are you thinking of?" she asked.

"Oh, nothing."

"I was thinking of nothing, too. It's going to be bad, isn't it?"

"It's going to be rough." Her understanding was part of this miracle, this sense of joining, of union, of oneness.

Yet there wasn't any possibility of marriage. The Department disapproved of love, altogether. Love was a force operating beyond the bounds of directives, protocol, rank, regulations, act of Congress, and even the taboos of nationality and race. It was an unpredictable plague that could smite a distinguished Career Minister, as well as a Class VI FSR, cause him to ship his family back home, and set him to doing the rhumba in a third-rate Rio dive. It caused couriers to forget their crossed bags, cryptographers to chatter of their codes, and Division Chiefs to make fools of themselves over Washington debutantes.

The Department took a dim view of marriage. If an FSO wanted to marry a foreign girl he had to submit his resignation, and usually he could count on its being accepted. And in that day there weren't many American girls loose outside their own land, except in Departmental staff. And it was absolutely forbidden that he marry a girl within the Department, a hangover from the Hoover economy years when it was considered a dangerous drain on the Treasury for both husband and wife to draw salaries from the government.

The Department trusted that an FSO would not marry until he was a Class II or III. Then it was hoped that he would go back to his home town and choose a wife who would not only be socially acceptable but who would have an adequate private income. A Class V, completely dependent upon his salary, and still in his probationary period, could not ask a girl to quit a job that paid as well as his own, and join him in a career that marriage would automatically limit and cripple. He wondered whether Susan had thought at all of marriage. He didn't dare ask.

They turned into Riggs Court, and Susan said she'd wait at the Circle and try to stop, and hold, a cab. He said that was fine. He knew that was a delicate way of saying she didn't want to go to his rooms, where Stud Beecham would see her, and know where his roommate had spent the night.

The apartment displayed the relics of a party—overflowing ash trays, glasses with water melted from ice cubes standing in their bottoms, the debris of sandwiches, olive stones. He shook Stud out of sleep. Stud said, "What time is it? Where the hell have you been?"

"It's five-thirty. I've been out."

"I'll say you've been out. We had a party for you. A surprise going-away party. All the old gang. The surprise was you didn't turn up."

"I'm sorry," Jeff said.

"Woman?"

"Uh-huh."

"Well, I guess you'll have to be excused. Who was she?"

Jeff was strapping the four-suiter. He grunted.

"If you wait a minute," Stud said, "I'll pull on my clothes and help you out with that stuff and take you to the airport."

"Oh, no. You stay in bed. I can handle it fine."

"She must be waiting downstairs," Stud said.

"Mind your own damn business."

"Why don't you take her with you?"

"You go to hell."

"I'll bet I know who it is," Stud said. "I'll bet I know!" He got out of bed and looked out at the sky. "Going to be good flying weather," he decided. "But I'm glad it's you, and not me. I hate airplanes. Airplanes are strictly for the birds. Man wasn't meant to fly. What are your stops?"

"Gander," Jeff said, "Shannon, Prague, Vienna."

"And sometimes," said Stud, "they stop in the middle of the ocean."

They carried the bags to the bottom of the stairs, and then a taxi driver appeared to help him. "Goodbye, chum," Stud said. "Remember to brush your teeth every day, and mail your laundry home Fridays."

"So long," said Jeff. "See you in three years."

"The lady," said the taxi driver, "says for you to hurry."

5

They didn't talk much on the way to the airport. He said the Lincoln Memorial was always beautiful at this time in the morning. She said wasn't it, but she thought the Jefferson Memorial was more graceful. He said he liked the Jefferson Memorial too, particularly when the cherry blossoms were coming out around the Tidal Basin.

They swung down to the Mount Vernon Highway, and she

grabbed his arm tightly, on the curve, and clung to him. "That'll be in April," she said.

"What'll be in April?"

"The cherry blossoms. I wonder where you'll be in April, who you'll be with, what you'll be doing?"

"I wish I could be right here," Jeff said.

"But you can't."

"No, I can't."

Then they were at the National Airport, clean and fresh from its pre-dawn scrubbing and yet surprisingly busy for the hour, and the porters had his luggage. They walked to the Pan-American counter, the uniformed ticket agent checked his name on the manifest, and he found himself caught up in the smooth conveyor belt that in twenty minutes weighs and loads exactly fifty-six thousand pounds of passengers, luggage, mail, and freight on a trans-Atlantic plane. He exhibited his ticket, his virgin diplomatic passport, his government immunization register. His next of kin, he was forced to recall, was Aunt Martha, in Chicago, whom he had neglected to write for six months, and who had no idea he was on the way to Europe.

"I suppose you'll carry your dispatch case with you, Mr. Baker," the ticket agent suggested.

"Oh, yes, of course." It had been stupid of him to forget that an FSO never checked his dispatch case along with the other luggage. A dispatch case was part of a man.

The agent brought it out from behind the counter. Its handle felt good in his hand.

Not until then did he realize Susan was no longer at his side. He was searching for her, his eyes sweeping the rows of benches facing the great windows looking out on the runways, when an airline captain touched his arm. "You're Mr. Baker, of the State Department?"

"Yes."

"I'm Bill Judson. I take your flight as far as Shannon. If you get bored, come on up front and I'll show you how our new flying machine works."

Jeff smiled. "Thanks very much. That's awfully good of you." He knew he had received the equivalent of a five-gun salute. He felt good all over.

Over the captain's shoulder he spotted her. Her arms were loaded, and she was looking for him. "You'll excuse me," he told the pilot, and then shouted across the waiting room, "Hey, Susie!" The pilot grinned, and other people turned and stared. But she heard.

She'd shopped the magazine stand. She said she thought he ought to have plenty of magazines—"They'll be welcome in the Mission so don't throw them away." And the new H. Allen Smith book. And cigarettes.

"Five cartons!" he said. "I don't know whether they'll let me carry that many through customs."

She dropped everything on a bench, and then tapped his dispatch case. "That's what this is for. Didn't you know?"

"I'm learning," he said. He sat down beside her, put the dispatch case across his knees, unsnapped the locks, and fitted the cartons inside.

"That's a lovely thing," she said, rubbing her fingers along the perfect grain of the leather. "I hope some day it carries—I'm not sure what. But something thrilling. Something extra wonderful. Something for all of us. Something to wipe our fear away."

"I thought you'd got over it."

"I've rationalized it, some, but I can't get rid of it. Who can? There isn't a person in this country, Jeff, who at least once each day doesn't think of war. It's a permanent hazard, tangible as a fog that never blows away. It colors everything we do. Nobody can make a decision—business or personal—without considering it."

"Susan, what's going to happen to us from here in—I mean you and me?"

She looked at the clock. "There is so much we could talk about—and no time. I don't think we'd better plan—do you, Jeff?"

"No, I guess not. I just want you to sit quiet. I want to memorize you."

She looked down at her fingers, locked together in her lap. "There's something else I have to say."

"Go ahead."

"I just wanted to tell you you don't have to worry."

"Worry? About what?"

"About last night. No remorse. No obligations."

He leaned over, and kissed her hair, and said, "I want obligations, darling," and the loudspeakers began to whine, and somebody coughed into the microphone. Then the loudspeakers said Flight 86 was loading at Gate 3 for Shannon, Prague, Vienna, and Budapest.

They rose and moved together towards the gate, becoming part of a funnel of people, the spout of which ended under a sign saying, "Passengers Only."

They were pushed close together, and she said, "I guess this is the end of the line for me." She kissed him once on the lips, lightly so as not to smear him.

The gate opened, and he was carried through it with the stream of people, and she was left outside.

CHAPTER SIX

1

Jeff Baker got his assignment his first night in Budapest. He had, of course, reported to the Minister the morning of his arrival; that is, he reported to Morgan Collingwood, the Consul General, who was senior Foreign Service Officer, and Morgan Collingwood had presented him to the Admiral, which was the proper procedure.

Mr. Collingwood's manner didn't fit his resounding name. Mr. Collingwood was a slight, balding man who looked like the oldest and most inconspicuous vice president in a bank—the one who sits farthest from the rail, and approves all the important loans. But the Admiral looked like an admiral. His hair was white as the crest of a breaker, his face red as if he had just stepped off a gale-swept bridge, and his eyes a deep and startling blue, as if they had absorbed the pigment of smooth tropic seas and unclouded tropic skies.

The Legation's offices spread through three floors of a modern stone and concrete and chrome and glass building on Szabadzag-tér off Bathory Utca. It was not far from the Parliament, the Bourse, and the Palace of Justice, and had once been occupied by the Hungarian Ministry of Foreign Affairs. The Admiral's office was on the topmost of the three floors. He sat behind an executive desk that might have been imported from America, and the desk was framed between the Stars and Stripes and the two-star flag of his rank. On the wall behind him were pictures of Theodore Roosevelt, reviewing the Great White Fleet, Franklin Roosevelt when he was Assistant

Secretary of the Navy, and the battleship *Wyoming*. If you could shut out the view of the Danube with its shattered bridges dangling their broken steel arms in the water, and ruined Buda on the other bank, the office could have been in Washington.

Mr. Collingwood said, "This is Mr. Baker, just in this morning from Washington. We had a cable about him a few days ago."

"Oh, yes," the Admiral said. "Glad to have you aboard, Baker."

On the Admiral's desk were tiny, perfect models of four destroyers, a cruiser, and an aircraft carrier. Before they all sat down he rearranged them, putting the cruiser in the van, and aligning the destroyers on each side of the carrier, in accepted flanking position. The Admiral inquired about his trip, and his lodgings. Jeff told him it was a smooth trip, and he had slept most of the way across, and he was staying at the Astoria Hotel, but that Quincy Todd had promised to find him a small apartment.

"Todd met the plane at Matyasföld, as usual," said Collingwood.

"Young Todd," the Admiral said, "makes an excellent flag secretary. Fine for the housekeeping chores. He'll show you around. Speaks the language. You don't, do you?"

"No, sir," Jeff said. "I've got Italian and French and German, but no Hungarian. I was going to take lessons."

"Won't need to," said the Admiral. "It's the same here as every place else. All the educated people speak English. Now you take me. I've been every place in the world. Spent my whole life traveling around the world. Never had to speak anything but English."

The Admiral asked how things were at home, and Jeff told him things were about the same, and the Admiral shook his head as if that were bad, and said, "I want you to come up to my place for dinner tonight. I want a first-hand picture of the situation in the States. Like my intelligence fresh. Besides, Fred Keller will be there. I want you to work with him. Sort of a special project."

"Is Mr. Keller in the building?" Jeff asked.

"You know him, don't you?"

"Yes, we've met."

"He mentioned it. He's not in the building. You see, Baker, he has a very, very special job. Very delicate. He operates entirely outside the Legation. Deals with people who can't afford to be seen going in and out of here. You understand, don't you?"

"Oh, yes, sir. You mean the Atlantis Project."

Jeff knew from the way Collingwood started, and from the Admiral's face, which lost all its affability, that he had said the wrong thing.

"Where did you hear Atlantis Project?" the Admiral demanded.

"In Washington, sir."

"God damned fumbling fools!" the Admiral said, slowly shaking his head from side to side. "Here we break our necks to insure security and those blabbermouthed bastards talk about it all over the place!"

"I was warned that it was extremely confidential," Jeff protested. "Naturally I wouldn't ever mention it except, well, here."

"Confidential hell! It's classified top secret! They had no right to tell *anybody*!"

The Admiral let out his breath, almost in a whistle, and said, "Well, I guess there's no damage, because I'm going to use you on the job. But it's just as I've always said—it's a mistake to have generals running the State Department. They don't know what security means. Ought to have Navy men."

The Admiral slapped his palm on the desk and capsized the cruiser. "Now look, Baker, from now on I never want you to mention the word Atlantis. Is that clear?"

"Yes, sir."

"And you'll be at my place at seven. Todd will see to your transportation."

"I'll be there, sir." He was glad to get out of the Admiral's office.

2

Jeff spent the rest of the day with Quincy Todd. Todd was a stocky man with pink, round, beardless cheeks, and brows and lashes so blond and pale that they offered no concealment to his

eyes, and forced him to stare out upon the world in perpetual astonishment. His face looked five years younger than Jeff's, but his
double-breasted suit strained to conceal a paunch, and Jeff guessed
he was older. He also was a Third Secretary and Vice-Consul, but
he had slipped into the job that some missions call "stableboy" and
others "donkey boy." This meant that he did a great many chores
that had nothing to do with diplomacy, except that if they were not
done the machinery of the Legation would stop.

He wheedled gasoline out of the Hungarian Ministry of Transport, argued exchange with the Finance Minister, and fought the
Ministry of the Interior, when employes of the Legation fell into
the hands of the police, or simply disappeared. He knew his way
around the Russian Kommandatura, and the intricacies of the Soviet
bureaucracy. If a truckload of canned food, or a correspondent, or a
typewriter, or a courier vanished on the road from Vienna to Budapest, he knew where to find it, or him. He did all these odd jobs so
well that there was no thought of replacing him. He was a square
peg tightly wedged into a square hole, and not an hour passed that
he didn't curse his knowledge of the Hungarian tongue, and his
talent for trouble-shooting.

He shepherded Jeff from office to office, presenting him to the
staff. As he introduced the men, and a few women, he identified
them by their jobs. He said, "This is Mr. Kovacs, our chief dis-
bursing officer," or, "This is Captain Reedy, our Assistant Air Attaché." But some he introduced simply by their names, without
referring to their jobs, and Jeff knew that this was because for one
reason or another their affiliations or assignments were considered
confidential. Eventually he would grow to know all of them, and
something of what they were doing, but in the beginning they would
be mysterious. These men seemed as much in a pattern as those in
blue suits, and those in uniform. They all appeared to own gabar-
dine trench coats and pork pie hats. And while their ages must have
differed, they all seemed the same age, like stones in a wall.

His mind blurred with the strange faces tagged with new names,
few of which he remembered. He knew this would soon change.

In a few weeks the faces would become all too familiar, like fellow passengers on a long cruise. When it was finished Todd said, "Let's have a drink."

Jeff said, "I need one."

Todd said, "There's an *espresso* around the corner where I can always get fair cognac. I'll cut you in on it."

He knew he was going to like Todd, but if he had been asked why he knew this he would only have been able to say, "He speaks my language." He hoped that as soon as they were seated behind their drinks Todd would brief him on the Legation. What he had seen was much more complex than indicated by the table of organization charts in Washington. Yet it had probably formed itself to meet the challenge of place and time. He was eager to know all about it, and become part of it, as quickly as possible.

Out on the street he put aside his preoccupation to begin his assessment of the city and its people. Pest was not a ruin like Buda. Here in Pest the streets were free of rubble. New plaster and unpainted boards, ugly as scar tissue, had grown across the wounds in the buildings. The people seemed as well dressed, generally, as you would see in the poorer sections of Brooklyn, or Baltimore, or Boston. But this was not a poor section of Budapest. This was the center of finance, and culture, and government. On the Bathory Utca he and Quincy Todd were by far the best dressed, the most prosperous of men. He was conscious that people noticed them, some with respect, some with envy or irritation or even a hatred open and hot. They were conspicuous. They were Americans. They had been born in a land that had picked this time to erupt its riches, and this accident of birth made them members of the time's aristocracy. His passport was the century's patent of nobility.

They turned into the broad Vaczi Korut, and then into an alley, and there was the *espresso* with its sign in flaked gold on the glass, "Café Molnar." They sat at a table with a top no bigger than a checkerboard, an elaborate steel and silver urn on the counter hissed and spat and produced thick Turkish coffee, and a girl brought them the coffee in tiny cups, along with the cognac. Jeff sipped the cognac, and then the coffee, and the combination was rich and warming. "It's good," Jeff said. "What do they charge?"

"Just one thing," Todd said.

"One thing?"

"A forint. When they changed from the pengo to the forint everybody called the forints things and I still call them things. You want to keep this place quiet. It's the only place in the whole section where you can get a drink for a reasonable price, and we don't want it overrun by the Dick Tracys."

"The who?"

"The Dick Tracys. You met some of them."

"Oh, I see. What do they do?"

"Oh, they do everything. We've got the MIS, the ONI, the CIC, the FBI, the CID, G-2 from USFA, Central Intelligence Agency, assorted Treasury agents, and our own security people. We're supposed to have more Dick Tracys," Quincy Todd added with some pride, "than any other Mission in Europe. Except, of course, Berlin and Vienna, and you can't count them, really, because they're occupation zones."

"Don't they get in each other's hair?"

"Well, they spy on each other, and they read each other's mail, and they try to scoop each other on hot intelligence, but they don't exactly get in each other's hair. Theoretically, the Admiral coordinates their activities. But they do get in my hair. They use all the transport, and eat all the food, and drink all the Scotch at the Park Club, and every once in a while one of them investigates me. It's the price I pay for the maintenance of democracy and Western civilization."

"The world being what it is," Jeff said, thinking of the Atlantis Project, and wondering whether Todd knew anything of it, "I suppose they're necessary."

"I guess so, but you can't be sure, because nobody knows exactly what they all do, because everything they do is secret."

Todd talked of the routine of the Legation. The Legation had a motor pool and a garage, and on the Kossuth Lajos-tér it maintained a mess. The mess was a carry-over from the days, back in 1945, when only a Military Mission had been in Budapest. But with the resumption of diplomatic relations it had been wise and expedient to continue it. "The Admiral," Todd said, "likes everybody to eat at the mess at lunch. The Admiral doesn't want people straying around in restaurants. He likes to keep his finger on things. You can have dinner any place you want, but it's best to turn up at the Park Club some time during the evening, so you can be seen. The Park Club is like a country club without golf. It was a hangout for British and Americans and French before the war and it still is but now it's mostly American. It once was somebody's palace, and it's very lush. The food and liquor are good and we've got a fair band and there's dancing every night. Now about women—"

"Before we start about women," Jeff suggested, "how about telling me about the Admiral? Why an admiral in Budapest anyway?"

"Nobody knows," Todd said. "Maybe it's because the Hungarians are used to admirals. They had Horthy, you know."

"That's not reasonable."

"All I know," Todd said, "is that when I came here we had a general, and then we had a regular Career Minister, and now we have an admiral. Maybe it's because they've got generals everywhere else, and the Navy thought it was being discriminated against, and so they put an admiral in Budapest."

"I never heard of him until I joined the Department."

"Didn't you? Out in the Pacific we heard of him. He had a task force. Lost a carrier and a transport. The Army claimed he screwed things up."

"Then what?"

"Then he was promoted to COMYDDOCSOUWESPAC."

"What's that?"

"Why, that's Commander of Yards and Docks, Southwest Pacific. He fought the battle of Sydney in Prince's and Romano's. Then he became a wheel in Navy Intelligence, and now he's here. He's not a bad guy. Just security-happy."

Todd signaled with his eyes, and the girl brought more cognac.

She had strong legs that were flattered by her brief dirndl, and she weaved between the tables, her body erect but her hips moving as if she danced. She spoke to Todd in a language that Jeff had never heard before, with a few French phrases surprisingly dropping out of the sentences. Todd replied in Hungarian, and the girl said, "Okay, okay," and smiled at Jeff, her teeth vivid white against dark lips, and patted his shoulder.

"What's going on?" Jeff asked. He'd heard tales in Vienna about the Budapest women. But way back in Naples, they'd talked about the women in Rome. When he got to Rome it was the women in Florence, and in Florence it was the women in Milan, and then the women in Vienna. The women were always more beautiful and more eager in the next city.

"She was just asking about you. She wants to know if you're going to be in Budapest long, and whether you'll come here often, and whether you have a woman. I told her you already have a woman."

"As a matter of fact I do have a woman," Jeff said. "At least I think I have."

"If you're not absolutely certain," Todd said, "you'll soon know it in this town." He smiled up at the girl as if they were discussing her beauty. "You've got to be careful about these women in Pest. Now you take Marina, here. She's a dish, all right, but she's a Rumanian gypsy, and if you ever got in the hay with her you'd find yourself involved with her six brothers, three sisters, and maybe her whole tribe. Anyway, she's a social impossibility. Morgan Collingwood would swoon. He'd have you shipped to the Ivory Coast, with a recommendation to file and forget."

"I guess you have the same trouble here," Jeff suggested, "that we had in Vienna. They all want cigarettes and chocolate and CARE packages."

Todd spoke to the girl, and she took away their empty coffee cups. "No," he said then, "that isn't it." He looked down at his glass. "All they want in Pest is a little happiness, and a little kindness. Those have become the rarest luxuries in Eastern Europe."

"I see."

"I don't like to be sentimental about it. You can't be sentimental about women in Budapest. When you find a girl, first be sure she's politically safe, and then be sure she hasn't got syphilis. The Russkies used Mongol divisions to take Budapest, and they ran wild. When I got here there were a hundred thousand untreated cases of syphilis in the city. Since then the hospitals have been getting some penicillin, and other drugs, but it's still a definite hazard of course."

"Very interesting, and instructive," Jeff said.

"The safest thing is to find a girl within the Mission. That won't be easy. Girls join the FSS for one of two reasons. Some of them want travel and adventure, and the others think it's a virgin forest for husband hunting. Most of those who want adventure have already been grabbed by the Dick Tracys, and the ones who want to marry have found out by now that there's practically a closed season on Foreign Service Officers."

"Well, I'm not going to let it worry me."

"You're not going to be a dedicated man like your boss, are you?"

"My boss? Who?"

"Fred Keller."

"How do you know he's going to be my boss?"

"My boy, in a Mission like this everybody knows everything. A Legation is a New England village transplanted into the middle of somebody else's country."

"Do you know what my job's going to be?" Jeff asked, in what he hoped appeared innocence.

"I've only a vague idea, except that it must be interesting, because it's been kept so quiet. I thought I was going to get it, and that you were going to have my job. But it looks like I'm stuck forever. Well, that's what I get for learning Hungarian, God damn that Berlitz!"

They left after another drink, and Todd dropped him at his hotel. "I'll have transportation for you at six-thirty," he promised. "Most of our vehicles are jeeps, but I'll pry loose a staff car for you tonight, because you're messing at the Admiral's. When you're finished with it, send the driver back to the motor pool."

3

While he shaved Jeff wondered what it was about Quincy Todd's speech that seemed so familiar, and yet so irritating and strange. It was not until he was on the way out the Andrássy Utca, which slices the city from the river to the suburbs straight as a sword cut, that it came to him. He had been taking stock of the passing traffic, noting that the cars and trucks were shabby as the people. Fenders were rusted out of the lend-lease Studebakers that the Red Army still used, and the Red Army's jeeps were misshapen as if by battle damage. The civilian automobiles looked as if they had been dragged from the back of used car lots. In all of Budapest there seemed nothing new, nothing fresh, nothing gay. And while he had been in Budapest only once before, and then only for a few days, he remembered this of the city—that it had lived and that it had smiled. Now the city had turned down its mouth, and gone into mourning for its past, and the color of its mourning was gray—the gray of unpainted boards and unsanded stone and unsmiling faces, the gray of Russian uniforms and Russian trucks and cars. In the whole length of Andrássy Utca, only the political posters splashed color, and red alone is depressing and monotonous.

Then he realized what it was that was familiar and yet queer about the way Quincy Todd talked. Automobiles weren't automobiles. They were vehicles, or transportation. A garage was a motor pool. He would lunch at a mess. Hell, he thought, it's like being back in the Army.

4

The Admiral lived in the austere Legation residence, standing behind its stately poplars and circular driveway in the embassy section that adjoins the Városliget, the big park that was like Rock Creek Park in Washington. A uniformed doorman bowed him out of the sedan, and a butler took his topcoat and black homburg and said, "You're Mr. Baker, sir? The Admiral is waiting for you in the library." He led Jeff down a long hallway, deeply carpeted, rich with murals and statuary that reflected the good taste of some former occupant, some peacetime appointee, who had inclination and money to furnish this dwelling so that it might properly advertise the wealth and culture of his country. The manner of his reception, and the grace and grandeur of the hallway, impressed Jeff, so that he experienced a pleasing sensation of excitement, and of being part of something important. Now his rank limited him to a hotel room, or a small apartment, but one day his government might make him master of a residence like this. One day he might *be* the United States of America in a foreign land.

The butler slid open a pair of double doors, Jeff walked through them, and his dreams were scattered by a quarterdeck bellow: "Watch where the hell you're putting your feet!"

Shocked into awkward immobility, he stood like a crane with one foot in the air. He looked down. He had almost stepped on a model battleship. It was one of a fleet that sailed through a narrow channel of leather-bound books across an isthmus of Oriental runner. The Admiral was on his hands and knees in the middle of another fleet on the other side of the room, glaring up at him like an angry bulldog. "All right, Baker, come in," he growled. "Don't stand staring like you never saw me before."

"Yes, sir."

The Admiral sat back and crossed his legs. That morning he had been wearing a tweed suit, but now he was Navy, his uniform coat across the back of a chair. Jeff guessed that he changed into uniform at the end of a day, for comfort, the way some men put on a dressing gown. "I'm working out a problem," the Admiral said. "Want to join me? Move some of these ships around?"

"I'll try," Jeff said, "but I'm afraid I don't know much about it."

"That's all right. I'll tell you what to do. Take that fleet there."

"The one between the books?"

"Yes. The one in the Bosporus. You've got the American fleet, which is in the Bosporus, and I've got the Russian fleet, over here in the Black Sea."

Jeff sat down on the floor, cross-legged like the Admiral, wondering what to do next. It occurred to him that some men play with electric trains, and others collect stamps, or ancient automobiles, and some men whittle, and play chess by mail, and do double-crostics, so he should not consider the Admiral childish simply because his hobby was holding maneuvers on the library floor. He picked up a carrier, admiring the workmanship, and said, "This is the *Midway* class, isn't it? It looks just like the *Midway*."

"That's right!" the Admiral congratulated him, appearing pleased and surprised. "These models are exact and scaled. I get them from Schwarz's—you know, the toy store on Fifth Avenue. Now put down the *Midway*, and I'll outline the problem."

The Admiral's voice and manner changed. He was no longer sitting on the floor in a Budapest suburb. He was in a great War Room in Washington hung with wonderful maps of many seas, and he was briefing the Joint Chiefs of Staff. "Gentlemen," he said, "the situation is as follows. Fighting has broken out in Berlin, and it appears inevitable that within forty-eight hours our land forces will be swept from the continent of Europe. But the Navy has used foresight. The Navy has mobilized all available ships in the Atlantic, and dispatched them to The Straits, for we know that the enemy's first thrust will be at Turkey. We have three battleships, six carriers, six cruisers, and suitable escort destroyers in The Straits. In the Black Sea the Reds have six battleships, ten carriers, fifteen cruisers, and an estimated forty submarines. Now the problem is—"

"Where did the Russians get all those battleships and carriers?" Jeff interrupted. "I thought they only had one or two."

"Oh, they've taken over the British fleet. The British are Socialists, aren't they?"

"Yes, but—"

"Quiet! Now the problem is, shall we go into the Black Sea and attack the transports which must now be loading at Burgas, Varna, and Odessa—risking annihilation if the Red fleet is operating as a single force—or shall we retreat to the Mediterranean and accept battle only when we have land-based air cover from North Africa?"

The Admiral stopped speaking and looked inquiringly at Jeff. "Well," he said finally, "what's your decision?"

"Me?"

"Yes, you."

"I don't know."

"God damn it," said the Admiral. "The alternatives are clear, aren't they? You can take a calculated risk, and try to smash the enemy before he gets started, or you can play it safe. Now, what are you going to do?"

Jeff rested his elbows on his knees, and propped his chin in his hands, and examined the fleets. "I'm the American admiral, right, sir?" he inquired.

"Correct."

"Well, I'm going to get my fleet out from between these books— out of the Bosporus, I mean—right now, and send them west as fast as they can go, and then I'm going to load about ten atom bombs on B-two-nines and B-three-sixes at our field in North Africa, and then I'm going to blow hell out of the Russian fleet, Burgas, Varna, Odessa, and maybe Belgrade and Moscow too."

"That's not fair!" the Admiral protested.

"Why not? If you can have the British fleet, I guess I can use my atom bombs!"

The Admiral struggled to untwist his legs, found it difficult, and then subsided. "I never use atom bombs in these problems!"

"They're available, aren't they?"

"It spoils the fun," said the Admiral.

He frowned, as if the subject burdened and troubled him. "Don't misunderstand me," he went on. "Atom bombs won't replace navies. Anybody who thinks the atom bomb will replace the Navy is a defeatist. As a matter of fact the atom bomb can only help the Navy. It's not enough to just make atom bombs, you've got to deliver them, and the best way to deliver them is by aircraft carrier. So we're going to have bigger and better and faster carriers, and they're going to be protected by bigger and better battleships, armed with rockets and guided missiles. The Navy always looks ahead. No atom bomb can stop the Navy. But we don't use atom bombs in these little problems."

So Jeff played according to the Admiral's rules. He sent his fleet into the Black Sea, where it was ambushed by submarines. He got his fleet wiped out. The Admiral did not seem displeased. He said Jeff should come around another evening and try again. The next time Jeff could have the Russian fleet, and he himself would take the American fleet, and they'd see what happened.

5

They had drydocked the warships in a bookcase, and the Admiral was putting on his coat, and remarking that it was about time for dinner, when Fred Keller arrived with another guest. Keller greeted Jeff warmly, and said he had been looking forward to his coming to Budapest, and that they had a big job cut out for them. He introduced Jeff to William Quigley, who said, "We met this morning."

"I'm sorry," Jeff apologized. "I met so many people this morning I didn't place you."

"Perfectly all right. I like people to forget me."

Jeff thought this a queer statement. As they made their way into the dining room he watched Quigley, and decided that if Quigley's ambition was to have people forget him, he'd be successful. Quigley was neither short nor tall, thin nor stout, young nor old. He might have chosen his clothes for protective coloration, for he blended into the background inconspicuous as a quail in autumn leaves.

"Quig is in the Department's Security and Investigation Division," Keller explained, "especially assigned to our project."

"Now, now," the Admiral said. "No talk of the project until after dinner. I never trust a woman or a servant—not even my own. I've had the same Filipino mess boy for twenty years. Never talk in front of him. Never talk in front of anybody."

The dining room table had been designed to seat forty at diplomatic dinners, but a fence of flowers cleverly set aside one end of it. The Admiral and Keller sat at the table's head. Jeff was on the

Admiral's right, opposite Quigley. The Admiral asked Jeff whether he'd seen the big heavyweight fight, and Jeff said yes, on television. The Admiral said television was wonderful, and he wished they had it in Budapest.

Jeff remembered something that the bartender at Harry's New York Bar in Paris had once told him—that when Americans met on foreign soil for the first time, their opening gambit of conversation was invariably prizefighters or women. It was the bartender's conviction that no bar was completely equipped without a copy of the *World Almanac*, to settle disputes about prizefights. It was something that had always stuck in Jeff's head, and generally he found it to be true.

So he talked about the fight.

The Admiral said he thought too many Negroes were winning fight championships.

Jeff felt pretty strongly about this. He said the prize ring was one of the few places where a Negro had an absolutely equal chance. "You never hear of Negro tennis or golf champions," he said, "because they're not allowed to join country clubs."

Keller said, "It's good propaganda to have colored champions. It counteracts the Russian line. When they start talking about our racial frictions, that's one fact the Reds can't get around."

"Well, Fred, there may be something in what you say," the Admiral admitted. "It may be an international asset, but it doesn't do any good at home. Ever since Louis won the title, the niggers have been pushing. Why, they're even giving them commissions in the Navy."

The white-jacketed Filipino brought in an enormous silver platter, with a hill of black caviar rising in its center. This was more caviar than Jeff had ever seen at one time before, and he said so. "It was a present," the Admiral said, "from the Russian Naval Attaché. Genuine Black Sea sturgeon."

"Really!"

"His name is Yassovsky," said the Admiral. "Met him in Washington in forty-four. Very decent fellow. Has a reputation as a brilliant tactician. That is, with submarines and destroyers. Not really a battleship man. Just sent me the caviar. For no good reason."

"Do you see him often?" Jeff asked.

"See him! Certainly not! I couldn't have him here, any more than he could invite me over to his place. Why, that'd be fraternization, wouldn't it? But he did send me this caviar, and I sent him cigarettes." The Admiral glanced at Quigley, who was listening without expression. "Anyway, I hear he's left the city."

"That's the report," Quigley said.

They ate curry, and a salad, and tiny pancakes swimming in a flaming sauce, and Jeff answered questions on the political situation at home, careful to give the facts without opinion. The Filipino brought coffee, and the Admiral told him, "You can go out now, Juan. Shut the doors and see that they stay shut." Jeff knew that they had reached the hour for business.

6

"I think the time has come," the Admiral began, "to go from the planning to the operational stage of Atlantis Project. So a general review is in order, not only to brief our young newcomer, but as a recap for ourselves. Right?"

"Right, Admiral," Keller agreed.

"Now as you know, I'm simply in charge of policy. With a war coming on I'd rather be on active service, naturally, but the powers that be have decided that I can be useful in this post. I'll admit that this is the most interesting shore assignment a man could want, and what makes it especially interesting is Atlantis Project. Do you know—" the Admiral drummed his forefinger on the table for emphasis—"that this is the first time we have ever really prepared intelligently for a war? We're doing things now that we don't usually do until the shooting has started. Usually, we get caught with our pants down."

The Admiral's voice became round and oratorical, exactly as it had been when he outlined the battle problem on the library floor. "Europe will be overrun. No doubt about it, and we might as well accept it. Some of our people in Germany and Austria may fight their way to the coast, but at best we can assume an American Dunkirk. Ordinarily I'd say that we ourselves would be captured and interned. Have to accept the fortunes of war, you know. But I have reason to believe—nothing definite, you understand—that key personnel in the Atlantis Project will be flown out when war becomes inevitable. I'm sure that Washington would consider you gentlemen—I won't speak of myself because I'm just an old war horse, and expendable—but you gentlemen will be too important to the war effort to let the Reds get their hands on you. Now our principal objective is the establishment of an organized underground in Europe to work for us after we're gone. Is that correct, Fred?"

"That's perfectly put, Admiral," Keller said.

"Suppose you carry on from there."

"Right." Keller began to talk, quietly as an actor underplaying his part, using his tanned, expressive hands in the most reserved of gestures. Hungary would be vital to the Russians. It would be a staging area and zone of communications for the Red armies moving to the West. He felt sure that the Reds would bivouac the bulk of their armies in the cities of Western Europe, in the hope that we would not drop atom bombs on these cities.

"They know we're soft-hearted," the Admiral interrupted. "They know we don't like to destroy friendly civilian populations."

Keller went on talking, and Jeff realized that he must have been the architect of the project, for he spoke with a salesman's glibness, answering all the objections before they could be presented. "Now I think the Hungarians are generally friendly to us. At this time a Communist government has been imposed upon them, but I think it is fair to say that generally the Hungarians are anti-Communist. They have fought for their freedom for a thousand years, and they will fight again.

"Our aims are fairly obvious. First and most important, we need a constant flow of intelligence and information. We need it on the strategic level for the efficient conduct of political warfare, and we need it on the tactical level for our military planners. Secondly, our people will lead passive resistance, and be in charge of simple sabotage conducted for morale purposes. They will operate an underground press, and clandestine radio stations. They will keep alive the flame of freedom. Third, when American forces once again invade the Continent, our people will become the nucleus of a resistance army that will attack the Reds in the rear. To achieve our objective we must work with caution and yet with imagination, among those groups which we know will be friendly and receptive to us, and hostile to the Soviet Union."

He turned to Jeff. "What do you think of it?" he asked.

"It's thrilling," Jeff said truthfully. "I feel that I'm watching history being made."

"More than that," Keller said. "You'll make history. You'll become a part of it."

"It frightens me a little."

"Because it is audacious? The Admiral will tell you that no political or military plan—and the two are as one now—can succeed without risk and daring."

"It isn't that," Jeff said, and found he was without words to explain his disquiet. "It is—perhaps that I'm afraid of making a mistake."

"He means the security angles," the Admiral suggested. "And he's quite right. Frightened all of us, at first. Frightened the Secretary himself."

Keller nodded, and now it seemed his words were directed at Quigley. "We are all aware, and must continue to be aware, of the dangers of penetration. The Secretary, as the Admiral says, was worried. If the Russians or the Hungarian Communists knew, or even guessed at, our plans, the results could be catastrophic. They'd slit the throats of our Hungarian friends, and smash our organization before it was born. They'd be alerted on the rest of the Continent. And there's no way of estimating the repercussions at home. It might make the Department look silly. And I don't know what might happen to us."

"I do," said Quigley.

They all looked at him questioningly. It was the first time he had spoken, except to reply to questions. There was a moment of odd, embarrassing silence, while they waited for Quigley to say something more. He looked up at the chandeliers, as if fascinated by the crystal winking in the candlelight, and as if there was nothing more to say.

"I wish you'd quit worrying, Quig," Keller said. "There aren't going to be any leaks, because nobody is going to talk, nothing is to be committed to writing, and our contacts with the Hungarians will be careful, careful, careful. Let's take Baker's assignment, as a model."

"Yes, Fred, let's get on with the job," the Admiral said. "Do you think the Russians worry when they flood our country with spies, and corrupt our labor unions, and spread their poison in our schools and radio and newspapers?"

"Right. We have divided the Hungarians into groups and occupations which per se we can set down as sympathetic and potentially useful. We can assume that what is left of the nobility wants no part of Communism. We can also assume that we will find friends among manufacturers, merchants, bankers, exporters and importers, most of the intellectuals and professional people, and the agrarian landowners. Eventually we will have a man assigned to each of these groups.

"We're going to give the world of the theater to Baker here. The theater is an important part of the life of Budapest, and one through which naturally flows a great deal of information about the Russians. It is an influential medium of propaganda. Furthermore, the Budapest theater is closely linked to the American theater. Hungarian motion picture theaters for many years have been dependent upon the United States for sixty per cent of their films. Many Hungarian actors and actresses have been successful in America. American plays have been popular here. It will be quite natural that an American Third Secretary be seen with the theatrical crowd, either for reasons of business—or pleasure." Keller allowed himself a smile.

"Especially a young, unmarried Third Secretary who knows how to handle himself with the ladies."

"Haw!" the Admiral laughed. "So that's why you picked him!"

Jeff felt uncomfortable, started to deny that he was attractive or a lady-killer, and then saw he would only appear foolish. Instead he said, "It sounds wonderful. But where do I get the money?"

"Atlantis Project has a reasonable amount of unvouchered funds," said Keller. "Now as to your procedure. You will approach what Quig here would call your 'targets' with the view of choosing those best qualified to carry out the aims and objectives I have outlined. You will sound them out most cautiously. You will gradually let them know what they can do to help us—and themselves—when war comes. You will never let them know that you are part of an organization, or that you talk or act for anyone but yourself. You must always give the impression that you are acting without the Legation's knowledge. They won't believe it, but it will allow us to repudiate you if there is a slip. Not until the last stages—when war is inevitable and a matter of days or weeks, will they be given definite assignments, and provided with money, equipment, codes, channels of communications, and definite instructions. Our job at this time is simply to find the completely reliable people who are not only on our side, but who are willing to act as our agents."

"It's going to be a tight little operation," said the Admiral. "A nice, tight little operation. And I want to tell you, Baker, that if we're successful—well, I'm not the kind of a commander who keeps all the glory for himself. There'll be plenty for all of us."

They talked until midnight, and Jeff could not help admiring Keller's capacity for detail. He understood why it was not necessary to risk the project's security by committing any part of it to paper. It was all in Keller's head, always secret, and yet marvelously available.

7

When he left the stars shone cold and blue-white like a handful of diamonds flung against the sky, and the wind blew steadily from

the east and cut through his topcoat, hinting·of the gales that would
blow out of the steppes in the winter to come. He got into the
car, and the driver slid the sedan down the Andrássy Utca. The
street lamps were dim, and there were great pools of black between
them. There was no other traffic.

They were halfway through the city when a man's scream of
terror filled the street. The sedan jerked forward, but Jeff turned
in time for one quick look down the side street. He saw two dark
figures running, and in the instant that the side street was in his
vision, one man leaped upon the other, and brought him to the
pavement, precisely as a wild animal drags down his prey.

The car spurted for three blocks and then slowed again. "What
the hell was that?" Jeff asked. The driver, his shoulders and neck
bent and tense, said something in Hungarian. Jeff tried German.

"The *unbekannte Menschen*," the driver replied without turning
his head. "The unknown men, so the papers call them."

"What's that mean?"

"Russian deserters. At this season they stop fools who are out at
this hour, and strip them of their clothes. So then they can hide
in civilian clothes, and perhaps try to escape to the West. Always
the papers call these clothes bandits the *unbekannte Menschen*, because the papers do not dare to mention Russian deserters, but all
Pest knows what is meant."

"Are there many of them?"

The driver moved his shoulders. "Who can tell?"

8

Jeff relaxed against the back of the seat, and lit a cigarette, and
then lit another for the driver. He discovered that his hands were
shaking, and he was glad when they stopped under the marquee
lights of the Astoria. He told the driver to return to the motor pool,
as Quincy Todd had instructed. He went to the desk, and the night
porter gave him his key, and a brown envelope. He turned it over

in his fingers, and saw that all that was written on it was "J. W. Baker" printed with pencil. "Who left this?" Jeff asked.

"I don't know, sir. A man, sir."

"What kind of a man? Someone from the Legation?" Ever since the war's end the Astoria had been used as a transient hotel by Americans, so the hotel people would recognize the Mission's couriers and drivers.

"No. I think a Hungarian, sir."

"Is the elevator running?"

"Oh, no, sir."

Jeff put the envelope in his pocket and walked upstairs, his legs heavy and aching. Their stiffness, he thought, was the result of his deep sleep in the plane the night before. A plane's reclining chairs are comfortable, but you cannot fully stretch out your legs, if the legs are extra long.

In his room he stripped off his clothes impatiently, climbed into his pajamas, and pulled back the covers of his bed. He remembered the letter, swore, and debated whether to fall into bed, or to walk across the room and open it. Then he recalled he had left his cigarettes in his vest, and he would want them on his bed table. He often woke in the night, suddenly, and when he did he always needed a cigarette. So he had to cross the room anyway.

He found his cigarettes, and then ripped open the envelope. Inside was a letter, neatly printed, but some of the letters looked queer, as if written backwards, or backhanded.

"If you are the Captain Jeff W. Baker who was at the Oriente Hotel in Bari," it read, "I would very much like to see you. If you are that Baker please be so kind as to leave a note at the apartment of János Donat, at Lovag Ut. 25, and assign a place of meeting. Any place of meeting will be okay with me but I do not wish to be embarrassment to you."

The letter was signed, "Leonides."

Jeff knew only one Leonides, and he was Leonides Lasenko, a major in the Russian Air Force.

Jeff read the note again, and shoved it under his pillow. He was too tired to think about it. He snapped out the light, and stretched his body until his feet touched the footboard. He rubbed his head into the pillow and thought how strange it was that the last time he had been in bed it had been Susan Pickett's bed in Washington. He tried to recall it, but he could not imagine how it was, for it was so long, long ago. She was two days and one world away.

CHAPTER SEVEN

1

QUINCY TODD FOUND him an apartment. It was only a room and bath, with its private entrance into the hallway, in Madame Angell's flat on the fourth floor of a reddish stone house on Revay Utca. Madame Angell had been letting out this room to British and Americans since the twilight years after the first World War. Her third husband had been an Englishman, and he had willed her his name and his nationality, which was her distinction and her pride. Madame Angell was an Istanbul-born Greek. Her first husband had been a Turk, her second an Armenian, and her fourth an Austrian, but she considered herself English, and kept a faded blue British passport conspicuous on the parlor table, alongside a photograph of Mr. Angell. While Mr. Angell had been something of a rake, and had never found it expedient or perhaps even possible to return to Britain, as the years passed she magnified his virtues, and made light of his peccadilloes. In that section of Budapest she was known as "the Englishwoman who lives on Revay Utca," and every year, in times of peace, she attended the King's birthday party at the British Embassy. During the war she had let the room to a German economic specialist, but nobody spoke of this now.

Quincy Todd had warned him of all this, and more. The building superintendent, Sandor, who also functioned as elevator operator, was a police spy. But that was to be expected anywhere in Europe. Madame Angell would use Jeff as a sounding board against which

88

to exercise her favorite among her ten or twelve tongues. Hot water would appear only at sporadic intervals, and heat would be unpredictable. He was not to leave candy in the room, for while Madame Angell was completely honest, she could no more resist chocolate than a drunkard could resist whiskey. And he should not leave whiskey in his room, because Sandor would search the room at least once a week, and Sandor was a drunkard.

However, there were compensations. His rent was six hundred forints a month, which was within his living allowance. The house on Revay Utca was fifteen minutes' walk to the Legation, and less to Keller's establishment. The furniture was comfortable, although old-fashioned. It had a telephone. This was important, since for ten years no new telephones had been installed in Budapest.

And it was a large room with plenty of wall space for his maps. When his friends the maps were on the walls he felt at home.

He discovered that Madame Angell stayed up all night maneuvering the dials of a large and intricate radio. Madame Angell was a propaganda fan. She maintained herself in a narcotic state of tension and excitement by absorbing the whole world's cacophony of violence—threats of war and rumors of war, news of fighting, bombings, assassinations, revolutions, plots, riots, coups, and the verbal marches and counter-marches of the heads of states. For her the end of civilization was something breathlessly postponed from day to day.

She was a soap opera addict on an international scale. For Madame Angell the troubles of Hungary were dwarfed by the monumental crises of greater nations, just as the troubles of the American housewife are dispelled as she is anesthetized by the agonies of Ma Perkins, Stella Dallas, Young Widder Brown, Helen Trent, Our Gal Sunday, Young Doctor Malone, middle-aged Dr. Jordan, the Second Mrs. Burton, and Portia facing life. Once daily her receptacle of disaster overflowed, she had to relay her tidings of impending doom to someone, and when he was at home Jeff was always closest to hand.

2

He had requisitioned a portable typewriter from the Legation, and each Wednesday and Saturday evening he wrote to Susan, for the diplomatic air pouches closed for personal mail at noon on Thursdays and Sundays. On the Wednesday of his third week in Budapest he was in his room, writing to Susan, when Madame Angell rapped, and jostled her way through his door, carrying a tea tray.

"A little tiffin, Mr. Baker," she said, "but no sugar. It would be nice if you could get some sugar."

"I'll try," Jeff promised reluctantly. He had provided her with five pounds of sugar, magically produced out of the mess by Quincy Todd, only two weeks before.

"Tiffin isn't tiffin without sugar, is it, actually?"

"I suppose not."

Madame Angell fitted herself into the big chair. She was a ponderous and billowy woman, and she must once have been even larger, for the flesh folded loose from her face. She was like a balloon that has been inflated almost to bursting, but from which some air has been allowed to escape, so that the surface is wrinkled and out of shape. "Poor Mr. Baker," she said. "Poor, poor Mr. Baker. I don't wonder that you look worried."

"Do I?" Jeff asked in surprise. He had been worrying, at that. He had not answered Leonides' note, and he could not push Leonides out of his mind. He had been enriched by Leonides' friendship, and now the Russian was calling the loan, and he could not be ignored. Jeff was, frankly, afraid of being seen with a Russian, or in any way becoming entangled with a Russian. Nobody in the Legation ever spoke to a Russian. It had been two years since a Russian had had a drink, or even attended a formal diplomatic dinner, at the Minister's residence or the Park Club. No single thread remained of the strands of mutual purpose that once bound them together as allies. All this he was writing to Susan. He found that his thoughts and logic clarified as he set them down on paper.

Madame Angell made a clucking sound with her lips, and shook her head. "Poor young man! Your country torn to pieces while you sit here. Who could ever imagine a revolution in America? Fancy!"

"A what!"

"The revolution. Surely you've heard of it?"

"No. Why, that's incredible."

"I've been listening to it all evening. All your southern provinces —the whole southern part of your country—is in revolt. The senators and governors of your southern provinces—or do you call them states?—have called for the overthrow of the President. The details are unclear, but it seems the revolt is led by a southern leader named Jim Crow. All the southern governors and senators have sworn they will uphold him."

"I begin to see," Jeff said.

"The revolt seems to have resulted from something called the Lynch Law. I think an attempt was made to declare this law not in accordance with your Constitution. I am not sure, except that everything is a bloody mess."

"That isn't a revolution," Jeff told her. "That's just politics inside a party. It's as if—" He searched for a simile in the political life of Hungary that would be understandable to her, and found that there weren't any. "Where did you hear this?" he demanded.

"First I heard it from Radio Sofia. I think they quoted a dispatch from Washington by way of Stockholm printed in *Pravda*. It was very plain. There is a revolution in America. My flaming oath!"

"Don't you listen to the 'Voice of America'?" Jeff asked.

"Certainly. I hear New York every night. I hear it between the BBC and Bucharest."

"Well, what did they say about it?"

"Nothing. That's why I know it's true. When I want to discover what's happening in Washington I listen to Moscow, and when I want to find out what's happening in Moscow I listen to New York. Isn't the world in a beastly state!"

"You must think so!" Jeff said.

He finished his tea, and Madame Angell picked up his tray, and then put it down again. "How forgetful of me," she said. "How bloody forgetful." She located a pocket in the folds of her dress and drew out an envelope. "Sandor brought this up as I was bringing the tiffin."

He put the envelope beside his typewriter. He could guess what was in it. "Thanks, Madame Angell."

She kept her eyes on the envelope, as if in hopes that Jeff would open it while she remained there. "Sandor didn't say who brought it, or when. Sandor is a bad type, you know. Sandor may have—"

"I know."

She shrugged her heavy shoulders. "You Americans have grown secret like all the rest. But with the troubles in your homeland, I can hardly blame you. Bloody awful, these revolutions. Now I must listen to Belgrade. Belgrade is always good. Did you know that Tito has his own atomic bomb? God's truth. Heard it on Belgrade last night."

3

Jeff waited until he heard her door close, and then he opened the envelope. The note, this time, was curt.

"You go often to the Espresso Molnar. I beg you to be there tonight. I will wait until midnight."

He re-read the last page of his letter to Susan.

"I met this Russian in Bari," he had written, "at the Fifteenth Air Force Headquarters. We were both there as liaison officers, and we were billeted together in the Hotel Oriente.

"I think I'd better explain a little more about why I was there, and why he was there. After I left the rest camp they didn't send me back to Division, but assigned me to Fifth Army Headquarters in Florence. I was the captain who moved the maps in the briefing tent—about as useful as a magician's assistant. Then, when they were planning the Spring offensive in 1945, they decided to use heavy bombers in tactical support of Fifth Army in the attack on

Bologna. Since I knew the ground fairly well, they sent me to Bari, and we figured out ways for the heavies to identify our forward positions so they wouldn't bomb our own troops. Leonides was in Bari for exactly the same reason, except his job was to protect the Russian army operating on the other side of the Adriatic. I remember now what a devil of a time he had wheedling a bomb line out of his own generals.

"But he did his best, and he was a swell guy. Everybody liked him, and he was the best poker player in the Oriente."

Jeff wondered why he had written to Susan that this Russian was the best poker player in the Oriente, and he guessed it was because there was no way of knowing a man like sitting at a table with him, night after night, and examining his play at poker. From these poker games at the Oriente Jeff could attest to Leonides' character. He could swear that Leonides was intelligent, and a keen student of human nature. He knew he was ordinarily patient, but at times impetuous and daring. Since Leonides did not gloat when he won, or lament overmuch when he lost, Jeff knew he was a gentleman, although he had been born in the slums of Moscow. He knew, further, that Leonides was honest and courageous.

The last paragraph he had written said: "Much as I would like to see him, I don't see how I can risk it. It would be sure to become known, and the Legation would consider me most indiscreet, and perhaps dangerous."

Jeff ran a string of x's through this paragraph, and wrote: "Although I know it is indiscreet, I am going to see him tonight. I just received another note from him. I think he's in trouble and needs my help. Anyway, what the hell, I'm a free American citizen, am I not, and can talk to whoever I choose? Or is that anarchism?"

4

Now that he had made his decision, he was in a hurry to go. He would finish the letter later, or in the morning. He put on his overcoat, stepped into the hallway, and went through the useless gesture of locking his door. Almost any key would fit it, and he was fairly certain his room had been visited on several occasions while he was absent. He remembered the letter, and swore at himself for his carelessness. He went back into the room, swept the first three pages of the letter off the table, plucked the fourth from the typewriter, folded them and put them in his inside coat pocket.

He rang three times for the elevator, and was about to use the stairs when he heard it grumbling its way upward.

Sandor Patek was fifty, bent and slight, with watery blue eyes and faded yellow hair that curled raggedly at the ends. He had a daughter in St. Louis. When Jeff was in the elevator he usually talked of her. For a year he had received no letters. He wished she would send him CARE packages. She had married a very rich man, and had an automobile and a house with two baths. "You go out this night?" he asked in German, as the elevator descended. "Is not this Wednesday, the night you remain upstairs? Perhaps the note I brought had something to do with it, *nicht wahr?*"

"You are absolutely right," Jeff said. "The note is from a beautiful woman. She needs my help."

"So?" Sandor said, blinking expectantly.

"She was seized by Rajk's secret police and now hangs suspended by her toes from the Franz Josef Bridge. I am on my way to rescue her."

The elevator jerked to a stop, and Sandor opened the door, his face showing anger and shock, as if Jeff had committed a desecration. Rajk was the Communist Minister of the Interior, and therefore Sandor's boss, and his name was not used loosely nor was the secret police ever ridiculed, although it might be hated. Sandor said something nasty in Hungarian, for he knew Jeff did not have the language. All the way to the *espresso* Jeff felt pleased when he recalled Sandor's face. People turned to stare at the tall American in the warm overcoat speeding on long legs past St. Stephen's, chuckling out loud to himself and incongruously wearing no hat.

5

He walked through the door of the Café Molnar and he saw Leonides immediately, for his was the only uniform there. Somehow Jeff had expected that Leonides would be in civilian clothes, and that the clothes probably would be shabby and ill-fitting, and that Leonides would be shielding himself in the darkest corner.

Altogether there were eight tables in the *espresso,* and there were groups of three or four around each one, for while there were few calories in the Molnar's fare, still there was quick warmth, and conversation, and the illusion of Kaffee klatsch relaxation. Only Leonides sat alone. He was at the most conspicuous table, the table closest to the window. His uniform was immaculate, the blouse smooth until it reached the belt, and evenly pleated below. His boots were black and shining, the stiff epaulets on his shoulders soft yellow. He was not so tall as Jeff, but built compactly, and when he rose he gave the impression of endurance and power, like a locomotive that has been still on the track, and then moves slowly ahead.

Thus he rose as Jeff threaded his way towards him, and held out his broad hand, and grinned so that the four steel teeth in the front of his mouth, which he used to display so proudly to the poker players at the Oriente, gleamed silver. "So you old bastard!" Leonides said. "You came! You have not declared war on me."

"Not yet," Jeff said, grasping Leonides' hand in both his hands. He was conscious that his words rang louder than they should. As he seated himself he heard no other sound in the *espresso* except the scrape of his chair. It is the custom, in a Budapest café, for the patrons to be openly and pleasantly curious about those around them. But not as curious as this. Not paralyzed. The *espresso* was hushed as in the emptiness of a Sunday morning. Jeff felt embarrassed, like a man who goes to the theater and is suddenly dragged out on the stage.

Then behind the bar Marina, the gypsy, set the coffee urn to spitting. She looked over at him and winked, and he knew what she was thinking, that at last something exciting was happening in the *espresso*, and she would soon bring the coffee and cognac, and find out all about it. By threes and fours the heads dropped at the other tables, and the hum and buzz of talk resumed, louder than before. The government clerks, musicians, money brokers, shopkeepers, and printers who frequented the Molnar had something new to talk about. With their own eyes they had seen something astonishing and without precedent. They were in attendance at a miracle.

"You look fine," Jeff said. "You don't look any older. Maybe it's that crew haircut, Kiev style."

Leonides put his elbows on the table, and his fists alongside his mouth so that only Jeff could see his lips, and when he spoke he spoke very softly, and his lips hardly moved. "I am older," he said. "And you are older, also. We are both so old that we will die very soon."

"Cut the drama," Jeff said. "Who's going to kill us?"

"Quietly. Quietly. What I have to say is only for you, not for the Pest rumor factory. You're going to kill me, and I'm going to kill you."

Jeff knew exactly what Leonides meant, and he had hoped they would not speak of this immediately. He had hoped they could bat the breeze about Bari, and perhaps get a little drunk, drunk enough to forget for a time this wall that stood between them. "What did you do after you left Bari?" he said. "You were going back to Moscow and burn your uniform. You were going to fly transport planes on the Moscow-New York run. You were going to marry that girl—what was her name?"

"Vilma. I didn't. She was dead."

"I'm sorry," Jeff said, and raced on from this unpleasantness. "What are you doing in Budapest now, Leonides?"

"Can't you guess?"

Jeff wished he had asked something else. This ordinary question was now as embarrassing and personal as inquiring about a man's religion, or his relations with his wife. "No, I can't guess."

"In this day, what would you do with a Russian who speaks English not badly, who for two years went to Cambridge, and who for another two years was a liaison officer with the Americans?"

"Propaganda?" Jeff ventured.

"Try once more. Remember that no other Russian in Budapest, not even the Marshal, would dare be seen in public with an American."

"In a place like Budapest," Jeff said, "you put him to watching the Americans and British."

"You win the sixty-four dollars," said Leonides. "See, I remember my slang. Yes, my job is to watch the Americans. Not the actual spying, mind you. That is the province of the foreign branch of MVD. I receive all their reports. That is how I knew you were here on the day you came. That is how I know, for instance, that last week you twice visited Zukats, the cinema exhibitor, and that you are more often in the Keller flat than in the Legation. Also I talk to those who know the Americans—the Hungarians, the Rumanians, the Swiss, the Swedes, the Austrians and Germans who are here. I examine all that you have done, and try to analyze why you have done what you have done, and predict what you will do. And once a week, or twice a week, I write a report for the Marshal of what is in the soul of the scheming Americans."

Jeff started to rise. "I don't like to have my soul examined. I'm sorry, Leonides."

The Russian put his hand on Jeff's arm. "Wait, dope. Wait for what I have to say. When your enemy watches you there is little to fear. When your own countrymen spy on you, then you are lost. That has been the curse of my country. Okhrana, Cheka, OGPU, NKVD, and now MVD—they are all alike. They suck the milk from my Russia, and fill her breasts with poison!"

Jeff sat very still. He knew now why Leonides had hunted him out, and the urgency of the summons. He knew even why he himself was here. "When I got your note tonight," he said, "I thought you needed help. I thought you'd become one of the *unbekannte Menschen* and needed clothes or money to run the border."

"I am one of the unknown men," Leonides whispered—for his quick eye had noted the girl coming with Jeff's cognac and coffee—"except that I am still in my uniform. There are many of us—many more than you think. There is even one close to Him. But we will talk of all this later."

Marina set the drinks down, and said, "Okay? Okay. See, I learn English."

"Who's the lucky teacher?" Jeff said. Her arms were bare and smooth and brown, and her vitality reminded him of Susan, and he wondered how long it would be before he had another woman, and what this would mean between him and Susan. She would understand, Susan would, that he could not be a monk for three years. She would ask him nothing, and he would tell her nothing, and his human and inevitable need would not stand between them.

The girl didn't answer him, but undammed a stream of Rumanian at Leonides, and the Russian rocked his head back and laughed with his mouth wide, so that everybody at the other tables looked. "I speak all the wrong languages," Jeff complained.

"She says," said Leonides, "that ordinarily she does not like Russians, because gypsies are individualists and Russians are sheep. She says she likes me better than any Russian she has ever seen, because obviously I too am an individualist. She also says for us to enjoy ourselves, because we will both be exiled in the morning, me to Siberia, and you to Alcatraz."

"Alcatraz? What's she know about Alcatraz?"

"They think it's the American political prison. There was an article about it in today's *Szabad Nep*."

Marina had been listening, but not understanding. "I learn English more. Okay," she said. Leonides patted her round bottom, and she whirled away, observant still over her shoulder, sure that Leonides still watched her.

6

"What was it we used to say at the Oriente?" said Leonides. "Stacked. Yes, really stacked. With such beautiful creatures in the world, why is it we must think of war?"

"So you're sure there'll be a war?"

Leonides traced squares in the moisture on the table. He frowned as he talked. "Yes. We are like two ships on a collision course with blind men stiff in fear at the wheel. Not only will there be a war, but I think I can tell you how it will start, and the course it will run, and how it will end.

"You will attack us. Your memory of Pearl Harbor will always be fresh and raw and you will not again risk surprise. You will attack us at that moment when your President believes we have the atomic weapon, and are ready to attack you. Your President will make this awful decision alone, without the customary reference to your Congress, because it will be a military necessity that he do so.

"He will have no choice. The pressures will be too great. Your Central Intelligence Agency will know when we have a stockpile of atomic bombs. Already he must have been informed of our progress in bacteriological warfare, in which we are perhaps farther advanced than you. Your reconnaissance will unmask our airfields. Your FBI will have penetrated our plots within your own homeland. Our actions in Germany and Austria and Manchuria and Korea and Greece will become intolerable to your Army. Our overt acts in the Mideast will frighten your Navy, which might starve without the Mideast oil, and the admirals too will clamor for war. And in that moment when he is certain your country faces another Pearl Harbor, then he will order the attack. He must."

Jeff drank his cognac in a gulp. "Go on," he said.

"In the first day your Air Force will destroy all our important centers. You will turn into radioactive powder Voroshilovgrad, Magnitogorsk, Gorki, Leningrad, Stalingrad, Odessa, Dnepropetrovsk, of course Moscow, and the new uranium cities beyond the Urals. How many millions you will kill I cannot estimate, nor will the number you kill affect the course of the war."

Jeff interrupted. "No, because by then you will have your armies in the cities of Western Europe, and you will drive the Western armies into the sea."

"Only in the beginning," Leonides said. "Later you will land on the Continent, and your armies will defeat the Soviet armies just as they did the Germans, and for the same reason. You will have overwhelming production and fire power and air power. Most of the Soviet armies will be destroyed, and what remains will retreat inside Russia."

"Then the war will be over," Jeff said.

"Oh, no," said Leonides. "That will be only the second phase. The third phase will come when you occupy most of Russia, and all of Europe. I should think it will take ten or twelve million men. Any general will tell you that victory is only achieved after you have occupied and pacified the enemy country. It will be extremely difficult and perhaps impossible. There will be interminable guerrilla warfare."

"And then we will have won the war," Jeff said.

"No, you will not have won. You will simply have performed a Russian tragedy. You will, out of fear for your own life, have committed murder and then suicide."

"I don't understand."

"Naturally, you will be under a military dictatorship: With so many ideological traitors, and Soviet agents, in your country you could not successfully conduct a war without such a dictatorship. Your jails will be bursting, and all your freedoms vanished. You will drain your natural resources to win this victory, and the drain will never end, for always there will be your millions of soldiers outside your borders, straining to maintain the victory and restore order. All of Europe and some of Asia will be in such ruins and chaos that it would be better to let it again join the jungle. But you will not be able to do this, because people will still live there, and they will all hate you. And eventually you will crack and break up, and your suicide will be complete."

Jeff signaled Marina to bring him another drink. "All of what you say may be true, Leonides," he said, "but there is one thing worse than winning a war, and that is losing it."

"That is true," said Leonides, "but there is not much difference in the end. The truth is, nobody ever again will win a war."

Marina came with Jeff's drink, and he swallowed it quickly, as he had the other, and it did not sting or warm him, but seemed innocuous as water. "Sounds silly, doesn't it?" he said.

"It is truly silly, but there it is, each day closer."

"And you have no hope?"

"I do have hope. If I had no hope I would leave here this minute and throw myself into the Danube." Leonides looked at Marina, and smiled at her, and she saw from his smile that what he had to say was serious and private and not her concern. She touched his shoulder and went back behind the bar.

"There is a saying here in Budapest," he went on, "that like many other Budapest sayings is funny and yet true. It is, 'The Dictator made two mistakes. He showed the Red Army to Europe, and he showed Europe to the Red Army.'"

Jeff laughed aloud, throwing his head back as the Russian had, and the others at the tables around smiled in understanding. Surely the Russian and the American were now telling each other bawdy jokes. Their friends would not believe it, when they had told what they had seen.

"As I say, it is true," Leonides continued. "It is the reason for all our desertions. Our soldiers have seen with their own eyes, and they know He has lied to them. What has been seen cannot be driven out of the mind or changed, like that which has been read, or only heard. They know that even in this beaten and cringing country the people live better than in Russia. They have more opportunity, more freedom. They have more things, like bathtubs and toilets and electric stoves. They are happier. Some can laugh. Do you know what it means not to be able to laugh, for fear that the MVD may see you laughing, and suspect you laugh at Him? In Moscow one smiles only for the camera."

"Go ahead," Jeff urged.

"Most important, in many places, such as Berlin and Vienna, the Red Army has been in contact with the American Army, and they have seen what the American Army has—what material and what privileges—and it is not believable. For my part, the happiest days of my life I spent in Bari. I think I know America, and Americans, and I like them and will do, am doing, my best not to war on them. There are many others like me, who know the West. There is even one high in our government, who is our leader.

"And we have talked with each other, and we are moving. Not quickly, for it would be swiftly fatal. We are the Second Russian Revolution." He reached out his wrestler-strong hand and gripped Jeff's arm. "Did you hear that, Jeff—the Second Russian Revolution!"

"I heard," Jeff said. The limitless possibilities opened before his mind. "I didn't think it was possible, but now I see I was foolish. We didn't think there was opposition against Hitler, either. But there was, and they very nearly killed Hitler."

"We will most certainly kill *Him*," Leonides said. "We will kill *Him*, and the other sour and crazy ones, and in Russia we will have a new government and a new country and there will be peace."

"Christ, I hope so," Jeff said. He must be composed. He must listen carefully.

"I pray so," said Leonides. "I pray so. We can do it alone, but with your help it will be quicker. Perhaps without your help it would not be quick enough. It is difficult for us to approach you. We tried before. Yassovsky, who was Naval Attaché, sent a present of caviar to your Minister-Admiral. He knew him well in Washington. What happened? The Minister-Admiral sent Yassovsky cigarettes, but no word. I don't understand it. It was a direct invitation. Or perhaps, as you fellows would tell me when we played poker, I have an Oriental mind."

"I understand, I'm afraid," Jeff said. "Yassovsky has gone?"

"He was recalled to Moscow. I don't know why. It worries me, and the others of us. Now there is no possible link between us, and you, except you, Jeff."

Jeff hesitated for the part of a second, the beat of a heart. "What do you want me to do?" When the question was out he knew he had turned his future into a path he had never expected nor intended. Once before he had made such a decision. It was like the day he had found the height commanding Futa Pass lightly held. He had moved his platoon up the height, without flanks, orders, communication, supplies, or the support of artillery. Up to this moment, it had been the most momentous, and really the only decision of his life.

"At this time," said Leonides, "you do nothing. We have many plans. We will need much help. There is, for instance, the matter of the radio station. It is progressing well, but we may need help. We will have a newspaper. Where can it be published? Pamphlets and leaflets. What press will print them? Money we will need, of course, and eventually perhaps air transport, explosives, arms."

Jeff choked back the questions he wanted to ask. Who was the leader? How many were they? How soon would they act? In time, he was sure, Leonides would tell him what he needed to know. "Leonides," he said, "you know my position. You know that I am only a Third Secretary, without influence or power or the right to make decisions or commit my government. Whatever you want, I will have to take to somebody higher up. You know this?"

"Of course. All I want now is the assurance that at the proper time you will transmit the news of what we are, and what we intend, and what we need."

7

"Sure," Jeff agreed. He balanced his chair back on two legs, and then let them bang to the floor. Quincy Todd had come through the door of the Café Molnar. It had been Jeff's understanding that Todd came to the *espresso* only during the daylight hours. But here he was, four steps away, pulling off his overcoat, peering through the tobacco smoke and uncertain light, seeking someone. "Hey, Quincy," Jeff yelled. The best defense was always an attack.

Todd turned, smiling automatically, moved towards their table, and then froze like a man in the woods who had almost stepped on a snake. He had seen the Russian.

"Come on over," Jeff urged.

"Just poked my head in to look," Todd said. "I have to leave right away. Thanks all the same." He glanced back towards the door, as if in fear his retreat would be cut off.

"Sure you won't have a drink?" Jeff asked. "Come on, pull up a chair."

"Sorry. Have to go," Todd said, and fled, his coat under his arm.

As he went out of the door from behind the bar Marina called, "Quin-see." But he was gone.

"Well, I'll be damned," Jeff said.

"This will get you into trouble?" Leonides suggested.

"I don't think so," Jeff said. "He's a good guy. I honestly don't see why it should get me into trouble. I'll just explain that I met you in Italy, and bumped into you here. That's reasonable, isn't it?"

"Yes, you'll be all right," Leonides decided. "You'll be able to—what do you say—swing it. I know you Americans. You are different."

They talked of how they should meet in the future. Jeff could always send a note to the house on Lovag Utca. "The apartment," Leonides explained, "is what is known as a letterbox. It is occupied by a Hungarian named János Donat. Whatever is left with him will reach me. But you should not go there yourself, except in exceptional emergency, for if an American were seen entering the apartment Donat might be compromised. On my part, I can always leave a message at your apartment."

"The Hungarian superintendent," Jeff warned, "is a Rajk spy."

"I know," said Leonides, "but so is the Hungarian who carries our messages."

"There is one more thing," Jeff said. "Can I communicate what you have told me to someone else, in case anything should happen to me—a transfer or anything?"

"I have placed my life in your hands," Leonides said simply, but in a tone that was almost a rebuke. "Not only my life, but many others'."

"I'm aware of it."

"It is true that it would be better if one other besides yourself should know what I have told you, and yet I am hesitant to give my sanction that it pass beyond you." Leonides looked down at the table, and Jeff knew that he was looking into the days to come, and estimating the possibilities. "If you have a friend in your government whose insides you know, who perhaps you have known all your life, whose lips cannot be opened by any means, then I agree. I say yes."

"You are very careful," Jeff observed.

"Your Department of State," said Leonides, "is not secure."

CHAPTER EIGHT

1

In the morning Jeff awoke thinking. When he awoke and wished himself asleep again it was because the day loomed dreary or unpleasant. But if he awoke thinking then the day invited progress and excitement. It was a good sign.

He showered and shaved and when he stepped out of the bathroom there was a pot of scalding water on his table, insulated by Madame Angell's tea cozy. He mixed his powdered coffee, and reminded himself that he must wheedle more sugar out of Quincy Todd. He wasn't happy in the morning without his coffee, with plenty of sugar, but no cream. He set the cup alongside his typewriter, and concluded his letter to Susan.

"Thursday A.M.," he wrote. "I saw Leonides. He looked fine." This sounded inane, but how much more could he dare tell her, or anyone, except the one person in whom he eventually must confide? "He is still in uniform. He is attached to the headquarters of the Soviet lines-of-communication troops here. Things being as they are, I don't expect I'll be seeing much more of him.

"Susan, I desperately wish you were here. Not only because I want you desperately, but because there is so much we would have to talk about. I want to share my life with you. I suppose that sounds corny, but that's what I feel inside me. It doesn't seem possible that I am homesick, because in the years in Italy and Austria I was never homesick. And my job here is much more interesting than anything I have ever done before. For the first time in my life I feel that I have the opportunity to do something that is really important—important to you, Susan. It must be that I'm just plain lonely, and that I need you. I'm getting your air mail letters in three days now. Write me often, for I love you, Susan."

It sounded stilted and incomplete, but it was the best he could do. He could not tell her of the cabal of which Leonides was a part. He trusted her, certainly, but he was afraid that if it became necessary for her to transmit Leonides' story to the Department, the story would not be credited. She was, after all, only the girl who took the nine o'clock conference. She was a very attractive and reliable recording machine. He could imagine the reaction if Susan approached, say, the Undersecretary of State, and remarked: "I got a letter from my boy friend in Budapest. He knows something of an internal plot to overthrow the Soviet regime, and he would like me to tell you about it."

When he shared Leonides' secret with someone it must be a person with access to the Department's higher levels, and probably with access to the Secretary himself. He doubted whether anyone except the Secretary would have the power or authority or the nerve to act in the matter. He knew that the hope on which the Department based all its policy was that the Soviet regime would change. Whether the Department would actively encourage a revolt against the regime, or whether the Department preferred to wait until the dictator died, in the belief that a more reasonable leader would replace him, he did not know. Nobody knew, except the Secretary. Perhaps even the Secretary, never having been faced with the alternatives, himself did not know. In any case, this was not a matter to be risked in the mails. If Atlantis Project was too secret to put on paper, then so was this, except in utter emergency and necessity.

He signed his name to the last sheet of the letter, and was typing the address on the envelope when there was a knock on his door. He hoped it was Quincy Todd. He would like to explain last night to Quincy, so he would not suspect Jeff of traffic with the Russians, and tattle to Morgan Collingwood. He didn't think Todd would do this. Todd would talk to him first. "Come in," Jeff called.

2

It wasn't Todd. It was a moment before Jeff realized it was Quigley. He had bumped into Quigley several times since his first night at the Legation residence, but Quigley was a man whose face always seemed like the face of someone else. Now for the first time Jeff was conscious that Quigley wore rimless glasses, and that the eyes behind them, although of no identifiable color, were hard like freshly cast metal.

"Is this room secure?" Quigley inquired.

"I don't know. Maybe there's a red-headed Russian under the bed. Why don't you look?"

"Don't be funny, Mr. Baker. You're in no position to be funny."

When he had last seen Quigley, at the mess, Quigley had called him by his first name. Now Quigley was calling him "Mr. Baker." That wasn't good.

"I see you were writing a long letter," Quigley said. "Do you mind if I look at it?"

"You're damned right I mind!" Jeff came out of his chair and put himself in front of the security officer. Quigley was a small man. The top of his hat came level with Jeff's eyes. He was not young, and he looked as if he had been absorbing his vitamins in capsule form for years, with no visible beneficial effect. He was just a little man in a trench coat and a pork pie hat who didn't move or blink or frown or in any way show that Jeff impressed him. He said, "I must insist."

"Do you *like* to read other people's mail?" Jeff asked.

"As a matter of fact, I do. It's the most fascinating part of my work."

"Well, you're not going to read mine."

"Yes I am," Quigley said quietly. "You see, Mr. Baker, you've committed a really astonishing breach of security. I've been in this business for a long time, Mr. Baker, and I've never heard of anything more brazen, and I might say stupid. For this day and time, Mr. Baker. For this day and time. You spent three hours last night with one of the most dangerous Russians in Pest. A clever intelligence officer. His assignment is to learn about the Americans, in case you don't know it. You have been entrusted with the most sensitive, and highly classified, information in this Mission. You drink with this Russian for three hours, and the next morning you write a long letter. I think you will agree that I must require a complete statement. And I must see this letter."

Suddenly Jeff felt awkward and out of place. He picked the letter from the desk, handed it to Quigley, and said, "Here it is. Hope you get a bang out of it."

"Do you mind if I sit down?" Quigley said. He took off his coat, laid it carefully across the foot of the couch, and dropped his hat on top of it. Then he found a chair, and moved it so the morning light would fall over his shoulder. He sat down, and read the letter, as methodically as if it were a new Department directive. Jeff could not sit down. He locked his hands behind his back, and took stiff paces in front of Quigley's chair. He was choking with scorn, indignation, and loathing. He was sure Quigley must feel his contempt, but if Quigley felt it, he didn't seem disturbed.

Quigley finished the letter. "Well, Mr. Baker, I think that explains everything very well. It doesn't seem to be so serious as I had imagined."

"You mean I'm not going to be hung, or boiled in oil?"

"This is still not funny, Mr. Baker. If the Admiral hears about it, he may want you flogged, keel-hauled and thrown into irons." The very smallest, most elusive bit of humor touched the corners of Quigley's mouth. It could not be said that Quigley smiled. It was simply that his face exposed an emotion. He rose, dropped the letter on the desk, and peered at the address on the envelope. "Susan Pickett, Bay State Apartments," he repeated. "Fine girl. Colonel Pickett's widow. Keeps her mouth closed."

"Do you know her?"

"No. I know of her. I know of almost everyone in the Department."

"I can see where you would," Jeff observed.

Quigley didn't appear offended. He looked around the room, and said, "Do you mind if I make a little inspection? I'm never happy in a room unless I know what's in it."

"Go right ahead. Make yourself at home," Jeff told him. "If you get bored, why there are some fresh personal letters, just arrived from Stateside, in the right-hand top drawer of the chiffonier."

"Thanks very much. I asume you have sense enough not to leave them in your room if they contain classified material." Jeff began to understand that Quigley could never be offended, or insulted. Quigley made a quick circle of the room, examining light sockets, the telephone box, peeping behind the radiator, testing the walls, sniffing with distaste at the locked door that once had made the room part of Madame Angell's flat. When he finished he said, "I suppose it is all right, but of course anyone could put a wire recorder on the other side of that door, and pick up everything that goes on in here."

"Do you think anybody would bother?"

"People do. In this day and time, Mr. Baker. In this day and time. If people minded their own business, Mr. Baker, I'd be out of a job."

Jeff found, to his surprise, that his indignation had burned out, and had been replaced by curiosity. "Tell me," he said. "How did did you know I met Major Lasenko in the *espresso* last night? Did Todd tell you?"

"No. Was Todd there?"

"He just poked his head in, saw the Russian, and then vanished as if we were carrying the plague."

"A very sensible man," Quigley said. "From now on, that should be a good example for you."

"Well, how did you know I was with Lasenko?" Jeff persisted.

Quigley sat down, placed a hand on each knee, and said, "Mr. Baker, I am a professional. There are some so-called security officers here—the ones whom Quincy Todd calls 'Dick Tracys'—who are not professionals. They are not fit to wear a Junior G-Man badge. They may once have been Alcohol Tax Unit agents, chasing bootleggers, or prison keys, or divorce snoops, or third-grade detectives in fourth-rate police departments. When war came they got themselves jobs in intelligence, or security, and now they have found a new bandwagon. They have discovered that it pays to be mysterious. They get a nice salary, and all-expense tours to Europe and Asia and South America, and unvouchered cash in large lumps, and neither the Congress nor Internal Revenue dare ask where the money goes because they are all chasing the Reds and anyone who questions them is meddling with national security and is probably a Red himself, or anyway a fellow traveler. They are wrecking my profession. I have been in the Department for thirty years, first as a courier and later as a security officer. Because I am a professional I know most of what goes on, and because I am a professional I cannot tell you how I know, because it might compromise my sources."

"I see," Jeff said. "Thirty years in the Department! I wonder if you knew my father?"

"Baker? Baker? The only Baker I knew was Nicholas Baker. He was an important man in the European Division."

"My father's name was Nicholas Baker, and he was in the European Division, but he was a clerk."

"So you're Nick Baker's son. I knew him very well. He was a friend of mine." Jeff noticed another subtle change in Quigley, hardly a change in expression, perhaps only a change in the cadence of his words. "And he was important. I'm sure that on occasion his influence directed policy. In those days the little, unknown men like your father insured the continuity of our policy. The Foreign Service Officers could take their weekends in New York, or Long Island, and their fortnights in Florida, or Bermuda or the Maine woods. But men like your father had to be at their desks every day, nine to six, and requests for policy from the Missions cannot wait. The Department is too big for that now, and the work too specialized. The little man can see only the smallest fragment of the whole. He should attend to his own job. I do. You should, too, Jeff."

"I am. I am doing the very best I know how."

"I'm sure you are. I'm sure Nick would be proud of you. You know, Jeff, Nick talked about you a great deal. We used to play cribbage together, some evenings after work, down in the tunnel that led to the White House from Treasury and he would talk about you. Now I think I'd better go. I'm going back to the Legation. May I suggest, Jeff, that you approach Quincy Todd, and ask him not to mention last night. I'd rather not have the Admiral know about it. The Admiral is sometimes hard to handle."

"I will," Jeff promised. "Do you mind taking this letter to the mail room, so it makes the pouch?"

"Not at all."

Jeff sealed the letter, and handed it to him, and said, "Thanks, Quig. Thanks very much." When Quigley was gone he flopped down on the bed and for a long time lay on his back without moving, staring up at the stains on the ceiling.

3

When at last he shook himself off the bed he knew something that he had not known before. The career for which he had prepared no longer existed, for him or anyone. The art of diplomacy, like many other things, lay buried in the radioactive dust of Hiroshima. Within Hiroshima itself there might be, within a few generations, mutations of the body. They would be shocking and ugly, but not dangerous. There had been more immediate mutations in the mind of man. His lobe of fear had abnormally grown, his confidence in a better future had disintegrated, his instinct for brotherhood and kindness was vestigial, his memory of the Sermon on the Mount was somewhere gone.

Even the character of the Department of State had changed. The Department had become a two-headed monster, and the head with a tongue was an instrument of psychological and political warfare.

It spoke of its power, its goodness, its planes, its ships, its bombs, and the weakness, the badness, the cruelty, and the totalitarianism of the enemy. The other head could only think, and dream—dream of the United Nations, and UNESCO, and world federation, dream of things that could have been, but which—like the Sermon on the Mount—were not practical.

He understood the way of it. There was the bomb, and there was this cold war. There was a saying: "When war begins, diplomacy ends," and the United States was at war. It was wrong to call it a cold war, as if it moved with a glacier's deliberation, or were safely encased in the freezing compartment. It was a war hot and consuming and dreadfully wasteful, a war fully munitioned with passion and hatred. Matson had been right. He had come here as a soldier. Once again he was a platoon leader out on the point, and he didn't like it any better than he had liked it before. Yet he would do his job, because it was in his spirit that he have pride in work well done, just as in the Army he had taken pride in Company, and Battalion, and Regiment, and Division, and later in the importance of his liaison between Ground and Air.

4

He missed Quincy Todd at the luncheon mess in the pension off Kossuth Lajos-tér, but he found him that night in the Park Club. The Park Club was at Stefánia Utca 34, not far from the Minister's residence, and the homes of Morgan Collingwood and others in the Legation. In the day of that economic cornucopia and political monstrosity, the Austro-Hungarian Empire, the cavalry of Franz Josef, plumes flying and breast plates gleaming in the sun, paraded this leafy avenue on Sunday afternoons and national holidays. In those days it had been the practice of the Hungarian aristocrats and foreign diplomats resident in Pest to step out upon the terraces of the Park Club—then an international casino—and admire the lancers and hussars.

Now the cavalry and the age had passed, but the Park Club itself miraculously had little changed, although there had been a remarkable shift in the nationality of its patrons. It was a social outpost of the West. Beyond the Park Club lay the East, and barbaric customs.

The Hungarian hosts were now far outnumbered by their guests, and the guests footed all the bills. The club was off limits, by mutual taboo, to Russians, Bulgarians, Czechs, Rumanians, Jugoslavs, and Poles, except those satellite nationals in disfavor with their Communist governments at home. These refugees were not seen often at the Park Club. One way or another, they vanished from Budapest, for them a perilous way station on the westward road. Most of the members were American and British, and there followed, in the order of their influence in the Western alliance, the French, Dutch, Belgians, Swedes, and Swiss. The Italians were split. The ones with titles preferred the Park Club, the others found their amusement elsewhere. The Hungarian aristocracy, and those business and theatrical luminaries who were socially acceptable, enjoyed the club's excellent cuisine and liquors, its dances and privately imported American films, whenever possible—providing they were already compromised by contact with the West, or in bravery or imprudence dared ignore the Communist displeasure.

Jeff found Quincy Todd in the cocktail lounge. George Fejer, the club's pianist, was rippling out "Civilization," and singing what he thought were the words. Fejer had a miraculous ear, and he could pirate a hit tune off American short wave, but sometimes the words escaped him and he made up other words which did just as well. Quincy Todd was dancing with Marge Collins, who was in cryptography, but they were entranced with Fejer's fingers and their feet were barely moving. Then Quincy Todd saw Jeff, and winked, and said above the music, "Oh, what you did!"

"I'm at Fred Keller's table. Come on over." Jeff saw the Collins girl's lips move, and saw Quincy shake his head, no, and continue shaking it, and so Jeff knew Quincy hadn't talked about the Russian.

He made his way across the dance floor, and Keller was at a table against the wall. "Come on over," he called to Jeff. "I've got someone here wants to meet you."

The someone must be the girl with Keller. "I'm on my way," Jeff said. She was the most striking woman he had ever seen. She seemed to illuminate the side of the room. It was apparent what kind of a body she possessed, for her silver lamé gown, which could only have originated in Paris, was slashed to the waist in unnerving angles. It was not her body which captured Jeff, but her face. "This is Rikki Telredy," Keller said. He held out his hand as a horticulturist might bring attention to a unique camellia. "Isn't she lovely? Rikki—Jeff Baker, one of my colleagues."

"Oh, I've heard of you," Jeff said, seating himself. "You dance at the Arizona."

"She is *the* dancer at the Arizona," Keller said. "I told Rikki last night that you were interested in the exchange of talent, and other cultural matters, between Hungary and America, and Rikki said she hoped you'd be here tonight, and here you are. I think you two will find a great deal to talk about together."

"I'm sure of it," Jeff said. Fred was bird-dogging a target for him. Fred was telling him that Rikki was a prospect for Atlantis Project. Fred was certainly generous with his women. He must be, as Quincy Todd had said, a dedicated man.

Then the piano's artistry ended, and a waiter brought fresh drinks, and Quincy and Marge came back to the table, and Quincy said, "Later."

"They've got secrets," said Marge Collins. "Those two have secrets together."

Quincy laughed and said, "Yes, we've got secrets—both of us."

Keller told the classic tale about the American correspondent who was pushed around by a Russian general, and his awful revenge. He cabled home reports that the Russian general—who actually was no more cooperative than any other Russian general, and less than most—was chummy with his Anglo-American opposite numbers on the Allied Control Council. The story was seen by the Russian Embassy in Washington, relayed back to Moscow, and the Russian was recalled, and presumably sent to Siberia. Jeff didn't listen. He had heard the yarn before, and anyway he was watching Rikki.

She was, he supposed, the perfect Magyar type, and in Hungary are born some of the most beautiful women in the world. The soft glow of the room fired her coppery hair with many tiny lights. Her cheek bones were wide and prominent, her face triangular, her skin golden as if she had carefully rationed her hours in the California sun, and yet there was no sun in Budapest at this season. Her nose was straight, and her nostrils so mobile that their movement changed her expression. Her full lips were never quite shut, so that she always appeared expectant. Her eyes were dark, and long and slanted. Jeff knew he was looking at a product of four thousand years of invasion and conquest, in which many armies and many races had rolled across the Danube at this gate to the West. In her he could see the Tartars, and the Mongol hordes of Genghis Khan; the Turk storming up the Balkan peninsula in a tide that ended only at the gates of Vienna; a trace of Byzantium, and a trace of Judea; Arpád the Conqueror leading his Magyars through the Carpathians out of the mysterious steppes; the arrogance of a Roman legionnaire; the chic of a French émigré; the legs of a Viennese actress. She was mixed by an old civilization. She was wonderful. She was European.

He asked her if she would like to dance, and she said not yet, that they should wait until the rest of the band came, and then they would do a *czardas* together. He said he didn't know how to do a *czardas*. He had always believed himself clumsy on a dance floor. He was of the jitterbug era, but he could never bring himself to try a dance strictly American, much less some wild Hungarian thing.

She said she'd teach him. He said, "You speak American English."

She said, "I've been dancing at the Arizona for ten years. The Arizona is exactly like an American club. All the tourists used to come to the Arizona, and when your Military Mission came to Pest after the war, it was their first stop. Even before food."

"I don't wonder," Jeff said. "I don't wonder."

He got a little drunk, because he was envious of Fred, and finally he dared a *czardas* with Rikki. Everybody laughed, and applauded, and Rikki said he danced very well, and he was drunk enough so that he believed her.

5

Then Quincy Todd summoned him with his eyes, and they left the table and went into the men's room. They were alone.

"All right," Quincy began, "give."

"You first," Jeff said. "Did you go back afterward and give her her language lesson?"

"Uh-huh."

Then Jeff told Quincy he had met Leonides in Bari, and run into him by accident, and there was nothing to do but bull with him about old times. Quincy Todd was satisfied. "I don't know what Morgan Collingwood would do to us," he said, "if he knew you were drinking with a Russian, and I was out with a Rumanian gypsy waitress. I really don't know."

"Just out with her?"

"That's all. She's a funny girl. Real moral. Nice girl, Marina."

"That Russian," said Jeff, "is a nice guy."

"So we both forget it," Quincy said. "Within these four walls."

"These four walls," Jeff pledged, and they went back to the table.

6

It was not until the evening was well along that Rikki spoke of the rumor. "I don't know whether any of you would tell me," she began, "even if you knew. But I heard it this afternoon at rehearsal. A high American official, flown secretly from Washington, had a conference last night with the Red Marshal. Here. In Budapest."

"Nonsense," Keller said.

"Oh, no, it is not nonsense," Rikki said. "They met in a restaurant. Some say a restaurant on the Vaçi Utca, and some say on Andrássy Utca. People saw them."

"Really?" said Quincy Todd.

"Yes. They talked of peace agreements."

"But there is peace," Todd said.

"I mean real peace."

"I can hardly believe it," Jeff said, because he was nervous, and because he felt he should say something.

"It must be true," said Rikki, "because all stocks went up on the Bourse this afternoon. And in the Black Bourse the forint rose. Yesterday the forint was twenty to the dollar, black. Today it is fifteen. Everybody is thrilled. Everybody is excited."

Quincy Todd looked at him in the oddest way, and Jeff asked Rikki to dance again, because he wanted her to talk no more of it.

7

It was two in the morning before he got to bed, feeling the fag end of his drink, and wishing he had another but knowing he'd be better in the morning if he took no nightcap. He dreaded hangovers. Not that his hangovers were any worse than anyone else's. It was that a hangover could kill your day. You couldn't think properly. Jeff liked to think. He liked the stimulus and exercise of thought.

He was turning out the light when Madame Angell came through his door. "The news!" she said. "The news!"

"What news?"

"I was just listening to Moscow broadcasting in Spanish to South America. Fancy what they said!"

"What?"

"They denied a report by the Swedish news agency that said the Russian Foreign Minister and your Secretary of State met here— in Budapest!"

"So what? So they denied it?"

"Then it must be so," said Madame Angell. "My flaming oath!"

"Don't you ever believe it!" Jeff said, and pulled the covers over his head. In a strange world, this was a strange city.

CHAPTER NINE

1

ONE DAY in mid-December the Admiral's secretary, a yeoman seconded to the State Department, called Fred Keller and said the Admiral would like to see him at once. Ordinarily the Admiral didn't issue such preemptory orders, through another party, to Keller. Ordinarily their discussions were informal, and held in the Legation residence over brandy or in the private corner at the Park Club which everyone called "admiral's country."

So Keller was disturbed. He was a little afraid of the Admiral anyway, although he was sure he never showed it, and certain that no one else could notice. When he forced himself to inspect this uneasiness, or fear, he only knew that the Admiral's hearty voice and didactic statements alarmed him. The Admiral could be wrong with loud and unchallengeable conviction. He told the Admiral's secretary he'd be right over.

2

Fred Keller was born June 1, 1909, in his father's town house. His father, who was always described as "the well known sportsman," was playing polo on Long Island at the time. This was to form the pattern between father and son henceforth. Fred knew his father only as a forbidding, overbearing, remote, and excessively masculine man whom he saw on occasions that grew less and less frequent. They were usually unpleasant occasions. His mother could not bear to punish Fred. This was exclusively his father's job when his father was around. In the end his father disappeared altogether with the woman Julia Keller called "that prostitute from Carácas."

Thereafter Fred never felt quite safe in the world of men. He never felt safe in the Admiral's office. The Admiral, now that he thought about it, reminded him of his father.

3

When Fred Keller walked into the Admiral's office he was careful to conceal his unease. It was necessary to treat the Admiral with respect, but also it was necessary to maintain equality. When the Admiral sensed that a man was afraid of him, or awed by his rank, then that man's life became miserable.

The Admiral pointed to a chair. "Sit down, Fred," he said.

Keller sat down. It was best to be silent until the Admiral showed what was on his mind. Keller was sure there was nothing wrong with his work. Everything was moving smoothly.

"Fred," the Admiral said, "I just got a confidential letter from a friend of mine in Washington. I can't tell you his name, but he's very high in the government. I've been thinking over what he said, and I think we'd better speed up our operations."

"You mean Atlantis Project, I suppose, sir?"

"Well, yes. That's about the only thing we've got going here that isn't routine. Everything else would rock along whether I was here or not, but I'd like to see something come of Atlantis in a hurry."

Keller knew that while the Admiral had his idiosyncrasies, he was politically shrewd. His career proved that. He had gone into O.N.I., which had once been regarded as the graveyard of ambitious officers, at precisely the right time. And now, when political and traditional warfare merged into one, he occupied a strategic post of command. Keller said, "I thought it was agreed, sir, that we should move slowly and with caution."

"Times change. Events move faster, and we have to speed up to keep pace. Besides, there's always the chance of competition." The Admiral leaned back in his chair. "What one man can think of, another can think of. I'd like to see us put this thing across first, wouldn't you, Fred?"

Now Keller knew what was up. In some other part of the world, somebody else was working on something approximating Atlantis Project. The Admiral, naturally, wanted the kudos that would go to those associated with the first success. Everyone remembered what Mark Clark and Robert Murphy had done in North Africa. Nobody remembered the names of those who built organizations behind the lines, later, in Italy, the Philippines, Belgium, and Burma.

"It may be dangerous to speed things up," Keller said. "We have to be sure of our recruits. We don't want to enlist any double agents. And remember that our own personnel isn't too experienced. This sort of thing is new to them, and—"

Keller hesitated, as he sought to frame words that would be clear to the Admiral, and yet not make him impatient and scornful. "And what?" the Admiral demanded.

"We have to remember that our own personnel is American. They have been brought up to believe there is something unclean about this type of work. Some of them don't like to use the Foreign Service as a cover. Fundamentally, they like to be frank and open."

"You have to fight fire with fire, don't you?" the Admiral said.

"Yes you do. But it takes a period of indoctrination."

"They've had enough indoctrination." The Admiral's voice showed the discussion was over. "I want to be able to report to Washington in one month that Atlantis has been formed, and is working. We've got to show results. You get that now, Fred, one month."

"Very well, sir."

"I don't want any slips."

"There won't be any, sir," Keller said, because he knew that was what the Admiral wanted to hear.

He felt relieved when he left the Legation. Nothing had gone wrong. The Admiral wasn't angry about anything. He was just requesting faster movement, as any commander might put ahead an invasion's D-Day. He shouldn't allow the Admiral to upset him like this.

4

One by one, that afternoon, Fred Keller called in the men on his team. They were, ostensibly, Commercial Attachés, oil technicians, financial experts, or in the offices of the Naval, Military, and Air Attachés.

He had assigned one to each likely field in the economic and cultural life of the country. They were seeking recruits against the day when there would be no American Mission in Budapest. They had been instructed to estimate these recruits carefully—estimate their political alliances, their balance, their discretion, their courage, their potential use and influence in the body of the city and the nation.

Keller, in keeping with standard security practice, called in the men of his team singly. It was not necessary or desirable that they know each other. This was protection against the possible unmasking of Atlantis from the lowest echelons. Each man on the team knew only what was necessary to form his own cell.

He didn't get to Jeff Baker until the following morning. He had purposely saved Baker for last. He had great hopes for Baker. For one thing the Budapest theater was traditionally a center of anti-totalitarian activity. And he had confidence in Baker's work. Baker seemed to show more imagination and perception than some of the others. Baker was a Princeton man.

5

Fred Keller lived in the Dohany Utca in an apartment which once had been the property of the Baron Toth. Wherever Fred lived he lived graciously. He knew the mechanics of travel and shipping, even in these difficult times. He had not been satisfied with Baron Toth's furnishings, and he had managed to get enough of his own stuff shipped across to do over the living room and master bedroom. He felt at home here. Surrounded by familiar objects—selected by his mother years ago—he felt secure and safe.

At nine o'clock he called Baker and told him to come over, "whenever you have the chance," but in a tone that would let Jeff know it was important. Baker said he'd be thirty minutes.

Keller told his butler to run up coffee. He himself preferred tea in the mornings, but he knew Baker drank an inordinate amount of coffee. He told the butler to dust the living room. He had the best butler in Eastern Europe, wooed away from the British Embassy by paying wages in dollars instead of pounds. But sometimes the butler was careless with the morning dusting. Keller could not abide a living room begrimed with ashes and disheveled with empty cups and glasses in the morning.

He changed his tie, and took off his lounging robe, and put on a sweater and sports jacket. He examined his hair in the bathroom mirror, and touched his temples with a dark liquid. He was too young to show gray.

He wondered how far Jeff Baker had progressed with Rikki Telredy. He discovered he had difficulty in imagining Baker as a lover. In one way Baker seemed only a lank and immature boy, and yet he possessed that lacquer of sophistication, that outer hardness, that comes to those who have been part of a conquering army. He found it difficult to estimate those kids. It was strange how little one man knew of the inner life of another man.

6

When Jeff arrived, the room was dusted and immaculate, and the coffee made. "Forget your hat again?" Keller greeted Baker.

Jeff put his hand on top of his head and said, "I did, didn't I?"

"There's really no harm to it, forgetting your hat," Keller said. "Except it makes you conspicuous. In this town a man without a hat, particularly an American, is conspicuous."

"I'll try to remember," Jeff promised.

Keller asked him how he was progressing, and Jeff told him fairly well. "Offhand," Jeff said, "most of the theatrical people dislike the Russians and like the Americans, and they aren't bashful about saying so. But I haven't been making any judgments on words alone. I've been trying to test their inner loyalties by presenting problems and situations and observing their reactions."

"That's smart," Keller agreed, "but we'll have to move faster from now on."

"I can't say," Jeff said, "that I'm sure of more than a few yet. Sure enough to ask them to join Atlantis." He had indexed them all in his head—the good, the doubtful, and the bad. Most were doubtful. Only a few were bad. Budapest had seen the Red Army. Perhaps it would have felt the same towards any army that in smoky-eyed anger and brute passion broke into the citadel of its civilization. Perhaps any army would have sacked and raped, and piled up its debt of hurt and hatred, had it rolled into the city over a carpet of its own dead, and with the memory of its own sacked and raped cities standing in its eyes. Jeff had seen Buda's suburbs of the dead—the acres of small wooden pyramids with the wood cracking and the red paint flaking off them as if they had been jerry-built in the boomtime of death. The army Budapest had seen was the Red Army, and Jeff deduced that was why most of the people were on the side of America.

"Well, how do they stack up—your theatrical people?" Keller inquired.

Jeff had listed, in his mind, something akin to a salesman's list of prospects. Now he ran through this list for Keller—the singers, composers, fiddlers, dancers, directors, playwrights, exhibitors, actors, producers.

"You ought to be able to do something with that Zukats," Keller told him when he had finished. "I should think he'd be completely dependent on Hollywood."

"He may be," Jeff said. "But he's a smoothie. I'm seeing him again this afternoon."

"And Miss Genghis Khan—what about her? You shouldn't have any trouble with her. She wants to get to America." Everyone in the Legation called Rikki Telredy Miss Genghis Khan.

"Oh, I'm sure she'll be all right," Jeff said. "Should I put the question to her? I'm seeing her tonight."

Keller smiled. "Seeing quite a bit of her, aren't you? All business, Jeff?"

Jeff wondered whether he had been poaching on private property in seeing Rikki so often. Sounded like it. Yet she always seemed willing to date him. "Well, you see," Jeff explained, "Miss Genghis Khan is especially useful because there isn't anybody she doesn't know."

"Now don't worry, Jeff," Keller said. "See her as often as you like. All of us have to sacrifice something, and I guess I can sacrifice Rikki."

Keller knew that Jeff would consider him most magnanimous. Baker would consider him a man who had so many women that he could give up a girl as beautiful and interesting as Rikki casually as he would hand a package of cigarettes to a guest who was out of cigarettes. Baker would look up to him as a man of the world, a man who was irresistible to women.

That was exactly what Jeff thought when he left the apartment.

CHAPTER TEN

1

JEFF WENT HOME and got his hat. He also changed his shirt from blue to white, and his tie to polka dot, and his suit from tweed to the best blue. Miklös Zukats, who owned five cinemas in the city, a stack of gold Swiss francs in a vault in Geneva, and a packet of RKO and Paramount stock in another vault in New York, regarded Jeff as a special emissary to him from Washington, and so Jeff dressed the part.

The masquerading always made him feel a little shabby, a little dirty. Along the Rakoczi and Andrássy Utcas Jeff had allowed it to become known that he was attached to the American State Department's Office of Information and Educational Exchange. He was interested in the showing of Hollywood's product, and the Department's own documentary films, in Hungary. He was interested in the exchange of theatrical talent, an enterprise that had once been normal and mutually profitable for both countries, but which now had become difficult and usually impossible. After the seizure of government by the Magyar Communists, the trickle of travel reopened in 1945 had steadily congealed, year by year, in the cold war.

Since his cover was readymade, perfectly fitted, and in the fashion of the times—for cultural propaganda was openly practiced by both sides—he was accepted without question for what he pretended to be. This made Jeff feel guilty, although he knew there was no reason for it. A cover was a normal device of political warfare. One couldn't go around announcing, "I'm trying to get people to form an anti-Communist underground." If you did that, all your friends would soon be dead.

2

Jeff was always welcome in Zukats' office in the Rakoczi, although sometimes Jeff suspected it was only because his presence boosted the exhibitor's ego. Zukats regarded himself as a cosmopolite and citizen of the world. His office was decorated in Italian modern, which is perhaps more modern and extreme than Los Angeles modern. Copies of *Life* and the *London Illustrated News* were carefully exhibited on the chrome-legged table. He read *Variety* every week, and consequently was considered the Hungarian authority on advancements in the English tongue and affairs of the theater in New York and London. If an American diplomat visited his office to talk films, then the darkness could not be closing in around him. The world wasn't going to pot. It was only his imagination.

"Well," Zukats greeted Jeff this day, "did you hear what's happened now?"

"You mean the fighting in the Near East?" Jeff said. "That's hardly news."

"Oh, that business!" said Zukats, waving it away with a gesture of two fingers. "Let's not talk about it. No. I meant Lana Turner."

When Zukats met a political subject face to face he averted his mind, and his conversation crossed the street. This annoyed Jeff, but Jeff knew he could not afford to be annoyed. Zukats was important. He was important because of his money power in the Budapest theater and his connections with Broadway and Hollywood. Jeff saw him as a potential financial clearing house for the cell Jeff hoped to plant within the city's organism—a cell that would come to life on the day when neither he nor any other American remained in Budapest. Jeff said, "I didn't hear about Lana Turner."

"Again she is in trouble with her studio," Zukats said. "And me twitching for her!"

"You what?"

"As you say, I have a twitch for her. I like her. She draws. She is B.O. Also in Hollywood three years ago I met her personally. Such gams. At the same party I met the great producer Goldwyn. Such a great man! Never plays the red board."

"What do you mean?" Jeff asked, and told himself he'd have to start reading *Variety*. He'd ask Quincy Todd to make some sort of deal with the airline, so he could get *Variety*.

"It is not money alone he wants. He is hep to art."

Jeff opened a plastic cigarette box on the desk and took out a Camel. "Do you mind?"

"Please. Every week I have them shipped especially." Zukats winked. "There are ways."

Jeff congratulated himself. The communications lines of business always have a way of bridging the fissures of world disorder. But his instinct reined him in. "You know, Mr. Zukats, I think you ought to follow Goldwyn's example. If he makes good American pictures, you ought to show good American pictures."

"Oh, that again."

"That again. From the crap you show in your theaters the people of Budapest must have a peculiar opinion of America. They must think that one third of us are gangsters who own night clubs, and the other third cowboys, and the rest of us the dipsomaniac sons and daughters of millionaires."

Zukats shrugged. "It's good B.O."

"It isn't good propaganda. You're making it easy for the Communists. When you show pictures like that you're making Moscow's line sound true."

"You know how it is," Zukats said. "All your big stars are barred. They go and yap about the Communists, so they get barred here. It is their own fault. Why don't they clam up—Cooper and Taylor and the rest?"

"Something called the right of free speech," Jeff said. "Remember?"

"Does it do any good to have free speech, and no foreign grosses?"

Jeff tried his technique of testing loyalty by forcing a decision. "I can get you good pictures if you've got the courage to show them."

"What? Documentaries? Do you want me to go dark?"

"We'd rather have you show no American pictures than the ones you show now."

Zukats leaned back in his chair and folded his plump, pink hands across his stomach. "You know that I am your friend. Why, I am almost an American. You know that without American pictures half the houses in Budapest would go dark. Do you want to ruin your friends?"

"The time has come," Jeff said carefully, "when every man must take his stand. What will happen to you if war comes—or even if relations are broken? Where will you get your films then? What will happen to you when the state not only tells you what pictures to show, but owns all the theaters, and takes all the profits?"

Zukats' hands jumped nervously. "When war comes, I may not be here."

"You'll be here. Do you think that even now Rajk's police will let you out of the country?"

Jeff knew he had touched a sensitive spot deep inside Zukats' shell, for his dumpy body came out of the chair, and when he settled back again his usually pliable mouth was thin and tight. Jeff guessed that Zukats had already tried to leave Hungary—and failed.

At last Zukats said, "Now I will speak to you truly."

"That'll be a switch."

"Six months ago I applied for an exit permit. You know our exit permits?"

"Yes." No Hungarian could cross his border without one.

"I said I had to go to Hollywood to arrange for more pictures. They said no. I tried, then, with money. One hundred thousand forints! They still said no. So then I asked myself, 'What would the big men in Hollywood do if they were in my position?' I thought about this much, and I found the answer. Do you know what it was?"

"I haven't the foggiest notion."

Zukats rocked in his chair, and half smiled. "They would do what was safe. They would go with the tide. For five years after Hitler came to power did Hollywood notice him? No. Does Hollywood attack Franco, or Trujillo, or Perón? No. It is not safe. It hurts the B.O. At this moment it is safe for Hollywood to be against Communism, just as ten years ago it became safe for Hollywood to be against Fascism. But if there was a Communist government in Washington, what would they do? Why, they would make and show Communist pictures, of course. They would say to themselves, 'If we do not do it, somebody else will.'"

"I don't believe it," Jeff said, but in his heart he did believe it.

"Ah, I know them," said Zukats. "So I will tell you what I am going to do. So long as I can book American pictures, I will take them. Also I hope this talk of war comes to nothing. After all, I have more funds in dollars than in rubles. But if war comes, if the government takes over my theaters, it will be so arranged that I can still run them. I will do what is safe."

Jeff put his hand on his leg and squeezed until it hurt, because a diplomat never lost his temper. "Suppose, Mr. Zukats, that I recommended that my department request the American producers to stop sending you films of any kind?"

Zukats didn't stop smiling. "Nothing would happen, my boy. I don't think the producers would pay to your Department any attention. True, the best American films I cannot show. But we have still a good market here, and Hollywood will think of its foreign grosses."

Jeff rose. "Goodbye, Mr. Zukats," he said. It was disappointing, and surprising too, in a way. Zukats had such close connections with America. He dropped Zukats into the slot marked bad.

3

That night Jeff didn't call for Rikki until eleven because the floor show bored him except for her number. The Arizona's time of ascendancy had been the late '20's and middle '30's, and in this period it had been described as being resplendent as Ziegfeld's Follies, cosmopolitan as Zelli's in Paris, and wicked as a Port Säid dive.

During the war it survived as a safety valve for Nazi and Hungarian officers on leave from the Russian front, and it enjoyed a brief revival in the wild days of the '45 inflation when American and Russian officers bombed the stage with bundles of million-pengo notes. Now it had assumed the city's gray mourning in this taut, still period while Pest waited, in the eye of the hurricane. For two decades it had not been redecorated. Its draperies and furnishings bore the stains of six thousand nights of revel. All that had been spilled— champagne, cognac, Scotch, raki, vodka, Kentucky bourbon and Munich beer, many tears and some blood—all in time made the same brown stain.

The first three times he had seen Rikki dance his eyes had not left her, but on this night he watched the others who watched her. While she danced nothing moved except the pulse and throb of the music and Rikki. The dance she did was called new, and original, but it was old as woman. It is done, in variations, by many races, from the Ivory Coast to the Central Pacific. It is a simple dance. It has a clear and simple story, the inception, progress, and climax of an act of love. After Rikki did it in the Arizona it was her custom to remain for fifteen minutes in her dressing room, alone. It was her claim that otherwise she would not be safe, for the Arizona was still wicked. It was Jeff's belief that the dance exhausted her emotionally. She did it that way.

The Arizona was amphitheater-shaped, the tables rising terrace by terrace from the circular dance floor. Jeff was seated at a table three terraces above the floor, a table that he now regarded as his table. For minutes before he could expect her, he kept his eyes on the curtained door to the left of the stage. Finally she came out, conspicuous in the silver lamé, her well-kept but by no means new broadtail coat over her arm. She moved directly to his table. When Jeff rose and pulled back her chair he knew that all those in the Arizona—the too-loud and buoyant operators on the Bourse, the Russian captains and lieutenants, the gloomy Finnish importers, dark and suspicious Turks, the Jugoslav delegation from Cominform, the Russian propagandists of *Agitprop,* the sleek and effeminate Rumanians more interested in conversation than in their women—all these were watching him, and envying and hating him.

"Well, where tonight?" she greeted him. "The Park Club, I hope. I am hungry."

"You're always hungry, Rikki."

"If you did my dance every night, and other dances also, and rehearsed the new show two afternoons a week, and carried everything up and down five flights of stairs because of no elevator, and walked everywhere because of no car, you would be hungry, too. It is true that I eat three thousand calories a day—four thousand when I can get butter or fats. But do you see any fat on me? Look! Look, you Jeff!"

Jeff looked, and said, "Don't get me wrong, Rikki. You're not fat."

"I will have a drink—a raki—and then we will go to the Park Club and have one of those wonderful club sandwiches with ham, chicken, and turkey. Is that possible?"

"You know, Rikki, I never see you alone. We never have a chance to talk alone, and I have important things to say to you, Rikki. You know that." In her way Rikki could be as important to Atlantis as Zukats could have been in his. She was known to all the city, had entrée to every circle, and possessed the faculty of accumulating information. News and gossip never flew past her. But what he had to say to her, and ask her, he could say and ask over this table so long as the waiters didn't overhear.

"You can see me alone if you wish, Jeff. I think you have misunderstood me." She raised her eyes, so queerly slanted, so wise and yet so sensitive to hurt. The music started, and Jeff took her hand and led her down the terraces.

The Arizona's dance floor revolved, and this created a pleasant illusion for the dancers. Even when standing still, they had the sensation of smooth movement, and the faces at the tables whirled past without effort. So Jeff stood still now, and tightened his arm around her, so that her face pressed against his shoulder, and the perfume of her hair was in his nostrils, and he could feel the whole lithe length of her body against his. She put her hand on his chest and eased him away. "Take it easy," she said. "No hurry. If you want me, Jeff, I will go to your place tonight. But first we will eat. You have food there?"

"Canned stuff," Jeff said. "And it isn't much of a place. It isn't like Fred Keller's. It's only one room."

"One is all that is necessary."

"I'm not rich, like Fred."

"Are you really worried about Fred? Have you jealousy?"

"I don't know. I suppose so."

"Do you know what I do when I go to Fred Keller's? You will laugh." He could feel the laughter inside her under his hand. "But do not tell him I told you. He would be furious, and I could not go there any more. I take sun baths."

"No!"

"It is truth. Fred has the only American sun lamps in Pest. How do you think I keep my brown? Can I go to the Riviera, or Yalta, or the islands on the Marmara? And how do you think Fred keeps his wonderful brown? Every day he has his lamp."

Jeff was irritated, and he thought he must be jealous after all. "Is that all you do there?" he asked, again standing still and allowing the floor to dance for him. "Doesn't he look at you—or something?"

"No. Not even that. Fred is a dear."

Jeff wondered where he had heard that before, and he remembered that Susan had said the same thing, and he wished he hadn't thought of Susan. "So he's a dear," he said.

"What do you mean?"

"You know what I mean."

Rikki ducked an elbow and guided him expertly to an open space in the floor's center, where the movement was not so giddy. She said, "It is not something one should say unless one is certain. Usually a woman can tell instantly, but about Fred I cannot decide. This I know, that he does not make love to women. He has such a polite way. He is always so gentle with women. Women seem necessary to him, yet he does not love women. Everyone must love someone. So who and what does he love?"

"Beats me, Lieutenant," Jeff said.

4

There were shadows along the Revay Utca. Some of the shadows were black and solid and poised for movement, so Jeff carefully chained his jeep. Unless one chained his jeep it would certainly vanish. Even with chains, sometimes a jeep vanished, piecemeal, or entirely if one left it in the streets the whole night. He drove his own jeep now. He had discovered it was simpler, and perhaps more secure considering his job, to drive the jeep himself instead of using a Hungarian driver from the Legation pool.

Jeff rang the night bell for the elevator, and it made a great clangor, and Sandor came out from his room under the stairs, belting up his trousers. Ordinarily Sandor was surly and disgruntled when disturbed after midnight, but when he saw Rikki his eyes became bright and observant, and he pretended courtesy. This was the first time the American had taken a woman to his room. It was therefore, for Sandor, an important piece of news. In the morning—or perhaps this night by telephone—he would inform his district supervisor, who in turn would report the matter to secret police headquarters. Rajk's organization would turn it over, since it was an international as well as an internal matter, to the Russian *Ministerstvo Vnutryennik Del*. In time he would get an extra ten or twenty forints, and a good mark.

"If you need me later," Sandor said in German as they reached Jeff's floor, "do not hesitate to ring."

"Oh, we'll use the stairs. It's not bad walking down," Jeff said.

"It is not necessary. Always I am at your service, Herr Baker."

"We'll see."

They went into the room, and Rikki said, "I don't like that man. He has bad eyes."

"He's a bad man."

5

Rikki looked around the room, and slipped off her coat and Jeff put it on a hanger in the closet. From the closet shelf he took a half loaf of round brown bread, a box of crackers, jars of cheeses, a can of chicken, and tinned butter.

Jeff marveled at how she ate. She ate like a puddler off the night shift. When they finished, and Rikki was wiping the crumbs from the table, Madame Angell came in and said she'd heard them talking, and would they like tea. The water was already boiling. Rikki said Madame Angell was very kind.

Madame Angell brought the tea, and said Radio Lyon was very exciting that night. Radio Lyon reported a coup in Azerbaijan, and Russian troops in the area, and also massing on the Kars frontier. It certainly looked as if war could not be far off. Jeff said that was very interesting. Madame Angell wondered whether Jeff and the young lady cared to listen to Radio Lyon. Jeff said no thanks. Madame Angell said the situation was critical, and they should listen. This week had been like the week of Munich. Jeff found a box of hard candies he had concealed between his shirts, and presented it to Madame Angell. She went away.

Rikki climbed on the bed, and piled the pillows against the wall, and leaned back against them. "Now what is this private thing of which you wish to speak?" she asked, jibing at Jeff with the word, "private."

"This business of your going to America," Jeff told her. "Suppose it falls through? Suppose you have to stay here, and you are still here when war comes?"

"When war comes—how lightly you say it! You know only one side of war, you Americans. You cannot imagine how it is to lose your cities, your people, your country, to be degraded like slaves and hungry like beasts. I think you made a mistake with your atom bombs. The second one, you should have dropped on Chicago."

"*If* war comes," Jeff amended. Twice this day he had said, "when war comes," and it worried him.

"What will I do? I will try to live, and survive, as I did before. Also I will wish for an American victory. It would be better." She reached across the bed, took an ash tray from the table and placed it beside her, and then added, with candor and simplicity, "You see, my Jeff, I was raped by a Russian. Perhaps rape is not the right word. A Russian came into my home, and there was nothing else to do, although I think in the end he did not enjoy it much. I think in the end he was ashamed. It did not harm me, except the embarrassment for my mother and younger brother. They were also at home."

Jeff thought, now any American brother would have beaten that Russky into a pulp. He said, "Your brother—didn't he—"

"No. I am glad. My brother still lives."

Jeff sat on the edge of the bed, close to her. The time had come for the question. "Rikki, would you do more than wish for an American victory? Would you act? Would you fight for our freedoms—yours and mine—after I was gone?"

"Do you mean would I be an *espione*—an agent?"

"Perhaps not that." Here he must choose his words carefully. She knew what he was doing too. He was asking her to lay her life on the line. "If there was a Hungarian underground, would you be in it? Would you help us? Would you be on the side of the West?"

She looked at him out of the corners of her Asiatic eyes, and Jeff wondered whether any man could long hold a secret from her. He thought, what an intelligent, what a perfect agent she would be. "I will answer you," she said, "but before I answer there are things I must say to you that you will not like."

"Go ahead. I can take it."

"Not about you. About your country."

He was silent. He didn't like people to be critical of his country when they had never been in his country, and he knew she was going to be critical.

"In the beginning," she said, "I must tell you how I once felt about America—like the Moslem dreams of Heaven, like that. I came here from Debrecen, a town in the east. You know it?"

"No." He wished she wouldn't get so serious so fast. She was like other European girls he'd known. They took their love affairs casually, but their politics seriously, which was just the opposite of most girls back home.

"It is a place of mud and swine and wheat. It is necessary to Pest, but it is not known to Pest. So why should you know it? I had danced in Debrecen—I was queen of the *czardas*—and an uncle gave me the money to come to Pest. First I danced at a little place which like the Arizona is on the Nagymëzo Utca. I danced there five years. Ten years I have been at the Arizona. I am thirty-four. Do I look it?"

"No. You look much younger." This was true.

"All this time I thought of America. You know how it is in my profession, Jeff. You can be the greatest dancer in the world outside of New York, but until you dance in New York you are nobody. So I thought of America, and I studied America—yes, your history, written in English—and I talked to Americans who came to the Arizona. They were so happy, so generous, so impetuous. They had such truth in them. Some were from New York and Hollywood, seeking talent. There is much talent in Hungary. I was offered jobs. I did not take the first offers. I had advice from Hungarians already in America. They would write me, do this; don't do that. Finally I took an offer. A year's contract. In that same week the borders closed. We became a province of Germany."

Jeff rebuked her. "That wasn't America's fault. That was your own lack of guts."

"You people—" said Rikki. "You have never had the pistol against your head! Anyway now I do not feel the same. We have talked much about me going to America, Jeff, but I do not know truthfully whether I wish to go. If I knew I could go tomorrow, I might not go."

"Why not?"

"You have changed. Something has happened to you. You are not the same." Rikki moved angrily. "All at once it seemed to happen. I was in Linz for a special engagement—yes, you Jeff, for a Nazi—when your troops came there. They were so wonderful, Jeff. You have no idea."

She put her hands over her breasts, and shook her head as if to toss out words that would not come easily. "What happened to those men, Jeff? Where did they go? Do you keep all your good ones at home? You will not answer me, no?"

Jeff didn't say anything. He could not help comparing the quiet dignity of the men of the 339th with the uncertain boys, afflicted with a conqueror complex, whom he had seen in the Vienna occupation.

"Later that same year—it was 1945—" Rikki went on, "I walked into your finance office—yes, the finance office here in the Mission on Szabadzag-tér—and I saw one of your officers. Do you know what he was doing, Jeff? He was looking at rough diamonds through a jeweler's glass. And the shelves of the office were lined with cameras, and watches, and binoculars like a pawn shop. This was the time for the pengo inflation, when we were stripping our fingers and our closets so as to eat, and it was possible for one with dollars to make a profit on our misery. I was sick. I cannot forget."

Jeff Baker had always believed in the intrinsic goodness of his country and his countrymen. America might make mistakes, but they were mistakes of judgment, not of the heart. This girl, Rikki, was saying his heart wasn't right, and he didn't like it. But all he could think of to say was, "There are bad apples in every barrel."

Rikki said, "It is not money that we ask from America, Jeff. It is something of the spirit. You had it once. Where did it go? You were climbing to the stars, and stretching out your hands to pull us up with you. But now, your eyes are on the ground just before you —not a meter more."

Jeff was growing angry. "What about ERP? What about that? You've been listening to Soviet propaganda, Rikki."

"Of course I listen to Soviet propaganda, to British propaganda, to American propaganda, to all other propaganda. We Europeans understand propaganda. We have learned to separate the fact, the motive from what we hear. We can smell what is hidden. We have been educated in propaganda by a master, Jeff—by Goebbels."

"Well, what about ERP?"

"It sounds good," Rikki said, "until one remembers the speeches in your Congress. One remembers how they haggled and bickered not only on how much should be given, but what should be demanded in return. I do not speak for Hungary. We have no right to your help, because we are in the Soviet orbit, and our stinking government would not and could not accept help and friendship if it was offered. I speak for your Western friends. What do you want of them? Would not peace and stability, payable to your children, be a fair rate of interest?"

"My Department isn't responsible for what is said in the Senate, as you are smart enough to know. You Europeans can never understand our free speech. You never believe that anyone in or out of public life, except in my Department and the Army and Navy, can say whatever he wishes about policy. That's what confuses you people."

Rikki made a face. "Your Department! Do you think anyone trusts your Department now? There were people who believed you. I did. What happened to the Four Freedoms? And the Atlantic Charter? And the United Nations? Do you know what I think now? I think your Department betrayed the United Nations."

"Rikki!"

"It is what I think. Your Department has no policy except the expedient, and fear of the Soviets. You can even be blackmailed by the Arabs. Your Department is the upholder of Franco, and the Argentine dictator. All over the world you support bad people. In China the corrupt ones, in Greece the worst of the reaction, in Turkey a police state as bad as we have here. Is it that your leaders are all old men, or cynics?"

"You like the Russkies better?" Jeff snapped.

"Don't be silly. There is one thing more. You. I thought you brought me here for one thing, and it is something else. Perhaps it is only my pride, but I did not come here to be enlisted as a spy."

He recognized that there was nothing more to say. He tried to keep his temper, but he said, "Okay, I guess this is where you get off." He took her coat from the closet, and she wormed into it with angry movements of her shoulders, and without speaking. They walked down the steps, she remaining one step ahead of him.

He helped her into the jeep, and then he got in himself, and wrestled with the heavy lock on the chain.

Finally he had the stubborn chain off the wheel, turned the key in the ignition, and jammed his foot down on the starter.

His next conscious action was raising his head and asking for water.

CHAPTER ELEVEN

1

It was not a big bomb. It was an absurdly small bomb. It was a petard, of no more power than an old-fashioned July Fourth giant cracker, and perhaps not as much as the plastic Red Devil grenades used by the Italians, so it is said, to frighten the enemy to death.

Its repercussions were felt in New York and Washington, but they were muffled by greater events and bigger bombs. For the world over, this was a bad week. The *Journal-American* got an eight-column banner out of it for one edition.

REDS BOMB U.S. DIPLOMAT

BUDAPEST, Dec. 17 (INS)—(delayed by censor)—Red goon squads today were blamed for last night's bombing of an American Legation automobile, and the wounding of J. W. Baker, of Washington, D. C., Legation Third Secretary. The bomb was planted in Mr. Baker's car while it was parked in front of his home on Revay Street. Baker will survive.

Admiral Randolph Blakenhorn, American Minister to Hungary, said, "This is an obvious attempt to frighten us out of the country. They won't get away with it. Baker is one of the most valuable members of my staff."

Admiral Blankenhorn will visit the Foreign Ministry to lodge a formal protest. He indicated . . .

The *Daily Worker* gave a different version, in a small box on page three.

BRITISH CAUSING TROUBLE?

BUDAPEST, Dec. 17—British agents provocateurs, or an aroused member of the Hungarian proletariat, were responsible for the bomb which damaged an American Legation limousine last night, Budapest police believe. J. W. Baker, a Third Secretary who was in the car, was unhurt.

Baker, police pointed out, was accompanied by Rikki Telredy, an actress. The bomb could have been thrown by a Hungarian patriot angered by Baker's attention to Telredy, or it could have been the work of British agents seeking to create an excuse for a diplomatic and economic attack on Hungary, according to the police theory.

The Minister of the Interior said the matter was of little consequence.

The *Herald Tribune* had the most complete story.

by Seymour Freidin

BUDAPEST, Dec. 17—(delayed by censor)—An American Legation jeep, clearly painted with American flags, was booby-trapped last night. Jeff W. Baker, Legation Third Secretary, suffered shock. His companion, actress Rikki Telredy of the famous Arizona Club, was uninjured.

A bomb was planted under the jeep's hood while it was parked in front of Baker's Revay Street residence. When he put his foot on the starter it exploded, blowing the hood back, and cracking but not splintering the windshield.

It is impossible to place responsibility for the bombing, and it is doubtful if the Communist-controlled Budapest police will make much of an effort. Anti-American Hungarians could have done it, or Red Army troops, or the police themselves. Or it could have been done by a gang of young hoodlums, or by frustrated car thieves who found the jeep securely chained.

Admiral Randolph Blankenhorn said . . .

2

When the explosion came Rikki could not see for a minute, and her nose and mouth were filled with smoke and fumes, and she was deafened, and if she screamed she did not know it. Then the first shock passed, and she thought of fire, and she groped for and finally found the lever that opened the canvas door and threw herself outside. Not until then did she think of Jeff. She didn't see him at the wheel so she looked in the back thinking he might have been blown backwards on the floor, and he was not there. She cried, "Jeff! Jeff!" and while she could not hear anything except a jumbled ringing in her ears she knew she was screaming as loud as she could.

She walked around to the other side of the jeep and she saw him. He did not look or act like Jeff. He did not look or act like any man she had ever seen. He was on his belly in the gutter and he was clawing at the dirt and stones in jerky, digging motions. He was saying words but what they were she could not understand, and in between the rush of words high-pitched sobbing sounds came out of his throat. She kneeled beside him in the slime and raised his head and talked to him in Hungarian as a panicky mother talks to a hurt child. She stopped talking in Hungarian, suddenly, and talked in English. "What's the matter, Jeff? What's the matter? Oh, be quiet, Jeff. Be quiet! I am here. I am here. It is all right. I am here. Oh, Jeff! Jeff! Please be quiet, Jeff. Please, please stop! Stop!"

He tore his head away from her hands and buried his face in the dark place between curb and gutter and Rikki rose and began to shout for help.

She shouted first towards St. Stephen's, at one end of the street, and then turned and shouted towards the Opera House at the other end, and then screamed at Jeff's house. In the short, dark length of Revay Utca there was no movement, no new light, no answering sound. There was only the babbling man, and the echo of her terror. She stopped screaming. She realized that the people of Budapest do not stir from their beds when there are loud and sudden noises in the night. When the lion roars in his kill, do the small creatures of the jungle venture out to see what has happened?

She turned to Jeff, and the noises still issued from him. She tried once again to lift his head, failed, and fell across his body, sobbing.

3

It was thus that the police from the station at 60 Andrássy found them. There were six policemen in this emergency squad. It was the squad that always went to the scene of bombings and shootings, and they knew how to handle it. They dropped off their truck alongside the jeep. Two men with rifles paid no attention to the jeep, but concentrated on the street and the surrounding houses, to guard against a trap.

The leader of the squad, a corporal, glanced at the girl huddled over the man. By his sound, the man was badly hurt. The corporal looked inside the hood of the jeep, smelled, examined the wires of the bomb, one twisted around a spark plug and the other attached to the starter wire. He saw how the explosion had blown the hood back against the windshield. The explosion had created its own armor, and he wondered how it was that the man was hurt. Perhaps he was shot. He saw the American flags painted below the windshield. This was going to be something, he could see. With this, he would have to be careful.

He took the woman by the waist and lifted her up and stood her on her feet, and when she continued to sob he shook her shoulders. "Shut up!" he said. She was quiet. Then he knelt on one knee beside the man and tried to turn him. The man resisted, and the man was tall and very strong. "Hey, I need help," he called. Two of his men came and the three of them forced the man over on his back, holding the arms so they would not be clawed. The man was a mess, and his eyes were wide in madness, and his arms and legs jerked and shook, but there was no blood. "I have seen this," one of the policemen said. "This is shellshock. This is battle fear."

"Yes," another said, "I have seen this too."

The corporal turned to the girl. "Were you in this Willys with him?"

"Yes."

"He is an American, is he?"

"Yes, he is American. This is his home here. Help me take him inside. He needs help at once."

"Not so fast," the corporal said. "He will live. How did this happen? Who is he? What were you doing in this Willys with him? Who are you?"

"I will tell you all that later. Help me get him inside. He must have a doctor."

"No, we will put him in the truck and take him to the station. A doctor can attend him there. We will take you too."

"*Mafla*—stupid ass," the woman said. "I am Rikki Telredy. I know Rajk. I know the whole government. You will do what I say or there will be trouble. I promise you."

The man was quieter now, and the corporal rose. "So you are Telredy?" he said. "Always you actresses go with the Americans. Why is it?"

"Perhaps they are better men."

"Or have more money," the corporal said. "All right, we will carry him inside. But we will wait with him until his own people come and give me a receipt for him. I will not be responsible if anything happens."

4

So they carried Jeff inside, and Sandor came out from under the stairs, his eyes blinking in excitement, and took them up in the elevator. They laid Jeff on the bed and wiped the filth from his face with wet towels, while Rikki telephoned the Park Club. She asked for Fred Keller and told him what had happened and he said he'd be right over with the Mission doctor.

Jeff was still babbling, but not so wildly now. When she spoke to him he still did not reply. She looked in the medicine closet in the bathroom. There were medicines there, but none that would help him except aspirin, and aspirin seemed silly. She saw a bottle of vitamin pills, and without thinking popped two of them into her mouth and swallowed them.

Until Fred Keller and Quincy Todd came with Major L'Engle, the Mission doctor, she sat on the bed, running her fingers along Jeff's temples, and shielding his wide eyes from the light. The policemen found Jeff's cigarettes, smoked, and grew bored. Every few minutes the corporal would think of a question, and she would answer in a monosyllable. When Jeff spoke now, she could distinguish words, but they did not make sensible sentences.

5

Major L'Engle was an Army Department doctor who had served in France and Germany, and later in a base hospital in England, and he knew combat fatigue when he saw it. "All right," he ordered, "everybody clear out!" He looked at Rikki. "You stay. I'll have to look at you later. Don't want any delayed shock."

The corporal wanted to know who was going to give him a receipt, and Fred Keller said he would. Keller said this was a most serious matter, and he trusted that the corporal would make a complete examination of the jeep, and make every effort to discover who was responsible. The corporal shrugged his shoulders and said it was always difficult in a bombing of this type. Also, once the criminals fled, it became a political matter, and therefore a matter for the secret police. No doubt the secret police would make an investigation. Keller and Quincy Todd both laughed. The corporal pocketed a pack of Jeff's cigarettes, summoned his men, and left.

"You two can stay if you want," Major L'Engle said then. "Just wanted to get rid of those monkeys."

He lifted Jeff's eyelids, and examined the palms of his hands. He loosened Jeff's collar, and pulled a blanket over his body. "He's got a bad dose of it," he said. "Look at his arms and legs. There's a lot working inside him."

"Bad dose of what?" Keller asked.

"Combat fatigue. Uncontrollable fear. It's a young man's occupational disease."

"It scares me," Quincy Todd said. "Can you catch what he's saying?"

"I wish I could use narco-synthesis," Major L'Engle said. "We're not equipped for it here. Looks like we ought to be, doesn't it? Haven't any sodium pentothal. But I'll cool him down with Blue Eighty-Eights."

"What's that?" Keller asked.

"Sodium amytal." Major L'Engle was a tightly knit man who wore a military mustache and he carried a military kit. In the bottom of his bag he found a fat, round, blue bottle. Into his hand he shook two pills, bullet-shaped, blue, and long as the end of a man's second finger.

"Can he swallow those?" Rikki asked.

"Sure. You get some water, Rikki. And you two fellows hold his arms when I'm ready."

The major cradled Jeff's head in one arm, forced the pills into his mouth and shook them into his throat, and made him swallow water after. It reminded Rikki of a veterinarian forcing medicine into an injured and frightened dog.

"What's he talking about?" said Quincy Todd. "Lot of Italian names, and something that sounds like fire coordinates. I never heard him swear like that before. Sounds like he's fighting a battle."

"He is," said Major L'Engle. "He's fighting a battle all over again."

"It must be hell to do that," said Quincy Todd soberly.

In thirty minutes Jeff's trembling was not so apparent, and his incoherent words were spoken thickly and slowly. Then at last he was silent, and his breathing became regular, and he slept.

Rikki began to cry, and Major L'Engle put his arm around her shoulders and said, "Now, honey, I'll have to find something for you."

She said, "I'm all right. I am perfectly all right. I want to stay here." Then she saw herself in the mirror. She looked her thirty-four years, and the three others she never mentioned. She looked all of them. "All right," she said. "I'll go."

"I'll give you a couple of pills. You can take them when you get home. Fred and Quincy will take you, and I'll stay here until he comes out of it."

"Is he going to be all right?" Keller asked. "I mean, this isn't permanent, it is?"

"No. Oh, no. He'll have to stay in bed for a few days, and rest for maybe a week. Then he'll be as good as ever."

"Suppose he has a recurrence?"

"He won't—unless he gets another bomb."

"We'll all have to be more careful. No more using a car without a driver. I'll get Quigley out of bed, and send him up here just in case."

"Yes," the Major said, "we'll all have to be more careful."

6

When Jeff lifted his head and opened his eyes his mouth was thick and parched and his head and face felt swollen and he asked for water. Then he saw L'Engle sitting on the edge of the bed, and Quigley in a chair close by. "Hello, Major. Hello, Quig," he said. "Christ, what a hangover! My mouth is full of goat wool. Can you hear what I'm saying? It's morning, isn't it?"

The Major had a glass of water in his hand, as if he had been waiting. Jeff drank, and said, "Where's Rikki? What happened?"

"You were booby-trapped."

"Oh. What about Rikki?"

"She's okay. Wasn't scratched. Wasn't much of an explosion."

"What happened to me?"

"Baker, that's something I can't tell you. You'll have to tell me."

"I don't understand."

"You must've had a pretty bad shock, in the war."

Jeff raised himself on his elbows. "Oh, that's it. I did have a shock, I suppose. No worse than others. Not as bad as some."

"Hospitalized for combat fatigue?"

"You mean did I crack up?"

"That's what I mean."

"No, I don't think so. They took me back to the station hospital in Florence, but then they decided I wasn't so bad, and they sent me to rest camp for a couple of weeks. You know the Fifth Army Rest Camp? The Hotel Imperial in Rome? Boy, was it wonderful!"

"Ever get any narco-synthesis treatment?"

"No. They didn't think I needed it." This wasn't precisely true. The medics in Florence had thought he needed it. But there were so many others in worse shape that when he'd pulled himself together, when his pride conquered his fear, they'd let him go to rest camp instead of base hospital.

Major L'Engle looked at Jeff's hands again. "I think they were wrong," he said, very quietly. "However, that's all past, and you are going to be all right, and Quig is here to see that nobody tosses any more bombs around. But if you were able to tell me everything that happened to you—the thing that sent you to the station hospital—you'd be better off."

"It wasn't much," Jeff said. "Some *Nebelwürfe* came into my position. That's all there was to it."

7

Of course that wasn't all there was to it, but it was all he could tell—all he could ever consciously tell.

When the 85th Division was assigned to take the heights commanding Futa Pass Jeff knew nothing of the grand strategy—nothing of the decision of the Combined Chiefs of Staff to order an offensive in Italy to contain the German divisions. All he knew was that the company would kick off at 0200 hours and his platoon would go first and their final objective was Mt. Altuzzo and he was to keep going until another wave leap-frogged him.

He also knew that he was afraid. He was always afraid in battle. There was no waking moment when he was in range of an enemy shell that he was not afraid. He was aware that he felt this fear more acutely than most of the others. It was his damned imagination that made him afraid. Whenever he was under the enemy's direct observation he could visualize a Kraut officer training his glasses on him, personally, and ordering a round. And he could imagine what he would look like after the shell had torn him up. He knew what shells could do to the frail and yielding flesh of man. He had seen.

And he was afraid because he was a smart soldier who kept track of casualty percentages in the combat infantry, and he could estimate his chances, which were never very good, and which got worse with every action. He was deathly afraid of mines and booby traps. He always tried to put his feet only on the fresh tracks of heavy vehicles. He never opened a door, or sat on a toilet in a newly captured village, without careful preliminary examination. His nerves were tuned to every sound of battle. The soldier who has an ear for battle—who can distinguish between all the sinister sounds with which death announces its arrival—lives longer.

He tried to conceal all his fears from his men. If his men guessed he was afraid, his platoon would go to pieces, and the company would suffer. The failure of a single small unit would cause trouble, and unnecessary casualties, all along the line. So every minute he was holding in his fear, for he had pride in his outfit and in the way his men regarded him.

In the late afternoon they rode in trucks almost as far as the regimental CP in Scarperia, hit the ground there, and immediately came under fire. You will remember that it was very dry in Italy that autumn, and the vehicles and the scuffling boots of the men raised a tattling cloud of dust as they pressed forward. Jeff cursed the dust, for he knew it invited shellfire. As he had expected, the German SP guns up in the mountains fired into the dust all the afternoon. At the crossroads in Scarperia Jeff lost his communications sergeant, who was an old and reliable friend, and from that moment Jeff was depressed, and had a premonition he would die.

In his progress up the Italian boot he had accumulated a number of fetishes. Twice, while whistling, shells had come in on him. Now he never whistled. He had shaved the morning of the first landing, and had come through the landing unhurt. So now he shaved before every battle, which his men thought curious and in some way proof that he was cool and reliable. In his pocket he carried a wrist watch that didn't run, because it had been with him in the first landing. And always, before battle, he said a prayer under his breath. It was very short and simple. "Please God, get me through this one time, and I won't ask again." The words were always the same, but he always knew he would ask again.

So they came to the jumping-off place, and flopped down in a little dry ditch shielded by dusty bushes. He had not known there would be a ditch there, and it was handy because the enemy's heavy machine guns were searching this ground, and his mortars were nervously working it over.

In the dusk when his silhouette could not be spotted he stood up on a mound and surveyed the place where he must go. It was the first line he had ever seen that looked like a line. In this light the mountains cleaved together, and became an unbroken wall, an escarpment that towered over him, so that he had to lift his chin high to see the crest. It did not seem possible that anyone could climb this wall in the night, much less fight his way up. "My God," he said aloud, "they're looking right down our throats!"

And he had then the conviction that even in this dusk with the mountains red in the west and black in the east they could see him. They were watching. They could see him coming. They were waiting.

His bazooka man said, "Ain't good, is it, Lieutenant?"

And Jeff said, "You never had it so good! Look at that sunset! Ever see a sunset like that?"

Jeff heard his bazooka man moving back along the ditch, and whispering, and he heard the muffled laughter of his men. He knew they would be repeating, "Did you hear what he said? We never had it so good! Ain't that rich!" So he believed his men were going to be all right, and he told them to eat and get their rest. He wished he could eat or rest, but he couldn't, for his imagination was leading him into black and fearful places.

Dark brought the storm. Behind him the earth erupted in barrage, and five hundred shells seared the sky, and the world trembled. He thought, thank God that stuff is going out. But whenever the fire slackened, he could hear the German shells come in with a crash like the short snarl of an animal. The one that landed in his platoon he did not hear coming. There was a crack and red flash and the whoosh of heated air and jagged iron. After he picked himself up and checked the line of men he found he must attack five men shy. And his own percentages had worsened.

He could not sleep, although the others seemed to sleep. He grudged each minute that slipped by on his watch (the one that ran), and he found himself wishing crazy things, such as how wonderful it would be if time would turn backward, and the minute hand would move the other way. He thought of yesterday, and wished he could live yesterday over again. He wished he could live it all over again, even the bad days, because no day could be as bad as this. He tried not to think of tomorrow, for there might be no more tomorrows.

The last hour was the worst, and his eyes hardly left his watch. Fifteen minutes before 0200 the guns all opened at once and he thought surely the sky must crack and fall in. The 4.2 chemical mortars beat their iron tom-toms not so far in front, and he was grateful for them, but he hoped they remembered to roll their fire up the mountains when he kicked off.

He sensed the men stirring around him, and he passed the word. When the minute hand touched the hour he said, "Okay, let's go." He climbed out of the ditch and moved forward, his body and mind concentrating on making himself small. Out of the corner of his eye he could see his men moving along with him, and he felt a measure of relief. Every platoon leader is relieved when he sees his men are with him.

Almost immediately he saw what would have to be done. There was a fence of tracer bullets across his path, coming from a machine gun on the left. He had been taught that tracers at night looked deadlier than they actually were, and you should ignore them and press on. This was probably a good theory until you actually saw the tracers. Then it was no good. He thought they should get that gun.

They did get the gun, and then miraculously there was no tracer wall to cross, and it seemed that they walked through a lane. There was fire and terror on both sides, but straight ahead miraculously it was not bad. So he walked straight ahead towards the deeper black that was the mountains. They went on until they were climbing, and Jeff wondered whether they had gone too far.

Then he saw the bulk of this hill and realized that he crouched at its very base. He thought it would be good if he went up this hill, although he had not been told to take any hills. He saw little red gouts of rifle fire from the top of the hill, and heard a burp gun working up there. He was surprised there was nothing else, but perhaps the shells had knocked out whatever else there had been.

His bazooka man said, "Where the hell you goin', Lieutenant?"

Jeff said, "Up the hill."

His bazooka man said, "I don't think we ought, Lieutenant."

Jeff said, "Come on."

Somebody in the darkness laughed and said, "You never had it so good, you lanky bastard!" And he could hear men laughing all around him and they went up the hill and at the top they found six Krauts, two of them wounded. They had to kill the Kraut officer, and the others gave up. The Krauts said they were from the Fourth Para Division, and had been expecting the attack for a week. They said they were all that was left of a company. The bombardment had killed all the rest. You could see that.

Jeff sent two men back with the three whole Krauts, and he instructed them to tell the Captain he had his platoon up on this hill, but he didn't know what hill it was. He was sure he had no flanks, so the hill would be hard to hold if there was a counter-attack and he suggested that the Captain bring up the rest of the company when the Captain found out what hill he was on. Also he needed a communications team. It would be best if they could get wire to the top of this hill, because he thought it would make a good O.P. But anyway he had to have a walkie-talkie.

He told his men to dig in.

In the early dawn he stared north and west until his eyes watered, and finally the landscape began to come clear. "Oh, Christ!" he said, and involuntarily ducked. It looked as if he could spit across to the top of Altuzzo. Directly opposite, on the level of his eyes, was the corkscrew road that ran up Altuzzo, and there were Germans on this road with tanks and self-propelled guns and queer-looking equipment. The guns were firing far behind him. He looked to the left, and there was Futa Pass, and it was below him, clear as an aerial photograph, and there was heavy traffic on it moving in both directions. He knew the Germans were using the last of the darkness to reinforce their positions. The men were now all looking at what he saw, and one of them said, "We never had it so good," but this time nobody laughed.

He did not fire on the Germans, because he did not want to attract their attention sooner than necessary. He waited for what he knew must come.

It came. They had received three salvos before Jeff realized from the color of the smoke that a battery of his own 105s was zeroed in on his position.

He was counting his dead, and shouting for the morphine syrettes for the wounded when heavier stuff began to come in, and this time the smoke was brown and he knew he had got his platoon under bombardment from both armies. He lay on the ground, the concussions hurting his belly, and prayed that the men he had sent back with the prisoners would get back. It turned out, later, that the men never did get back. They were never seen again, and were listed as MIA. Probably they were killed.

The bombardment grew worse. Steel fingers were tearing the hill apart, and digging for him—digging for him personally. For another hour they somehow lived, but by no means all of them lived. Jeff felt that each succeeding shell was creating a chemical change within him. He felt he would never leave this evil hill. He sent three more runners back, one at a time. Then the bombardment began to slacken. Jeff saw that the white and gray shells had moved on and were now breaking against the face of Altuzzo, but not on the road from which the German tanks and SP guns were firing.

He did not know that he was sobbing, and praying.

What finished him were the six heavy rockets, the *Nebelwürfe,* that fell around him. He was on his hands and knees when they came. The blast and concussion crushed him into the earth as a man's hand swats a fly.

After that he did not know anything until he awoke in the station hospital in Florence. They told him his men held the hill against a counter-attack, but this he did not remember. People called the little hill Baker's Peak, because it turned out to be important enough to deserve a name. People said we might not have got Futa Pass when we did, except for Baker's Peak.

Jeff stopped shaking after his two weeks in Rome. But for a long time a car's backfire, or the casual shooting that goes on in war even behind the lines, would send him face down and quivering in a ditch. So they made him a captain, and gave him a Silver Star, and attached him to Army HQ, which found good use for him as liaison officer with the 15th Air Force in Bari in the spring.

8

Of none of this could he speak, nor could he articulate his hatred of the insensate force that had pounded his will and courage from his body.

Major L'Engle understood all this very well, and he gave Jeff another Blue Eighty-Eight, and watched him until he again was fully asleep.

The Major put his things back into his bag, and washed his hands. "I'll be back in the afternoon," he told Quigley. "If he gets wild, call me at the Mission."

"Very well," Quigley said.

Jeff Baker rolled over on his side, and for a moment words gushed out of his mouth, and then he relaxed and slept again.

"Poor boy," Quigley said.

"Yes," said the Major. "Poor boy. He has a wound that will not heal, and for which there is no Purple Heart."

CHAPTER TWELVE

1

JEFF RECOVERED QUICKLY, as the Major had predicted, but they made him stay in his room. When his hands stopped trembling without the sedation of the Blue Eighty-Eights, Major L'Engle told him he could soon get back to his work. "But don't step on any more starters," he warned, "and don't get shot at unless you can't help it."

Jeff said he wouldn't, and Major L'Engle asked him whether he'd like to try the narco-synthesis treatment, which might help him. The Major could get the necessary drugs shipped out from the States. Jeff asked the Major whether he thought it was necessary. The Major said it couldn't do any harm, and might do some good. "Of course," he admitted, "you're never likely to have a shock like that again, so you'll never black out again the way you did. But if there's another war, Baker, I wouldn't like to be you."

"If there's another war," Jeff said, "I wouldn't like to be you either." The Major laughed at that, and Jeff said he'd think it over. Privately, Jeff didn't believe any more treatment would be necessary. Somehow he believed he'd licked this thing. He didn't believe he'd ever be quite so afraid again. Man was superior to explosives. Man had made bombs, and if man so chose man could banish bombs from the earth. He was better than a bomb.

2

Everybody was nice. Almost everybody in the Legation came to see him, or sent flowers. Except the Admiral. Jeff wondered why there was not so much as a note from the Admiral. Then Morgan Collingwood, the Consul General, dropped in on an afternoon, bringing with him a jar of Stateside jelly and some bouillon cubes.

Morgan Collingwood said he was glad to see Jeff was so much better. He said that as senior Foreign Service Officer on the post he would like to be sure that Jeff was comfortable, and safe, and if Jeff wished he could move into the Consul General's residence for a time. Jeff said this was very nice of Mr. Collingwood, and thoughtful, but he was perfectly comfortable here. Also, it was Quigley's opinion that the booby-trapping was an act of hooliganism, or general resentment, rather than a specific and deliberate attempt on his life. Jeff saw his chance to ask Morgan Collingwood about the Admiral. He tried to be casual, and remarked, "I haven't had any word from the Admiral."

Morgan Collingwood looked uncomfortable, as if his Herbert Hoover collar was suddenly a size too small. "It's most unfortunate about the Admiral," he said.

"What's unfortunate?" Jeff asked.

"Well, the way he looks at things. After a man has been shaped for four years at Annapolis, and forty more in the Navy, then he looks at things differently than we civilians."

"I don't get it, Mr. Collingwood." But Jeff could guess.

"Well, Baker, the Admiral isn't happy about your behavior. Do you want me to speak frankly?"

"I certainly do."

"The Admiral heard—from whom I don't know—that you did nothing to protect the woman you were escorting. He heard that you cowered in the street. Of course the Admiral hasn't said anything publicly or officially about his feelings. As a matter of fact he praised you at his press conference the other day. The Admiral called a special press conference. He wanted to be sure that a constructive version of the affair appeared in the press at home. But privately the Admiral is chagrined at your conduct."

Jeff tried to keep silent, but he couldn't. "That's too goddam bad," he burst out. "He can take one of his toy battleships and he can—"

"Now, now!" said Morgan Collingwood. "That sort of talk won't do you any good."

"No, of course not," Jeff said, "except it makes me feel better. Didn't Major L'Engle explain—didn't he explain to the Admiral?"

"Yes, he explained, but it only made it worse." Collingwood leaned over the bed as if what next he had to say was confidential. "You see, the Admiral said he didn't believe you'd had an injury in the war, because there was nothing in your record to show it. And anyway, he claims there isn't any such thing as combat fatigue. He quoted General Patton, and he said General Patton ought to know. Remember, Baker, I'm only telling you what the Admiral said. This isn't necessarily my opinion. As a matter of fact it is not in accord with my own feelings. He said combat fatigue was only malingering, or cowardice."

"Well, he can have his opinion," Jeff said, "and I'll have mine."

"Now that's being sensible," said Morgan Collingwood. "Just continue doing your job, and say nothing about it, and I'm quite sure he'll get over it. I understand you received a decoration. It might be a good idea to wear it at our next formal function—I think we're entertaining the French and British in a few weeks."

"You mean one of those little enamel dingbats?"

"Yes, a little pin for your lapel."

"I don't know where mine is," Jeff said. "I'm not sure I packed it."

He didn't say he had never worn it, because he could never be certain he had the right to wear the Silver Star.

3

He received cards from most of the Missions in Budapest, but none from the Russians, the Jugs, the Bulgars, or the other satellites. The Hungarian Ministry of Foreign Affairs sent him a stilted, insincere note of regret.

He received two cables. The one from Horace Locke said:

RELIEVED HEAR YOU NOT BADLY INJURED STOP WOULD APPRE-
CIATE LETTER.

Jeff felt guilty because he had not written to Horace Locke, and a little foolish for not having thought of him as a confidant, now in this time when he needed an utterly reliable friend in the Department. Should he confide Leonides' conspiratorial plans to Horace Locke? Could Horace Locke get to the Secretary, if necessary?

He should imagine that Horace Locke could get to the Secretary. After all, Locke had once been a Chief of Division, and an important man in the Department.

He thought Horace Locke might be his man. There was about Horace Locke an almost Biblical aura of unswerving decency and righteousness. Just like his father.

But there was the difficulty of secure communications with Locke. It would be so much easier if he could tell someone in Budapest. The Admiral he must count out, now. Morgan Collingwood, he feared, would be shocked because it was unorthodox and without precedent. Collingwood might be frightened into blatting it through the whole Department, or freezing it forever inside himself. Quincy Todd and William Quigley were reliable, he was certain, but they would have difficulty in conveying the information to the high quarters where it could be evaluated and a decision reached. Perhaps Fred Keller was the man. He had brains, imagination, and he was top level. But in Leonides' words, he did not know Keller's insides.

The other cable said:

> DISMAYED HEAR OF ATTEMPT ON YOUR LIFE STOP JEFF PLEASE
> PLEASE DONT LET ANYTHING HAPPEN STOP AM WRITING FULLY
> LOVE
>
> SUSAN

This cable worried him, and yet in a way it made him feel good. She had committed herself entirely. She wasn't just shocked. She was dismayed. He had become part of someone else.

4

Every afternoon when she was not rehearsing Rikki came to see him. Sometimes she brought flowers, and sometimes books from her own library, books printed in the United States, their pages limp from much handling. Some, like *Look Homeward, Angel,* had been published twenty years before; Jeff had read it but it was good to read again. She wondered why no new American books could ever be seen in the stalls, and Jeff explained to her that in this new kind of war books were considered weapons. They were time bombs planted in the minds of men. Wherever the Soviet controlled, American books were dangerous, and were if possible exterminated.

She came to see him on his last day in bed. He marveled at her chic, her smartness. She wore a blue suit labeled Fifth Avenue but without a Fifth Avenue label. She told him it was an American Army blanket, traded in the black market in Vienna, smuggled across the frontier, sold at a fantastic price in Budapest, and then cleverly dyed and cut by men who loved their craft, and who would use all their skill on blanket wool, for it was the best material available. He wouldn't believe it. She took his hand and made him feel the cloth.

"It is blanket," he admitted. "It's amazing." He took his hand away.

He was sitting up in bed, with the pillows piled behind him, and wore a robe of white toweling. She leaned towards him, and plucked at the threads of the robe. "This matter of which we were speaking," she said. "This matter over which we quarreled—"

"What about it?"

"I will do what you want me to do, Jeff."

"That's fine, Rikki."

"Anything you want, I will do."

"There isn't anything to do right now. I just wanted to know how you felt." He knew what she meant.

Then she sat up straight, her head resting exactly on her straight spine, in the manner of dancers. "Every time I think I understand you Americans," she said, "I find I am mistaken. The ones with wives and four children far away across an ocean, they will chase me. They will tell me they will divorce their wives and forget their children for me, which of course I do not believe but that is what they will say. But you, who have no wife, you hesitate, you shake —look at your hands—you have disturbances of the brain, you have a churning inside you. What is wrong, you Jeff? What is this woman you have back there?"

"She's just a girl."

"What is her name?"

"Susan."

"Susan." Rikki considered the sound. "So plain."

"She isn't plain. She's very complicated."

"And all the time you are here, she expects you to have no other woman?"

"I don't think so, she's very liberal, and broad-minded."

Rikki smiled, and showed the tip of her tongue between her teeth. "I would like to meet that Susan!" she said. It was afternoon by the clock, but the night comes fast in Budapest's winter, and the darkness had come.

Soon Rikki would leave, and he would be alone, and lonely with the loneliness of one who is hurt and far from home, the deep double loneliness of the traveler in a strange city and the alien in a foreign land. He said, "Rikki, come here."

She said, "Wait." She turned off his bed lamp, and in the blackness he could hear the rustle of her clothes, and then he felt her weight upon the bed.

5

Jeff was up and dressed when Major L'Engle came in the morning. The Major gave him the usual examination, and then he told Jeff to hold out his hands, palms up. Jeff held out his hands, and the Major laid a newspaper across them. The edges of the paper did not tremble.

"You've progressed a long way in twenty-four hours," the Major said. "All of a sudden, you're completely relaxed. Haven't taken any drugs, or anything, have you?"

"Oh, no," Jeff said.

"You look fine."

"I feel fine."

"I didn't think you'd be this relaxed in a month."

"Didn't you?"

"No. You can go out of the house today. Take a little walk. Not too far. Your legs will be a little wobbly. You can go to work tomorrow."

"Good."

Major L'Engle put on his muffler and overcoat, and felt in his coat pocket. "Almost forgot. I brought your mail from the Legation." He brought out a fat packet of airmail, compressed by rubber bands. "These ought to keep you busy a while. You must have a lot of friends back home."

6

Jeff opened them, starting from the top, with the impatient eagerness of a small boy tearing through a pile of Christmas presents. There were a surprising number of letters from people he didn't know. Most of them were warm and sympathetic. They wanted him to know that the people back home were behind him. If worse came to worst, the Reds would be paid back tenfold for every injury and insult to an American. They hoped for his speedy recovery.

There were others who wanted to know what he was doing wasting the taxpayers' money gallivanting around with a Hungarian actress. If he got killed, he probably deserved it.

Three letters, from women, enclosed photographs, and suggested that what he needed was a good, wholesome American girl. Would he correspond with them?

There were letters, and cards, from old friends in the 339th. They wondered what had ever become of him, and hadn't he had his bellyful of war?

There was a forgotten bill, a year overdue, from a Washington flower shop, with a curt note saying, "We see by the papers that you are in Budapest. Unless this account is settled, it will be referred to your employers."

There were two notes from strangers requesting small loans.

There was a letter from Susan.

"Dear Jeff—

"I was in New State cafeteria, having my coffee before the nine o'clock conference, when I saw your picture looking at me from the front page of *The Post,* and all I could see in the headline was the word, 'bomb,' and for a long time I didn't dare read it. I thought, 'This can't happen to me—not twice in a lifetime.'

"But I hear from Gertrude Kerns—she's my friend in the Balkans Division—that a dispatch came in saying you were getting along fine, and would soon be back on your feet. Thank God! Oh, please, Jeff, be careful!

"I am enclosing clippings from *The Post, Times-Herald, Star,* and *News.* What really happened? Every story is different. Who was responsible?

"You will notice that the *T-H* has a photograph of that Hungarian actress, Rikki something-or-other. She looks sort of slinky. I'd never trust a person with eyes like that—man or woman. Now don't get the idea that I'm questioning you about her, because I'm not.

"Jeff, you know we didn't do much talking about us. We never had time. I don't know when we ever will have time. Judging from the news, time is running out on us.

"Terrible things could happen, Jeff. If it came, you might be captured and interned. That would be a terrible thing, but bearable. I would wait for you, dear. But with so much violence already, who can say whether anyone will pay any attention to the laws of war, and the Geneva Convention, this time?

"Remember how fearful I was? How afraid I was to have you?

Now I have changed. I want you, while time remains. I think of the line from Omar: 'The Bird of Time has but a little way to flutter —and the Bird is on the wing.' I find I'm beginning to agree with Omar now.

"I am going to make a suggestion. I don't know whether you will like it or not. It is by no means a démarche. If you do not agree, I will still be here. I will always be here for you.

"Jeff, I am afraid there is nothing left for you to do. We both feel the same way, dear, but there is nothing either of us can do. All the words have been said at Lake Success (what an ironic name for the place) and all the speeches have been broadcast, and all the notes sent and rejected, and all the treaties made and broken.

"I despair.

"And so, Jeff, I suggest that you resign from the Department and come to me.

Come to me, Jeff,

Susan."

He put the letter with the others on the leather-topped Italian desk, and yanked his overcoat out of the closet. He felt that he must get away from that letter. Why had she written it? Why had she put into hard, clear, written words what he dared not even think? And anyway he felt like a heel and wanted to get out of the room. Logically he shouldn't have a conscience about Rikki because he had only done what any other man would do if he had the chance. Yet he did feel ashamed. Susan's letter made him ashamed and he needed to get away from it.

7

Outside, he turned to the right on Revay Utca and walked towards St. Stephen's. He stopped before the butcher shop to look at the rabbits and hares dangling head down from the hooks in the window. Every day the smell of rabbit goulash oozed under his door from Madame Angell's kitchen, and when he looked at the rabbits he could still smell it. Rabbit had become the staple meat of the city. The Hungarians said it was better than the year before. Last year rabbits had been scarce.

He tried to push Susan's letter out of his mind, and consider the economics of food. The rabbits were in the window because there was a schism between farm and city in Hungary. There were many schisms in the world, and each new one seemed to open another crack in the elaborate machinery of civilization, like chain reaction. They all stemmed from the primary schism between East and West. Hungary was of the East. Its forint was no good in the West. Its forint could not buy anything outside its own borders. Would the British and Americans accept forints for automobiles, and tractors, and machine tools, and blankets? Of course not. The canny Hungarian farmers did not trust the forint. The farmer wanted only enough forints to buy what could be bought inside Hungary, and this was not much. It was no use hoarding or saving forints. Remember what had happened to the pengo? It was better to hoard the solid things that come out of the ground. So the farmers sent to Budapest only what they were compelled to send. They held as much as they could. It was said there was more grain buried under the barns of the *holds* than ever came to the city. Like everyone else in the world, the Hungarian farmers were looking out for themselves. Because in Moscow there were secluded, badly informed, frightened men possessed of a mad vision, and in other capitals were small men of small vision and perhaps equal fear, because of this he had to walk around Budapest smelling rabbit.

It was all sort of crazy. It was as if the inmates of an asylum had locked up their keepers and formed a bureaucracy. And it could get worse. When war came—if war came—it would be like a football game played with Schmeisser machine pistols. At the end of the game all the players would be dead, most of the spectators would have holes in them, and the score would still be 0-0. Perhaps, as some of his friends hopefully predicted, they wouldn't use atomic weapons, or germs, just as in the last war they hadn't used gas. Well, in that case the war wouldn't settle anything. It would be like playing without putting in the first string team. It would simply mean that it would be necessary to play the game all over again.

If it was going to happen, it would be the smart thing not to go up that hill. It would be smart, while time remained, to resign and have what fun he could. And his mind was back to Susan's letter again.

8

He saw St. Stephen's enormous dome looming above him, and in a way it reminded him of the Capitol, for the dome was almost as tall and just as massive. He knew, then, that he was going to go into St. Stephen's. He had not been inside a church, to pray, for a long time. He had visited the abbey at Cassino, which had seemed like a planned Roman ruin with its skeleton whitened by two weeks of shellfire and bombs instead of two thousand years of weather. He had looked at quite a few ruined churches, and he had used two or three as O.P.s. But he had not been inside a church to pray for, oh, twelve or fourteen years. St. Stephen's wasn't his church. He was Presbyterian. But it was the nearest church and he needed to pray inside a church.

The climb up the marble entrance left his knees watery, although there were not many steps. Inside he paused to remove his hat, and found that as usual he had forgotten his hat. He walked to the central pillars, and examined the statue of Saint Ladislaus. He felt self-conscious, but no one was watching.

He walked towards a side altar and there were backless wooden benches before the altar, all unoccupied, for this was not an hour of Mass. He became aware of the quiet, the peace. There was a murmur inside St. Stephen's, there was even music from the other side of the nave, and yet it was wonderfully quiet, and he drank gratefully of this quiet.

9

He did not know how long he had been there when he heard the creak of a man's shoes coming down the aisle behind him, and was aware that somebody moved towards him along his bench. He thought, with all the other benches, why does he have to come here. In the soft light he was aware that the man knelt and crossed himself. He turned his head, and said, "Good Lord!"

"Shh!" said Leonides.

"Don't do that to me!" Jeff said.

"That bomb did your nerves no good, eh, Jeff?"

"I'll say not," he managed to whisper.

"Yes, keep your voice low. We will attract no attention, praying here, unless we make noise."

"What about the bomb?" Jeff asked. "Who did it?"

"Not us. The MVD was concerned because of it. They have orders not to unbalance things here. Not now. The situation is too tense. He is not quite ready. He will carefully choose his time, but the time, I am afraid, is short. We must somehow begin our operations. We must somehow divert Him."

From the other end of St. Stephen's there rose the chant of a choir. "Is that why you came here?" Jeff asked. "How did you know I was here anyway?"

"I have been watching. This is the third day I have been watching. It is important for you."

"You mean your operations? Sure it's important."

"No, there is something more immediate. This girl, Telredy, who comes to see you—do you like her?"

"Yes, I like her. Why?"

"Then do not see her again. Never again see her."

"Why shouldn't I see her?"

"Because if you see her, she will die. Your Atlantis Project is known, Jeff. It is known that you are in it. Any Hungarian who you often see will, sooner or later, die or wish he were dead."

Jeff had the queerest feeling, as if he and Leonides had been through this before. He looked at Leonides, sitting on the bench beside him, his big hands clasped, his round, cropped head bent. And when he looked he made a conscious effort to control his own features, and the effort made him realize that this was like the poker games in the Orient. "What kind of project?" he said. "I don't understand you, Leonides."

Leonides half turned his head to meet Jeff's eyes. "You don't?"

"No."

"You are a bad liar, Jeff."

"That may be," Jeff said. "But I remember you are a good liar. I'd like to have a nickel for every pot you pulled in with a busted straight."

The chant died away, so that when Leonides spoke next it was only a whisper, "I am not bluffing, Jeff. If you think I am bluffing, continue with this Atlantis Project and see what injuries are caused. But do not continue, Jeff. Stop it quickly. I do not ask you to say yes, or no, only listen to what I have to say. The MVD knows of it all. The MVD knows that Keller is at the top, and you and a number of others below. I don't know the MVD source exactly. I know it is from the United States, and probably from the White Russian colony in the United States. It is easy for the MVD to operate among White Russians. The Communists and their follow- ers your FBI automatically suspects. The White Russians your FBI automatically trusts. Your FBI forgets that often the White Russians have primary interests in their motherland—family, estates, sweet- hearts. And a Russian is a Russian. The Germans learned that. They learned it when we emptied our political prisons, and formed the prisoners into divisions, and sent them to Stalingrad. The politi- cal prisoners fought well. They hated Him, but they loved Russia more."

"Shhh," Jeff said. A robed priest walked towards the altar, and did not glance at them.

"It is all right," said Leonides. "It is not unknown for a Russian to empty his sins in church."

Jeff said, "I have listened to what you had to say, Leonides. Now what about your operations? What's cooking?"

"We are fearful for Yassovsky. He was sent to the Crimea from Moscow, and we have not heard from him since."

"Anything else?"

"Our radio is set. We have it in a truck in the Hochschwab. You know the Hochschwab?"

"The mountains in the British Zone in Austria? Yes. I've driven across the Semmering."

"Not even the British patrol the Hochschwab. It will be safe for quite a time. It will do more harm to Him than all your wireless, and the BBC. We will call it RFR—Radio Free Russia."

"How soon can I tell my Department?"

Leonides bent his head until his heavy chin touched his chest, and he appeared deep in prayer. His lips moved. "Soon now, please God." Then he asked, "Have you yet told your one person?"

"Not yet."

"Who will he be? I should know, if anything happens to you. Remember, something almost did happen, Jeff."

Now, Jeff knew, he must decide. "Would Keller be all right?" he said.

The choir began a new chant, and Leonides raised his head and stared at the great painting of St. Stephen, offering a crown to the Virgin, over the altar. Jeff knew that Leonides was searching the files of his mind for what he knew of Keller. He was going through all the reports. He was evaluating intelligence. At last he said, "I do not think it should be Keller, Jeff. At first, one thinks Keller would be the right man. He is discreet. Until this information came from the United States, the MVD could discover nothing about his mission here. He is intelligent. For one his age he has risen fast in your Department. He has no vices, and no weaknesses. Perhaps that is why I do not like him. He is not quite human, and this news is for a human man, Jeff, a man of compassion."

"Very well," Jeff said, "I will tell someone else. I'll tell Horace Locke, back in Washington."

"You can communicate with him in secret?" Leonides repeated aloud, "Horace Locke."

"I'll find a way."

The priest walked back from the altar, and this time he looked at the two men silent on the bench, and smiled. It was a strange thing, an unprecedented thing, to see a Russian and an American side by side in St. Stephen's. He prayed for peace each day at this altar. Who could tell, perhaps his prayers were being answered?

CHAPTER THIRTEEN

1

WHEN JEFF GOT BACK to his room he fell across the bed. The short walk, and the hour spent in St. Stephen's with Leonides, had tired him. In the morning he had been perfectly calm, but now his fingers tingled and the muscles in his arms and legs jumped at disconcerting intervals. He forced calmness upon himself. He had to think—think with logic and without emotion—think of Susan, think of Rikki and her danger, of the compromising of Atlantis Project, and of Leonides and his conspiracy.

He buried his face in the pillow, as if by shutting out the light his brain would become accustomed to the darkness of the future and peer through the darkness. But his brain wouldn't operate properly. His imagination insisted on racing ahead of his logic, like a child breaking away from its mother, and pursuing the fleeting ghosts of possibility. Suppose Leonides was an *agent provocateur,* loyal to the MVD and the Politburo. Suppose Leonides was cunningly pumping him to confirm nebulous MVD information? His instinct and his judgment told him Leonides was an honest and decent man, but his imagination shouted beware. Suppose Rikki was in the pay of the MVD, or of the Hungarian secret police? Suppose the leak about Atlantis was not in America, but here in Budapest? He fell asleep when his mind, lost in the labyrinth of possibilities, curled up in exhaustion.

2

When he awoke he knew from the sun that it was afternoon.
Rikki was there with a bowl of soup from Madame Angell's kitchen.
"Look what I brought you," she said. "I hear this morning at the
Legation that you are much better. Perhaps I cured you, no?"

"Hello, Rikki," he said, swinging his legs off the bed and shaking
the sleep from his head. Now he must act. He must act at once and
decisively, so there would be no mistake. "Thanks for the soup,
Rikki. It was very thoughtful of you. I'm hungry and I'll eat it. But
put it down on the table and get out of here, Rikki. I can't see you
again."

He observed the impact of his words on her face. He was saying
it the wrong way. Her mouth opened, and her eyes were dark and
wet with pity. "Jeff," she said, "what is wrong? You are sick
again?"

"Rikki, it's dangerous for you to be here. I can't explain it all, but
you'll have to get out. Right now. Go on now, Rikki."

She put the soup down on the table so that it slopped over the rim
of the bowl. "What kind of man are you!"

"This is for your own good, Rikki."

She saw the pile of opened letters on the desk. "Now I see," she
said. "Now I see." She smiled as if nothing was funny. "My Jeff
has a letter from his Susan. He has remorse. You Americans, you
are funny. Not funny ha-ha. Funny peculiar. The happier you are
the bigger your conscience."

"Nothing of the sort," Jeff said. He was on the defensive. This
was going badly.

"Last night were you thinking of your Susan?" she demanded.

He stood up, and tried to say what he had to say quietly, without
affront or anger. "Rikki, this isn't a matter of Susan. This is you,
Rikki. This is your life."

She came close to him, and her hands touched his chest and crept
up to his shoulders. "You Jeff! You silly! I understand. This

Susan, she is no doubt a lovely girl. And you can go back to her, Jeff. I will not hold you. I want nothing from you, Jeff—nothing. I only wish to give. When you go back you can have your Susan. I will even talk of her with you, without jealousy. I know how you Americans like to talk of your women. I will look at her pictures. I will agree that she is pretty. But now, while you are here, you will have me."

Jeff took her hands in his hands, and thought how helpless they seemed in his hands, and said, slowly so there could be no misunderstanding, "You would not do me much good as a corpse."

Her expression changed. He had frightened her. She didn't say anything. She was beginning to understand.

"You can't come up here any more, Rikki. We can't meet anywhere any more. You should not go to Fred Keller's again. You should not eat or dance at the Park Club. You should never enter the Legation."

She lowered her head, and said, "Why not" but she said it as if she already knew the answer.

"Americans are poison for you, Rikki." He thought, this is the worst thing I've ever done in my life. This is the worst. America had been the important dream of her life, and he was excising that dream. He was banishing her. He was creating an exile in her own land. It was like giving her a lift, and then dumping her off in the desert.

"This thing of which we talked?" she asked, without raising her head. "This Hungarian maquis? Cannot I be in that?" It was as if a little girl had been ordered to take off her party dress because she was not welcome at the dance. and who begs at least to be allowed to serve in the kitchen.

He knew that as soon as he talked to Keller there wouldn't be any Atlantis Project. "No. You'll have to forget that."

"So you have given up, you Americans?"

"I have given up that idea. Can't you guess why? Can't you guess why I can't see you any more? Why you shouldn't be seen around any Americans?"

"Yes, I know. But it is very discouraging, Jeff. I am sick. I am empty. You know, all my life was with your people. I thought I was one of you. Now I am alone." She turned away from him, and went out into the hallway, and presently he heard her footfall on the stairs, and the diminishing sound was slow and heavy, and not that of a dancer.

3

Jeff looked at the soup. He was no longer hungry. Then he realized he must see Fred Keller at once. He should have called Fred before he fell asleep. His carelessness disturbed him. How many other lives besides Rikki's were in danger he did not know. He did not know how many others in the Legation were working on Atlantis Project, or who they were, or how many Hungarians might be suspected, and under observation of the MVD and Rajk's outfit.

He picked up the telephone. When the operator heard his voice she shifted him to another operator, who spoke English, and at the same time he heard a tiny, annoying hum. When he spoke again there was a hollow reflection to his voice. The call was being monitored. This was S.O.P. Everyone in the Legation assumed that all their calls would be monitored. But Jeff hated it. The intrusion on his privacy enraged him, so that sometimes he shouted horrid things into the phone when he knew the call was being recorded. He knew this was indiscreet and not according to the rules, but it relieved his feelings.

Since it was assumed that all calls were overheard, conversations were always oblique, monosyllabic, or rich in slang peculiar to this one Mission in this one nation at this time in history.

When Fred answered the phone Jeff said, "It's me."

"Hi-ya?"

"Okay. I've got to see you."

"I'm pretty well tied up."

"Got to see you right away."

"You can't. I've got appointments with Lower Slobbovians all

afternoon, and I expect Miss Genghis Khan for dinner." Lower
Slobbovians were Hungarians.

Jeff said, "No she's not."

"Why not?"

"She's sick and can't get well." That meant that she was suspected
by the MVD.

"Oh. That's too bad. Yes, you'd better come up at eight."

"That's not all," Jeff said.

"What else?"

"Wait until you hear. You should see me right now."

"I can't. That's all there is to it."

And then Keller hung up.

4

For Jeff the waiting until eight o'clock was painful. To be a
bearer of bad news was unpleasant enough, but to have to do it by
appointment was intolerable. He tried reading the Toynbee he'd
borrowed from the Mission information library a month before.
The history of civilizations had stirred and fascinated him, and at the
same time had awed and humbled him with realization of his own
ignorance. A future Toynbee would be able to dismiss his century
and all its wars and hatreds and mass aberrations simply as a Time
of Troubles, to be measured in the space of man's full journey upon
the planet only as a single step backward in unnumbered miles of
progress. If you absorbed Toynbee you became a philosopher. Yet
he found himself rebelling against his own conclusions. He didn't
want to admit that he was fated to live in a bad time. He didn't
want to admit the inevitability of the descent of his time into darkness.

He found he was pleased with himself because in this moment he
could concentrate on Toynbee.

At six-thirty Madame Angell brought him a tray, and the latest
news. The BBC quoted Drew Pearson, whom Madame Angell called
"your spokesman," as saying the Russians would soon be able to har-

ness cosmic rays, and cosmic rays would kill more people quicker than atomic bombs, biological warfare, or radioactive clouds. Radio Moscow said a Trotskyite plot had been crushed in the Ukraine. This sounded more factual, and potentially as interesting. A Stockholm dispatch to Berne quoted travelers from Finland as saying the Reds were testing trans-polar V-2 rockets. That wasn't unlikely. The uranium production in the Czech mines in Bohemia had doubled since the Russians placed German engineers in charge. He didn't doubt it.

He forced himself to eat. His stomach protested each mouthful, but he made himself eat because he needed strength.

It may have been the food's impact on his raw nerves, or the uranium, or the cosmic rays, or simply the tension of waiting. Jeff's hands began to shake again. With both hands he had difficulty lifting his coffee to his lips. He knew that in this condition he shouldn't see Fred. Fred would think he had gone to pieces. He telephoned the dispensary and asked for Major L'Engle. He wasn't there. He tried L'Engle's house, and the Park Club, and the mess. He wasn't at any of those places.

Jeff put on his overcoat and went outside. The walk and the air should help him. It should untangle his guts. He turned towards the Szabadzag-tér, with its old monuments to the four lost provinces—and the new one to the Red Army towering over them. The dispensary was on the second floor of the Mission. Maybe he'd find L'Engle there now. He hoped so. He needed him.

At this hour—it was seven o'clock now—the Mission was usually empty except for the doorman and guards and charwomen and the people in the code room and radio monitoring section. He went up to the second floor and tried the door of the dispensary. It was open, and the lights were on inside, but L'Engle wasn't there.

He sat on a white metal stool and tried to read a month-old copy of *Newsweek*. The type kept jumping out of focus. He wished L'Engle would hurry up and come back. He looked up at the rows of square bottles on the shelves. Probably better stocked than any hospital in all Pest, he thought. His eyes stopped at the bottle of

Blue Eighty-Eights. There was no mistaking them, and the label was plain—Sodium Amytal.

He wanted one of those Blue Eighty-Eights.

Maybe L'Engle would be out for another hour. Maybe L'Engle wasn't coming back at all. He couldn't wait.

Jeff slid off the stool and reached up and took the bottle of Blue Eighty-Eights and Miss Ellis, the nurse, opened the door and said, "Put that down, God-dammit!"

Miss Ellis had had a hard day. As a matter of fact Miss Ellis had had a hard year. She had volunteered for overseas duty in the belief that she would find a husband, for certainly the American men in such an unlikely place as Budapest would appreciate an old-fashioned American girl, even if she was a bit thick through the middle and in the ankles. She found she was mistaken. The competition was rougher than in New York, or St. Louis, or Omaha. It was even rougher than in her home town, Hyannis, Nebraska, where the slim and pretty girls outnumbered the eligible males two to one. It looked as if she would never find a husband in Budapest —unless she married a Hungarian anxious to emigrate—and she had developed a grudge against the men in the Mission.

And here was one of them—Baker who had never even asked her to dance—stealing her drugs. He was standing there looking at her with his mouth open, caught red-handed. A filthy hophead. "So you're the thief who's been taking my morphine and penicillin!" Miss Ellis said.

"Now wait a minute, Miss Ellis," Jeff said. "I just came up here to find Major L'Engle and get a Blue Eighty-Eight. I need it and I know he'd give me one if he was here."

"Put that down!" Miss Ellis tried to get her hands on the bottle.

He saw that there wasn't any sense arguing with her, and he turned his back so she could not interfere and shook out a Blue Eighty-Eight and popped it into his mouth and swallowed.

"Why, you filthy thief!" Miss Ellis spat at him.

He couldn't answer because he was having a hard time swallowing.

"I hope they put you in Leavenworth for ten years. You'll never get away with this, you know. Why, it's the most brazen thing I've ever seen!"

He got it down, but it still felt like a lump under his breastbone. "All right, Miss Ellis," Jeff said, "just take it easy. When you see L'Engle tell him I came up here and took one Blue Eighty-Eight. Just one, mind you! And I don't think you talk like a lady, Miss Ellis."

He hurried out. It was quicker to walk to the motor pool than call and wait for a vehicle. If he walked right over he'd be at Keller's on time.

5

Miss Ellis didn't scream, because there wasn't anyone on the floor to hear her, and anyway Miss Ellis wasn't the screaming type.

She sat down at the desk in the dispensary and began to write a report for Major L'Engle. She tore it up and started again, this time addressing it to the Admiral. For months she had complained to L'Engle that the drugs were being stolen. You could get a thousand dollars, counting the forint at par, for 300,000 units of penicillin— enough for one Romansky shot—on the Black Bourse. Also she was sure some morphine was missing. When she had beefed about this, Major L'Engle hadn't paid proper attention to her. Sometimes she even suspected L'Engle. She'd bet he'd been passing out her drugs to the indigenous personnel. She's seen Major L'Engle with some very pretty indigenous personnel. It was absolutely forbidden to allot the medical stores to the indigenous personnel. Now that she had something definite to squawk about she might as well squawk to the Admiral himself and get the whole thing off her chest. Maybe next time—if he was still here—Major L'Engle would pay some attention to her. She made her report hot. She concluded it with:

"In my professional opinion Mr. Baker behaved like a drug addict crazed by an uncontrollable desire for narcotics."

6

When Jeff walked into Keller's apartment he found Fred at ease in a maroon lounging robe, the faultless lapels faced with black satin. Fred was smoking a pipe and there was a brandy snifter and an open book on the table beside his big chair. He was wearing horn-rimmed glasses. Jeff had never·seen him with glasses before. He seemed like a man whose thoughts were only on a book and an undisturbed evening, until you looked closely at his face. Then you saw all the muscles were taut, and new lines showed around the mouth. "Hello, Jeff," he said. "Do you want to eat first, or talk?"

"I've eaten, thanks," Jeff said. "I think we'd better talk."

"I haven't any appetite, myself," Keller said. "My man ran up some chops for me. Wasn't able to touch them. Now what's this all about?"

"Your butler still here?" Jeff asked.

"No. I sent him home."

"All right," Jeff said, "here goes." He folded himself into a chair and lighted a cigarette. He was relieved to see the Blue Eighty-Eight had dispatched his jitters. "Atlantis Project has been penetrated. The Russians know about it. We've had it, Fred."

Keller's tan faded to yellow. "How do you know?"

"A Russian told me."

"I don't believe you!"

So Jeff told him the story. He started in the beginning at Bari. He told him everything, but he did not mention Leonides' own secret. He didn't mention Leonides' anti-regime resistance movement. He was still mindful of Leonides' warning.

As he talked he became aware of a change in Keller's expression. The unnatural calm vanished. Jeff thought, he's taking this terribly hard. The penetration of Atlantis was a blow, yes. But it could be infinitely worse. At least the project, in this stage, could be called off without catastrophe. The friends of the Western powers here would not be compromised. Henceforth the MVD would waste its men and its time watching a scheme that no longer existed.

7

What Jeff could not know, of course, was that for Keller the news was the most terrible of personal disasters. Keller had staked his career on Atlantis, and his career was his whole life. There was nothing else.

Keller's career had been happy from the beginning. The Department delighted and fascinated him. In the intricate supra-world of diplomacy everyone was polite and gracious, and culture and breeding were understood and welcome. The world that was sordid and violent and treacherous was another world with which he had severed contact. The Department was made for him. It provided the catharsis for all his energy.

He was lucky in the Department. He was lucky enough to get in on the ground floor when the New Deal came. His basic political, social, and economic beliefs were superficial, but he found it easy to get along with the men who came into power with the New Deal. For one thing, under the New Deal the Department expanded and increased in importance, and Fred liked that.

He was lucky to get the Berlin assignment. In Berlin one could see the way the wind was blowing and judge what was to come. His reports on Nazi ambitions went to the very highest levels. He was promoted to Second Secretary before he was thirty, and sent to Budapest. After that there was Bucharest, Paris, and Istanbul.

After Pearl Harbor he was brought home. He worked on the North African desk in Washington, an assignment involving the greatest discretion and secrecy. When Paris was captured he was one of the Department's team sent to reorganize the American Embassy. He remained overseas for the duration of the war, and became a FSO, Class I. From this springboard there was no limit to where he could go. He could become an Ambassador, an Assistant Secretary, perhaps even the Undersecretary of State.

Fred was one of the first to recognize and analyze the Soviet danger. He had developed a finely tuned perception of public opinion, and he early forecast Russian designs in the Balkans, Germany, Austria, France, and Italy. He was the first man to make a study of the parallels between Soviet expansion and the Haushofer theory that had been Nazi dogma. It was a startling document.

By the beginning of 1948 he was climbing steeply up that perilous incline that separates those who make national policy from those who only carry it out. He was no longer one of the Department's "bright young men." He had become an adviser to those at the top. Soon he would be at the top himself.

It was Fred Keller who conceived the Atlantis Project. As a model and precedent (should anyone be squeamish about using such tactics in preparing for war) he had Bob Murphy's operations in North Africa. Murphy's Consuls and Vice-Consuls had worked among the Vichy French in much the same way Keller's team now worked among the Hungarians.

It had not been easy to sell Atlantis to the Department. It had been necessary to use all his persuasion, and stake all his influence. There were doubtful ones. Some felt Atlantis might commit the Department too far. It was in the nature of a military operation, and a military operation is not a flexible thing. Once started, it is difficult to stop, as every commander knows at H-Hour. There were others who said it was premature, and some who complained it was too late. A few even questioned its usefulness, but these were of little importance.

He had found a powerful ally in Matson. Matson claimed Atlantis was essential immediately, not only in his own area, but throughout Europe. It was Matson who had nominated Hungary for the experiment, and suggested that Fred take charge in the field. So Fred had told the Secretary he would assume full responsibility.

If he failed—but failure was not possible. He could not face the Secretary with a failure of such magnitude. Atlantis had to be successful. He had to prove to them all that he was a successful man.

8

Keller's pipe was out when Jeff finished talking, but he was still puffing at it. He looked at Jeff, estimating, analyzing, searching. He said, "Well, it's not as bad as I thought. I really don't see any reason to discontinue Atlantis."

"You don't!" Jeff didn't think he'd heard correctly.

"No, I don't. But I do see reasons why if what you told me became known—say, to the Admiral—you'd be fired. I'm surprised, Jeff, that a man of your background and experience should fall into such an ancient trap. I'm honestly surprised."

"Are you sure you listened carefully to what I told you?" Jeff asked.

"I digested every word. I'm only worried about one thing. How much did you leak to the Russian?"

Jeff knew he was growing angry. "Leak to the Russian! Nothing, of course."

"I hope not. I wouldn't like to lose you, Jeff. I think you've been doing a good job, except for this one thing."

"But don't you see that this one thing finishes us?" Jeff demanded.

"You *are* dense," Keller said. He rose and paced to the bar, and poured a measured ounce of brandy into the fat-bellied glass. He swished it around, and warmed the snifter with his long-sinewed hands. He seemed to have forgotten to offer a drink to Jeff.

"Don't you see?" Keller continued. "Don't you honestly? Don't you see that the Russians are on a fishing expedition? Oh, they may know something. They may even know the name of our project, although I honestly don't see how they'd even know that."

"It seems to me that they know everything," Jeff said, "and they picked it all up right in Washington."

"That's ridiculous. As I said, they may have heard the name. So they assign this chap—what's his name?"

"Leonides Lasenko."

"They assign your friend Lasenko to pump you. Why did they

pick you, and not me, or one of the others? First of all, you're fresh out here, and obviously don't know enough to stay away from Russians. And secondly, Lasenko knew you. That's the important thing. Lasenko got your name from customs, and he recognized it, and went after you. Perhaps you were the only approachable American in Budapest."

"I'm sure of that, anyway," Jeff said. He wanted desperately to tell Keller the rest of it. He wanted to tell how Leonides felt, and what Leonides was doing. But if Keller believed Leonides was lying about the MVD penetrating Atlantis, then Keller would also say Leonides was lying about the rest of it. Keller would only say Leonides was very clever. Keller would say Leonides was trying to get Jeff's confidence by pretending to be a member of an anti-regime revolutionary group. And Keller's reasoning would sound logical. That was the hell of it. It was all so perfectly logical. There was no use saying any more.

"Now I'll tell you what I'm going to do," Keller said, and Jeff could see he was composed again. "You're just to forget about this whole thing and let me handle it. You're not to mention it to anyone else. You're just to forget about it. And nothing is going to happen to you, except for God's sake, Jeff, don't see that Russian again."

Jeff was silent, but he knew what presently he was going to say.

"Yes, I'll handle it all," Keller went on. "I'll change the name of the project. If the Russians have heard anything about Atlantis, and are trying to find out what it is, we'll just eliminate the name."

"It won't work," Jeff said. "They're not watching a name. They're watching people."

"Nonsense. I'll just tell the Admiral it's best for security that we change the name. Time we changed it, as a security measure, anyway. You go right ahead with your work. How're you getting along with Miss Genghis Khan?"

Jeff said, "I'm not going to see her again, and you're not going to see her again."

"Now Jeff, don't be difficult."

Jeff leaned back in his chair. He was quiet and calm now, and it wasn't the Blue Eighty-Eight that had given him this steadiness. "It's easy for you, Keller," he said. "You know the Russians won't kill you. You're safe, because if you were killed that'd be an incident, and at this time they don't want such an incident. But if they grab Rikki, and snaffle out her life, that doesn't hurt you, Keller. Back home the papers will just mention that the Hungarian police arrested a Hungarian girl, and there was a closed trial, and she was hung for treason. And all you would say would be, 'Too bad.'"

"That's enough, Jeff!"

"No, it's not enough. You known damn well the way the MVD operates. You know damn well you're safe. You know they'll watch—are watching now. And every Hungarian you see often enough, or I see often enough, that Hungarian is as good as dead. Do you want to be a murderer, Keller?"

Keller said, "One last chance, Jeff. I know you're unstrung. The bomb—that explosion."

"I'm not unstrung."

"I'd hate to believe that you were a coward. The Admiral thinks you're a coward. One last chance, Jeff. I directly order you to continue with your work."

"I'm not going to do it."

Keller shook his head. He seemed older than forty, now, and he had lost his spruceness, his straightness. "You will go to your apartment. I will have to see the Admiral."

As Jeff walked out of the living room he turned his head. Keller had both hands on the fireplace mantel, and was staring into the mirror, and his lips moved as if he called on someone for help.

CHAPTER FOURTEEN

1

JEFF HAD A BAD three days. It would be much better if he himself
went to the Admiral, he believed, but he could not violate the
unwritten protocol governing affairs of this kind within the Department. He couldn't go over the head of his immediate superior. He
couldn't speak of the matter to the Admiral, or the Consul General,
until he was summoned. There was ingrained in him a respect for
this protocol, and its reasons were apparent, like going through channels and following the chain-of-command in the Army.

The first day, nobody called him, or visited. This in itself was a
bad sign. It indicated he was leprous with trouble. He spent the
day typing a letter to Horace Locke. The letter was a careful summary of everything Leonides had told him of what Leonides had
called the Second Russian Revolution. He could not, of course, mention Atlantis Project, but he did think it was safe to say:

"I have had trouble over my job, and I have a premonition that
I may not long be in a position to convey this information officially.
Therefore I am passing it along to you. I am sure that with your
long experience in the Department you will know what to do."

He had no idea how he was going to get the letter to Locke. He
knew that any letter he dropped into the pouch, from now on,
would be suspect. And he had the same premonition Susan had.
Time was running out. The letter to Horace Locke was three pages
long. He folded it and put it in his inside coat pocket. That night

when he undressed he took it out of the pocket and lodged it under his pillow. He woke up several times in the night and felt under the pillow to be sure it was still there.

The second day Major L'Engle came to see him, looking harassed. "The Admiral ate me out," he said. "He's wild. What happened?"

"You mean in your dispensary?"

"Sure, in my dispensary."

Jeff told him what happened, and the Major nodded and said, "That's what I thought, but nobody is going to believe me, or you."

"What do you mean, won't believe you?" Jeff asked.

"Well, you taking that Blue Eighty-Eight is only part of it." The Major twisted his hands together as if what he was saying were difficult. "Baker, that thwarted, lard-faced harridan in white reported other drugs missing. I knew they were missing before she did. You see, I took them."

Jeff said, "I suppose they blame that on me too."

"Oh, no, the Admiral lets me have all that. You see, I told him. I told him the truth, but he thinks I sold the stuff on the Bourse, and I'm under charges."

Jeff took out the bottle of cognac he kept locked in his dispatch case and gave the Major a drink, because obviously the Major needed a drink. Then he took one himself. "I'm confused," Jeff said.

The Major drank the cognac in a gulp. "If I had just been smart enough to lie! If I had just told the Admiral that some of the G.I.s in the M.A.'s office had gonorrhea, or some of the staff had been sick, or even that I was sick myself, nothing would have happened. But I told the truth. You know the Hunyadi Home?"

"I've heard of it. The home for boys."

"Yes. It's near my place, and every once in a while I drop in there. I don't have any sons myself. But I like boys. Their infirmary is deplorable. No equipment at all."

"So?"

"So for the last six or eight months I've been helping them out. I've saved three pneumonias, and one meningitis, and some others. I told the Admiral the truth about it. In the first place, he doesn't believe me, and in the second place he ate me out anyway because I'm not supposed to use the Mission's drugs for indigenous personnel. He's right, of course. No getting away from it. He's right, officially."

"I'm sorry," Jeff said. "I'm sorry that I started this."

"Oh, I told him about you too. I told him it was perfectly okay if you took a Blue Eighty-Eight because there wasn't anybody there to give it to you. I explained the stuff wasn't habit-forming unless you took it for a considerable period. Did it do any good? No. Every time I mentioned your name he just sputtered. I don't know what else you've done, Baker, but whatever it is, you've got him wild."

"You know what I think?" Jeff said. "I think you did just right."

"Well, thanks, I really think so, too. But it's not going to do any good."

"I hope he'll cool down."

"He won't. I'm on tomorrow's plane, going home under charges."

"Jesus, that's too bad." He tried to think of something cheerful, because he liked L'Engle. "You'll be all right," was the best he could do.

"No, I won't. There'll be an I.G. investigation, and anyway a reprimand, and they'll look on their maps and find either the hottest place in the world or the coldest place in the world and they'll say, 'We've got a new post for you, L'Engle, where there are no black markets. Goodbye, bub.'"

Jeff poured another drink, and when he handed the glass to L'Engle he looked deep into his face. L'Engle's face was like rock, but rock weathered and mellowed by his years and his profession. "So you're going on tomorrow's plane," Jeff said. "And you're a decent guy. I know you're a decent guy."

"You don't have to feel so damn sorry for me."

"I wasn't feeling sorry. I was just thinking. Will you deliver a letter for me, Major?"

"Depends where it's going. I'm going to Washington."

"That's where the letter's going, Major."

"So long as it doesn't contain classified material, sure."

Jeff said, "This hasn't been classified, yet. There isn't any classification for it."

"Now that sounds interesting," the Major said. "That sounds mysterious. It won't get me in trouble? I'm in enough trouble now, Baker."

Jeff finished his drink. He wished he had time to think it all over, weighing and measuring the chances as he had been taught to do. But there wasn't time. Almost all the time was gone. Well, there was such a thing as a calculated risk. Once in a while, a man had to take a calculated risk. Eisenhower had taken a calculated risk when he spread his green divisions thinly through the Ardennes. Marshall had called ERP a calculated risk. Now he would take his. "This letter might get you into trouble, Major," Jeff said. "I want you to read it, and make your own decision."

He handed the letter to L'Engle.

The Major started reading it, and then he took a pair of glasses from the inside pocket of his blouse, and put them on, and started again. When he finished he handed it back to Jeff. "I'll deliver it," he said. "You got an envelope?"

"Yes." Jeff sat down at the desk and wrote, "Horace Locke. Old State. 17th and Pennsylvania Avenues, N.W., Washington, D.C." He said, "Here you are."

Major L'Engle dropped the envelope into his doctor's bag. "You don't have to worry about it," he said, "because this bag always goes with me, and I never forget it."

"I'm not worried," Jeff said.

"Yes, you are," said L'Engle. "You're worried that I might talk. You don't have to worry about that, either." He took the bag in his hand. "I guess I'll be going now."

"So long."

"So long. Look me up—if you ever get to Alaska."

And he was gone.

2

The morning of the third day Quincy Todd phoned and said, "Hey, where you been?"

"You know damn well where I've been."

"You don't have to act like an untouchable. You're not, you know."

"No, I didn't know."

"Well meet me at our place at noon and I'll tell you."

So at noon Jeff walked to the Café Molnar. He was strong again now. The weakness that comes with confinement to bed had gone, and his nerves were good.

Quincy Todd was sitting at the table which by custom was theirs. But Marina wasn't there to serve them. Another girl was there, and Jeff said, "Where's your girl friend?"

"I don't know," Quincy said, "and she's not my girl friend any more. That Russky beat my time."

"You mean my Russky—the Major?"

"Yes, your Russky."

"I thought she didn't like Russians?"

"She likes that one. Every night that I've been here for the last two weeks, there she is with the Russky. So what can I do? Can I go over and try to ease him out of the picture? No. I just sit here and it comes closing time and he takes her home—or somewhere. What's he got that I haven't got?"

"Nothing. He just gets here first. If you got here first, he'd be the one who'd have to sit alone."

"I've got to work. I don't think that Russky ever works."

"Don't worry, he works."

Quincy dumped his cognac into his coffee. "First today," he said. "Do you know what we call the second floor of the Legation now? The Whispering Gallery. And do you know what they're all talking about? About you, Jeff."

"I'm not surprised."

"Now, Jeff, I don't want you to tell me anything about this. I know you're in a jam, and I know the whole thing is extra secret. I just want to tell you what's been going on, and I want to pass along a little advice."

"Okay."

"In the first place they've been having conferences about you every day—I mean the big boys—the Admiral, and Morgan Collingwood, and Fred Keller, and Quigley. That means they can't agree. So you can figure you've got a friend or two, or there wouldn't be any argument."

"Maybe," Jeff said. "Maybe they've already decided what to do, but they haven't agreed on how to do it."

"No, I don't think they've decided, because they haven't sent any cables about you. I know, because I've had a couple of dates with Marge Collins. She'd never tell me what was in a cable, but she'd say if one went."

"That doesn't mean much," Jeff said. He knew that Atlantis Project could not be mentioned in a cable. It was absurd to be optimistic.

"And another thing, they're going to call you in tomorrow. I don't know what you've done, but whatever you've done they'll probably give you a chance to explain."

"I've already explained."

Quincy Todd stared out of the window with his blue eyes that couldn't seem to blink. On this day it was snowing, but there was no cheerfulness in the snow. There was no longer beauty in a snowfall in Budapest. It was only added misery. "I don't want them to boot you out of here, Jeff," he said. "You're human."

"I've got a girl back in Washington," Jeff said.

"Don't we all?"

"I suppose."

"I've got a hunch, Jeff, that if you go into this thing tomorrow and say, 'Okay, I've been a bad boy and I won't do it again,' why nothing will happen."

"I'll think it over," Jeff promised.

3

On the afternoon of that third day Jeff's phone rang again. At first he thought it was somebody at the Legation, because when he used only simple phrases Leonides' voice was without accent, and almost American.

"I've got to see you right away," Leonides said.

"Who is this?"

"Don't you know?"

"I'm not sure."

"The night you had four fives, I had four tens."

"Oh. Okay. Where?"

"The same place as last time. In about thirty minutes. But you start right now."

"Sure. In thirty minutes."

It was a sensible precaution that he enter the church quite a time before Leonides. He rang for the elevator, waited until it was on the way up, and then raced down the stairs. He didn't want Sandor to see in which direction he went.

On this dark day St. Stephen's was darker, even, than it had been before. On this day there was no choir, nor music from the organ. In the gloom he could see small groups of women silent on the benches. They had come in from the cold, or rested here a while, their baskets beside them, before trudging through the snow to their homes and their stoves.

There were some women on the bench he and Leonides had occupied before, so he found a vacant bench two rows closer to the altar. He genuflected, and made his mouth move, so as not to be different and attract attention, and then he sat down, his head bowed. He looked at his watch. Twenty minutes.

Exactly on the minute he heard the scrape of boots on the stone corridor, and felt someone brush against the bench. He did not raise his head until Leonides sat down close to him. Then he saw that the trousers were not Russian uniform trousers, but worn, shabby flannels.

But the face was that of Leonides. He was wearing a civilian suit much too small for him. The trousers climbed up the heavily muscled legs, and the thick wrists extended six inches out of the cuffs as he bent his elbows. He looked like a boy in the year of his greatest growth, whose family cannot afford a new suit. "What happened to you?" Jeff whispered. "Where did you get that outfit?"

Leonides didn't raise his cropped head an inch, and when he spoke Jeff could detect no movement of his lips. "I am a fugitive. I don't speak of how I got these clothes."

"Your plan?"

"Is known."

"How?"

"They questioned Yassovsky. They questioned him for one month before they killed him."

"What're you going to do?"

"Run the border. Run the border across the Raab into the British Zone. Then to the Hochschwab and our transmitter. We do not quit. We fight."

Jeff tried to analyze the risks, the possibilities, the terrible dangers. "Those clothes won't do. I'll get one of my suits. They'll fit better."

"No. It is better to be badly dressed. To be well dressed is fatal."

Jeff said, "I don't think much of your chances, Leonides. You know how they watch the border. You know how they watch for deserters. And they'll be after you. You know they'll be after you."

"There is no chance here. Here my face is too well known. I must go quickly."

"Do you need anything?"

"Perhaps some American money. It is wanted everywhere. If you have it, Jeff?"

Jeff reached in his pocket and took out his wallet. He had five twenty-dollar bills in an inner pouch. He handed them under his knees to Leonides. "I still think it's terribly dangerous. You haven't papers, or anything, have you?"

"Papers are no good for me," Leonides said. "Today nobody can safely cross a boundary even with an endorsement from God. Only the gypsies travel today. Only the gypsies laugh at passports. Only the gypsies know the safe ways, for they have been doing it for two thousand years."

"I see," Jeff said. "I see."

A woman with a shawl over her head moved in beside them. She set down a market basket, and in the basket was a single loaf of black bread with snow on it. She was very tired. Leonides looked at her, and whispered, "She is okay. She has too many worries to be curious of others. Now I called you for a reason you must have guessed. We will not see each other again for a long time, Jeff. So I give you the name of another, with whom you can have liaison. Zatsikeffsky, the Civil Air Attaché."

"How do you spell it?"

"You'd better write it down. Have you a pencil?"

Jeff moved very slowly, raising his hand to his chest. He found a pencil in his vest pocket. Leonides gave him a brown paper envelope, and spelled out Zatsikeffsky, slowly and in whispers.

"And in case something happens to him, too?" Jeff asked.

"He is the last of us here in Budapest."

"Elsewhere?"

Leonides was silent.

"Can't you tell me, Leonides?"

"It is forbidden. I am pledged never to mention the name. Yet on occasion one must take a chance, and I must now take it. I know the names of few important ones in other places. We do not wish to know. It is not good to know, for it could happen to any of us what happened to Yassovsky, and there is no man who will not talk. Only when a man is dead is he truly silent. I know one in Moscow who is above me." He mentioned a three-syllable name, and Jeff wrote it down. "You spell it," Leonides observed.

"I've heard it before."

"He is a great man."

"He must be. And a brave one." Jeff thought of his own troubles, and wondered whether he should tell Leonides, and decided he wouldn't do it, because Leonides had enough worries now. He did say, "I've sent a report to Washington, Leonides, to the man I completely trust."

"That's good. It's not so important that you be secret now, except with the names. As to the plan itself, it is known because of Yassovsky. Now I will go, Jeff. The quicker we start, the better."

"So long, Leonides."

"Goodbye."

Leonides rose and moved away, his hands in his pockets, and his head lowered.

Jeff remained in the church for another half-hour. The first time he had come to St. Stephen's to pray, and had forgotten to pray. But this time he prayed.

CHAPTER FIFTEEN

1

THAT WAS THURSDAY. At ten o'clock Friday morning Lieutenant Commander Phelan, of the Naval Attaché's office, came to Jeff's room. He was dressed in his best uniform, and wore his ribbons. Jeff guessed that what he had to say would be formal. Jeff was prepared for him. Jeff had dressed in his best blue suit.

"Mr. Baker," Phelan said, "the Admiral sent me to inform you that you are wanted in his office."

"At what time?"

"Immediately, if you don't mind, Mr. Baker."

"I don't mind, Commander. Do you have transportation?"

"I do."

On the way to the Mission they talked about the weather.

2

When Jeff entered the Admiral's office he could see that this was not to be so much a trial as passage of sentence. He could tell by their stiffness. The Admiral was behind his desk, and the others—Keller, Collingwood, and Quigley—were seated in a semicircle with their backs to the light. There was an empty straight chair in front of the desk, and Jeff knew he was supposed to take that chair. He did not want to sit there, however, because the light would be in his eyes and he could not clearly see their faces. "Sit down, Mr. Baker," the Admiral said.

"If you don't mind I'll move this chair," Jeff said, and he did move it towards the end of the desk. Then he sat down. In the better light he could see the Admiral's face growing red.

The Admiral picked up a sheaf of papers, rustled them into a pile, and put them down again. The model cruiser, carrier, and four miniature destroyers still sailed across his desk, but in disgraceful formation. "Now, Mr. Baker," the Admiral began, "you know why you're here. No matter what my personal feelings may be, I want to be fair with you. It's always been my contention that every man deserves a hearing. I'd give a hearing to a seaman, second class, and I'll give one to you. Now what have you got to say for yourself?"

"Nothing, sir," Jeff said.

"Don't you have any statement?" the Admiral asked. He seemed surprised. "You know, Mr. Baker, this is a very serious proposition."

"I'm aware of it, sir. I've already made my statement to Mr. Keller. I'm sure he reported it to you accurately." He knew that Fred Keller's training made it impossible for him to lie, or omit any word of what Jeff had said, in an official statement. He looked at Keller. Fred's face still seemed distraught, as it had looked when he left the apartment. Keller nodded, almost imperceptibly.

"It is absolutely incomprehensible to me," the Admiral said, "that you would consort with a Russian, and be taken in by such a cock-and-bull story. Not to speak of your other actions. Not to mention your shameful public display before the Hungarian police simply because there's a little harmless explosion. Why I've seen men stand up under a sixteen-inch salvo and grin. Done it myself."

Jeff thought the Admiral must be one of those born brave soldiers —a MacArthur or a Patton—naturally contemptuous of death. Other men were different. Other men didn't like war, didn't like any part of war. They saw no glory in its rituals or its panoply. Of course the Admiral couldn't understand this. All Jeff said was, "I can only envy you, sir."

The Admiral obviously didn't like the answer. "And you plundering drugs from the dispensary. L'Engle calls it secondary shock.

Lot of bushwa. I say that you're an addict, and I say that L'Engle's a thief and a black marketeer. That's what I say."

Jeff sensed that the Admiral was baiting him. Jeff felt that the Admiral wanted him to lose his temper. He looked at the little fleet in disarray on the desk. He kept his mouth shut.

"If it were entirely up to me—which it would be if the Department of State believed in maintaining taut ship—you'd be on the way back to the United States today with L'Engle. But the Consul General here tells me I've got to be polite to you, because you're a Foreign Service Officer." The Admiral enunciated "Foreign Service Officer" in what he thought was a babyish treble.

Jeff remained silent. He knew that nothing, now, could upset his poise, his independence, his serenity. They could put a grenade under his chair and he wouldn't budge.

"Yes, I've got to be very polite," the Admiral went on. "I can't fire you myself. I can only ask Washington to recall you. And I have to prefer charges. Well, that I'll do."

Jeff said, "I don't think it matters very much what happens to me. But what happens to Atlantis Project does matter."

"I don't think it's necessary for us to discuss the project," the Admiral said. But Jeff could see that his words were automatic, and not in accordance with his thought. "We'll keep Atlantis out of this."

"No, we won't," Jeff said.

He watched Keller. Fred was in trouble with himself.

He looked at the others. Morgan Collingwood was very still, very attentive. Jeff knew that Collingwood, as an experienced diplomat, would be projecting the situation far ahead and beyond the walls of this office.

William Quigley hadn't said anything. He was sitting with his hands in his lap, wooden as part of the furniture. Now Quigley felt called upon to speak. "If you will pardon me, Admiral," he said, "I want to point out that I am responsible to the Department for the security of Atlantis Project. Mr. Baker says that this project has been penetrated."

"I don't believe it," the Admiral said.

Quigley said, "It is not possible for anyone to say arbitrarily that it has or hasn't until there has been an investigation. I propose to conduct such an investigation."

The Admiral's office was quiet now. William Quigley raised his colorless eyes. "Jeff," he said, "it is my opinion that you haven't told us everything."

"You're right, Quig," Jeff said.

"You've seen your Russian friend again, haven't you?"

"Yes, I have."

The Admiral interrupted. "Mr. Baker, it strikes me that you have been deliberately treasonable. To our knowledge you have twice seen this Russian, and twice you've been warned. Now you say you've seen him again."

"There are two kinds of treason," Jeff said. He discovered that his voice was level and steady. "There is treason to your country and there is treason to civilization. I tried not to commit either kind."

"Then you did see him again?" the Admiral demanded.

"Yes, I did. I saw Leonides Lasenko again. I saw him yesterday afternoon. He was wearing civilian clothes, and he was trying to get across the border into the British Zone. He has become one of the *unbekannte Menschen*. He is a leader in a resistance movement against the Soviet regime."

The Admiral leaned his big frame across the desk. "Do you make this all up as you go along?" he inquired.

Jeff said, "May I continue?"

The Admiral glared. "You can say what you want. We don't have to believe it, you know. We aren't children."

"Before he left Lasenko gave me two names," Jeff went on. "One here. One in Moscow."

Quigley stirred in his chair. "Where's he going? Where's this Lasenko going?"

"He's trying to get to the Hochschwab. They've got a transmitter up there. They're going to call it RFR—Radio Free Russia."

The Admiral planted a hand on the desk. "Mr. Baker, I don't

want to hear any more of your fabrications. I think you have a twisted or diseased brain."

"I don't," said Quigley.

The Admiral turned on him. "Quigley, remember that you're not concerned with policy. You're strictly in operations, and only in security operations at that."

"I'm remembering," Quigley said.

"Can I go now?" Jeff asked. "Have you finished with me?"

"I have, Mr. Baker," the Admiral said. "You will go to your quarters."

3

When Jeff was gone the Admiral growled, "Did you ever hear such balderdash?" But nobody said anything, and the Admiral spoke again. "All right, come on. Let's get on with this. What's to be done? First send a cable to the Department, I say, asking for his immediate recall. Then we'll draw up the charges and send them in the pouch."

"We can't send them by pouch," Quigley objected. "You'll remember, sir, that nothing about Atlantis Project was to be committed to writing."

"In my estimation," the Admiral replied, "it's not necessary to go into this business of Atlantis being compromised. Fred Keller said yesterday he didn't believe it, and I don't believe it either. It'd just cause a useless flap in Washington. You know how they panic in Washington."

Now Keller rose. He stood behind the chair and gripped the back of the chair. He wet his lips. "I'm afraid I've changed my mind, Admiral," he said. "I'm afraid we've failed. Whether Jeff Baker leaked, whether the leak was in Washington, or whether it was somewhere else I don't know. But I find I must conclude that Jeff Baker is telling the truth, until proved otherwise."

"I agree with you, Fred," said Morgan Collingwood. "I don't think we can reach an arbitrary decision here at this time. I think there should be a complete investigation in Washington. I think

Quigley should go on Sunday's plane, and lay the whole matter in the lap of the Department."

"I think that would be proper procedure," said Keller. "Meanwhile I feel I should discontinue Atlantis operations."

The Admiral straightened the fleet on his desk. He pushed out his lower lip. He was thinking. The Admiral had not become an admiral by disregarding the advice of his staff. The Admiral knew what to do when he sighted unexpected enemy strength. "You certainly changed your mind in a hurry," he fired at Keller.

"Yes, I suppose I did," Keller said. "But now I am certain of how I feel."

The Admiral shook his impressive, white-maned head. In his day the world had been understandable. We had fifteen battleships, the British had fifteen battleships, the Japs nine, and the rest were second-rate powers. A man spent his life learning Mahan, and then heretics came along who said the battleship was just a fat target. The heretics talked of psychological warfare, and political warfare, and battle by radio. He had tried to learn this new type of warfare, but he had found it difficult and even unbelievable. How did it fit in with Mahan? How could a man disregard the Bible? The world would be better off if it got back to battleships. With battleships, a man knew where he stood. "Well, I suppose I'll have to go along with you," he said.

"May I suggest, sir," Keller said, "that Mr. Collingwood and Quig and I prepare a report on this matter without referring to the Atlantis part? Quig can catch Sunday's plane and take the document safe hand, and fill in the Department orally on the Atlantis section."

"Yes, I suppose that's the way to do it," the Admiral agreed. "It should go to Matson, or the Undersecretary, or the Secretary."

"The correct channel," said Morgan Collingwood, "would be to tell Matson first, and then allow Matson to inform the highest levels."

"Very well," said the Admiral. Now that he had thought it over, he could see that it was probably best to pass it along to Matson. It would be necessary to discontinue Atlantis for a time. This was disappointing. He suspected that the Navy would soon recall him to active duty, and it would be nice to go back with a third star. But if there were a security scandal during his administration of the Budapest Mission, he might not get active duty. The safe thing to do was lay it in the lap of Washington.

4

On Saturday Jeff didn't leave his room, even for a walk. He was afraid to leave because someone might telephone, or drop up to see him, and he wouldn't be there. He concentrated on his Toynbee, but his mind kept wandering to the letter he had sent to Horace Locke.

He tried to imagine the course of that letter. If L'Engle's plane was right on time, and if L'Engle cleared customs in a hurry, and if he went directly to Old State, then Horace Locke might have received the letter Friday afternoon. But if anything happened—any delay at all—then he wouldn't get it until today. He wondered whether Horace Locke worked Saturdays. There wasn't any reason for him to work Saturdays because there wasn't anything for him to do. Maybe L'Engle would find Locke at home if he wasn't in his office. He thought Locke lived in the Metropolitan Club, but he wasn't sure. He was sure that L'Engle would deliver the letter. On that he would gamble his life.

Quincy Todd called him late in the morning and said, "I see you're still here."

"Barely," Jeff said.

"Lonesome?"

"Uh-huh."

"I'll come up tonight and bring some local talent."

"I'd rather not." He had been trying to write Susan, and found there was nothing really he could say, and anyway there was the chance he might find himself back in Washington before the letter.

"Just for laughs."

"Okay, for laughs." It would be good, anyway, to see a human face.

5

And Saturday afternoon Quigley visited him. Quigley sat down in the prim way he had, and dropped a worn dispatch case, its lock askew and its seams leaking threads, at his feet. "Going somewhere?" Jeff said.

"Yes, I'm going to Washington. I suppose you can guess why."

"I suppose I can. Do you think I have a chance?"

Quigley considered the question. "I have been in the Department for thirty years," he said finally. "If I could guess what the Department was going to do, it would be necessary for me to be Secretary of State, and not a security officer. On occasion I believe that not even the Secretary knows what the Department will do, until it is done. That has been my experience."

"That's a helluva answer, Quig."

"You're in a helluva situation, if you will pardon the language."

"Am I?"

"Yes. You see, you have nothing to substantiate your story. It is true that your friend Leonides doesn't seem to be in Budapest. That I've discovered. But it doesn't prove anything. He might have been transferred, or on a trip, or down at Balaton for the skating."

"It's true."

"I believe it, Jeff. But who else will? Will Matson? Will the Secretary, if it goes to the Secretary? Do you have a friend in the Department, Jeff? It might be better if you had a friend in the Department."

Jeff thought it over. "I suppose you'd call him a friend. You know Horace Locke?"

"Certainly I know Horace Locke. It was a terrible blow to the Department when it lost Horace Locke. It was like losing Sumner Welles."

Jeff drew in his breath. "Lost Horace Locke! He's still there, isn't he?"

"If you mean is his name still on the Foreign Service List, yes he is still there. But he has no influence, and almost no job. I feel very sorry for him, and I'm afraid he won't be able to help you."

"He is the only friend, except Susan Pickett, of course."

Quigley struggled with the twisted lock of his dispatch case, said, "Darn it! Darn it!" and finally it opened. He took out a notebook. "Now, Jeff, I want you to tell me the rest of the story about Lasenko —every detail—everything you can remember."

So Jeff told everything he hadn't told in the Admiral's office the day before—except the two names—the survivor in Budapest and the one in Moscow, the big one. He knew that Quigley was going to ask for the names, and when he did ask Jeff said:

"I'm sorry, Quig."

Quigley nodded. "I understand. As a matter of fact I think you're very discreet, Jeff, and I won't press you. You say you sent a confidential report on Lasenko to Locke. Of course the Department doesn't consider that proper, Jeff. On the other hand it is done very frequently, and usually the reasons are excellent, as in this case. So I shall say nothing of it. But I do urge you also to send the names to Locke. As you pointed out to Lasenko, in case anything happens to you."

Jeff smiled. "In case anything happens to me. How will I get the names to Locke?"

"I'll take them."

"Really?"

"Certainly I'll take them. They'll be in Washington Monday. Just sit down at your typewriter and write a note to Horace Locke. You can't mention your own affair, of course, because that is restricted Department business. Just write the names, and say if anything happens to Lasenko, these other men can be contacted."

A man couldn't do everything himself. A man had to trust other men. He found he trusted Quigley as he trusted L'Engle. He moved across the room and sat down at the typewriter and wrote one brief paragraph.

Then he signed his name and addressed an envelope. He folded the paper and slipped it inside the envelope and handed it to Quigley. "Here you are."

"Aren't you going to seal it?"

"No."

Quigley took the envelope and dropped it into his dispatch case on top of his notebook and other envelopes garnished with red wax. He didn't say anything. He spent an absurd length of time fussing with the lock.

Jeff watched him. He seemed at this time so ridiculously small and inefficient. Jeff went to the closet and found his own dispatch case, which since he arrived in Budapest had been used for nothing except a liquor cache. He removed the half-empty bottle of cognac, and the pint of emergency rye. What was it Susan had said about this case? She hoped it would bring back something to wipe her fear away? Was that what she had said? Well, this was the only chance the case would get. "Quig," he said, "how about trading cases? Yours has had it, and I never use mine."

Quigley, still bending over, looked up. "That's an awful good case. I wouldn't think of taking it. This one is shot, but I'll get another in New York."

"Come on, take this one," Jeff argued.

"No, you keep it."

"I wish you would. I've got reasons."

Quigley stood up and took Jeff's case and ran his fingers along the beautifully turned leather and picked at the seams and inspected the lock. Then he took his envelopes and notebook out of the old case and transferred them to Jeff's case. "This is awfully good of you," he said. "This is the best case I've ever had."

"You're really doing me a favor when you take it," Jeff said.

Quigley shook hands, and Jeff said, "I guess I won't be seeing you again."

"I hope you'll be seeing me very soon and very often. You've done a very nice thing for me, Jeff. I don't think anybody ever did such a nice thing for me. Now goodbye."

Jeff thought it was very strange that a hard little guy like Quigley would be so upset, and even have tears in his eyes, and he wondered why.

CHAPTER SIXTEEN

1

QUIGLEY HAD CROSSED the Atlantic sixty-four times by ship, and this was his fiftieth crossing by air, and therefore something of a milestone. He kept a notebook to record miles traveled, and times of departure and arrival, and amusing non-official incidents en route, so that when he got home he would have something to talk about with his wife. This record was also useful when he made out his expense vouchers, and figured his per diem travel allowance. No Department finance officer or general accounting office auditor ever questioned the figures of William Quigley.

On this day, after he was seated in the Constellation, and had wedged his dispatch case against the plane's cushiony side with his leg, he took out his notebook—the thirtieth of identical size and shape that he had used up since joining the Department—and wrote, "December 25, 1949." December 25th. Another Christmas away from home.

He waited while the stewardess brought him chewing gum, and asked whether his seat belt was fastened, and did he want a paper or magazine. This was always the most enjoyable part of the trip home. When the neat, clean stewardess smiled and spoke to him, and he smelled the washed, engineered air inside an airplane, he was already back in America. America sent shining, metal slivers of itself through the air, filled with America's conveniences and luxuries and speed and efficiencies, to bring its wanderers home.

The motors showed their power, the plane began to move, and when he was sure they were airborne he wrote, "Took off from Budapest 9:32 A.M. Central European Time." He looked again at the date. In a few days the first half of the century would be gone. It had been some century, so far. In this half-century—in his life-time—the wonders he had seen! The electric light, the telephone, automobiles, airplanes, radios, all the new sciences, the new drugs, television—they all belonged to his century. None of them had been around when he was born. What a century it could have been, but what a century it had been. He wondered whether the second half would be any better than the first. It couldn't be much worse. Or could it? What would the school children, oh, in two thousand years, remember of his century? Would they recall all the wonders, or would they recite, "The Twentieth Century was the century of the atomic bomb and the beginning of the Second Dark Ages?"

He wondered whether he had done anything to help things along and he was still wondering when he fell asleep. While he slept the pressure of the dispatch case was comfortable against his leg.

He slept from Budapest to Vienna and he slept from Vienna to Prague and from Prague to Shannon. In Shannon he ate roast beef sandwiches and drank a quart of rich Irish milk. It was when they were halfway across the Atlantic that he put his dispatch case across his knees, opened it, and checked the envelopes within. When he came to Jeff's letter to Horace Locke he balanced it on his fingers and it was very thin and fragile, not at all like the other bulkier envelopes with their heavy red seals. He put it back in the dispatch case. Then he slept again.

When the plane touched down at National Airport he took out his notebook and wrote, "December 26, 1949—arrived Washington 10:57 A.M. E.S.T."

Customs and Immigration knew him, of course. As he got into a cab a newsboy was yelling about a new crisis, but he didn't buy a paper because he didn't want to know of any more crises. He debated what to do first, and decided that business must come first, and said, "New State."

"Virginia Avenue entrance?"

"That's correct."

2

While he waited in Gerald Matson's secretarial office he wished he'd stopped at the airport restaurant for coffee. People came in and out of Matson's office as if they were attached to an endless chain. He said to the receptionist, "I beg your pardon, but did you give Mr. Matson my name?"

"Mister—" the receptionist hesitated—"Quigley, was it?"

"Yes, Quigley. I just came in from Budapest. Didn't the Admiral cable that I was coming?"

"I really don't know," the girl said. He could see that she hadn't been long in the Department. He classified her as a CAF-4, engaged to a CAF-5.

"Well perhaps," he suggested, "you'd better tell Mr. Matson that I'm here from Budapest, and I have to see him on important business."

"All our business is important," she parried. She thought he was a peculiar little man, who probably sold insurance. She rummaged in a drawer until she found a handkerchief, wiped her lips off, and did them over again, wider.

Into the mind of Quigley there crept a pixie. "You will, eventually, tell him I'm here, won't you?" he inquired.

"Oh, yes, eventually."

Quigley thought, I've never done anything like this before, and why I should start at my age I don't know. But it might be fun and I think I'll try it because at my age one doesn't have much fun. "When you decide to present my name to Mr. Matson," he said, "would you also give him a message? Just a few words?"

"Okay, Mister Quigley. See, I remember your name."

"So you did. Just say, 'Atlantis has been penetrated.' "

She thought it over, and said, "That sounds dirty to me. Who's Atlantis?"

"Never mind. Just tell him."

She repeated, " 'Atlantis has been penetrated.' Okay, Mr. Quigley, as soon as Mr. Soukis has conferred with Mr. Matson, I'll go in there and say, 'Atlantic has been penetrated.' "

"Atlantis."

"Oh, sure. Atlantis."

A man came out of Matson's office, and the receptionist said, "Well, there goes Soukis. He's a big Greek. But I mean, big. Now I'll tell Mr. Matson you're here."

She came out again almost immediately. She didn't stop in the outer office, but fled into the hallway. Behind her was Gerald Matson, his dark eyes blazing like beacons in the pallid desert of his face.

3

Quigley's interview with Matson lasted through the lunch hour, and into the afternoon. Quigley presented the documents, and then told what could not be put down on paper. He told everything, because he was a perfect reporter. He mentioned everything except the letter he had for Horace Locke. This he classified as a personal matter.

When he had finished Matson asked, "And what did the Admiral recommend?"

"He wants Baker recalled."

"I don't blame him, but what about Atlantis?"

"He's laying that in your lap, Mr. Matson. Keller has discontinued operations."

"He's not going to put it in my lap. It's Keller's baby."

"Isn't it your baby, too, Mr. Matson?" Quigley asked gently.

Atlantis was his baby, of course. It was true he had not conceived it, but he had adopted it, nurtured it through the infancy of planning, presented it to all the best people, and pushed it into active maturity. He displayed it in the Department's higher levels with a parent's pride for a genius son. Atlantis multiplied his importance in the Department. It placed additional personnel under his control, and gave him access, at any time, to those who decided national policy. It had won him a place on the Planning Board. It had elevated the Balkans Division, so long a Department stepchild, almost to the level of Western Europe, and certainly to the level of Central Europe and Far East. If Atlantis succeeded he would share the credit with Fred Keller. He could look forward to an important Embassy. Perhaps even Paris. Anya would love Paris.

If Atlantis failed he would lose ground. If the circumstances surrounding the failure smelled of carelessness or scandal, it could be—Matson had a horrible vision. "This Baker," he remarked, "has certainly fouled things up. Not that I didn't expect it. I expected it all along. My opinion is that he got himself into trouble and concocted a story, and as he became more involved he piled one lie on another, in the manner of all liars. Furthermore, I think he was deliberately malicious."

"Whatever mistakes he may have made," said Quigley, "I won't believe Jeff Baker is malicious. I'm not even sure he made any mistakes."

"Oh, yes, he's malicious!" said Matson. "He knows very well that my wife is a White Russian! So he cunningly contrived to quote this so-called Russian turncoat as blaming this so-called penetration on White Russians here in the United States. You know what I think it is? I think it's a plot!"

Quigley crossed his knees, and seemed to be absorbed in adjusting the crease in his trousers. "You know," he said, "I hadn't thought of that."

"You don't think my wife would be indiscreet, do you?" Matson said.

"Anybody can be indiscreet—even me."

"Oh, come on now!"

"What do you intend to do, Mr. Matson?" Quigley asked.

"I'm not sure—yet. But I expect to do something fast."

"Are there any more questions you wish to ask me?"

"No. I'll call if I need you."

"Goodbye, Mr. Matson." Quigley was in a hurry to leave.

When he was gone Matson picked up the telephone and called his wife. "Anya," he said, "where's Iggy?"

"Why, he's still in Hollywood."

"That place is full of Reds."

"What are you talking about?"

He hesitated, while he tried to frame the question safely. "Anya," he said, "now don't be angry, but I want to ask you something. Do you remember when Iggy was in Washington and we were discussing something very important, and I told you not to talk in front of him?"

"Of course I remember it. Why did you bring it up?"

"You didn't talk to him any more, did you?"

There was that infinitesimal moment of hesitation, that the lie detector can diagnose but the human ear can only sense, and never with sureness. "Why, of course not, dear."

"That's good, dear."

"Why, what's this all about, Gerald?"

"Never mind. Forget it."

"Now, Gerald, don't tell me forget it! You call up with these mysterious questions and want me to forget it. I want to know what's the matter. After all, I'm a woman, and a woman is a curious creature."

"Can't talk about it over the phone. Just remember that you never mentioned anything to Iggy."

"Why, I didn't, dear," she said, and hung up.

Gerald Matson made up his mind.

4

And Quigley was walking up the stairs of Old State, on the Pennsylvania Avenue side.

He found Horace Locke at his desk. They had not seen each other for two or three years, but their greetings didn't show this. In the space of their service and acquaintanceship two or three years was not a long period of time. They greeted each other as if they had lunched together at the Occidental only a week or two before.

Quigley unsnapped the lock on his case and Horace Locke said, "That's a nice case you've got, Quig. Your old one finally collapse?"

"I traded," said Quigley, "with young Jeff Baker." He brought out Jeff's letter and handed it to Locke. "I brought this letter from him."

Horace Locke took the envelope and turned it in his hands. He saw that the flap was unsealed—saw that it had never been sealed. "Do you know what's in here?" he asked.

"No. Not exactly. I know it contains two names. Two important names. I don't know what they are. I presume you got Jeff's other letter, safe hand?"

"I did." Horace Locke allowed his mind to search its experience and reach a conclusion. The conclusion was that Jeff trusted Quigley implicitly. Jeff had left the letter unsealed for a purpose. Jeff wanted him to know that Quig was a friend. So Horace Locke could ask the question. "What kind of trouble is the boy in?"

"I'm going to tell you," Quigley said. "I don't know what's come over me. Everything about this case is classified, some of it confidential, some secret, and some of it top secret, and I'm still going to tell you."

"I used to be allowed to keep secrets," said Horace Locke.

"So you did. So you did. But I feel you'll have to take action, as well as use discretion."

Horace Locke looked out of the window at the White House, and the Capitol beyond. It was his view. He had seen it a long time. But it always fascinated him, for somehow it seemed always to be changing. It was almost as if the buildings changed with the character of the people inside them. "I've known ever since Friday that I would have to take action," Locke said. "I knew Friday why I had been waiting here all this time."

"I don't think it will be easy for you," Quigley said.

"I will do what is required."

"I know you will." For the second time he told the story. It did not differ in so much as a word from the story he had told Matson.

It was dusk when Quigley left Old State. He should have called his wife. If she knew that he had arrived in the morning, and still hadn't called, she would be angry. And she would know what time his plane landed, because of the notebook. He crossed to the Willard, and bought twelve roses. Roses in mid-winter Mrs. Quigley could not resist.

5

Horace Locke considered his first step. Eventually the affair would have to go to the Secretary. Of that he was sure. Certainly the news of this Russian fission should go before the Secretary at once. The news was not unexpected to Horace Locke. He had been awaiting news of this kind. He knew the history of dictatorships. They always appeared colossal and monolithic from the outside, but inside they were hollow. They were like the buildings erected for fairs. They didn't last. By his very form of suppression, the dictator invites and compels violence from his opposition. And no ruler lives without opposition. Daggers had dispatched Caesar, bullets Mussolini. There are not enough spies to watch a whole people nor enough jails to contain a fraction of a dictator's enemies. So the Soviet dictatorship, too, would come to an end.

But more pressing was the predicament of Nicholas Baker's son. If Jeff Baker were discredited, and tossed out of the Department, his story of the Russian resistance would never be believed. It might not be believed in any case, but once he was deprived of his official standing Jeff would have no chance. Not even the newspapers would touch it. They'd label him a disgruntled young man who had been fired from the Department, probably as a security risk, and not to be believed.

The best thing was to sound out Matson. He didn't like Matson, but he understood him. He deduced it would be in Matson's interest to get rid of Nick's son. If Matson discovered that Jeff had a friend—perhaps of little influence but still of sufficient voice to be heard in some circles of the Department—Matson would hesitate. He knew Matson.

He dialed the Balkans Division. A girl, probably the receptionist in the outer office, answered. "I would like to speak to Mr. Matson," he said. "This is Horace Locke speaking. It's urgent."

"Who did you say?" the girl demanded.

"Horace Locke." He could not say, "I am Adviser to the Diplomatic Monuments and Memorials Commission." That didn't mean anything to anybody. He said, "In the Department."

"I'm sorry," the girl said in a sing-song Tennessee twang, "but Mr. Matson has gone for the day."

"Has he gone home?"

"How do I know? He's gone." The receptionist clicked off her key. Well, she thought, it was sort of a white lie. Mr. Matson was already running into overtime, drafting one of those cables. And the longer he stayed, the longer they'd all have to stay. This guy whose name she'd never heard before called up and said something was urgent, and if she put him through to Mr. Matson they might be all night. So she had done her boss a favor, and herself too. She had a dinner date and she didn't want to be late because her fellow would soon be a CAF-6 and then they would get married and she could get out of this damn nine-to-five slavery. Nobody would know, and she wasn't hurting anybody.

Horace Locke called Matson's home in Alexandria. He wasn't home yet. Anya Matson didn't know when he would be home. He must be working late at the office.

Horace Locke waited thirty minutes, and dialed Balkans again. The receptionist was still there, and he thought it strange that she would be there if Matson had left for the day. "Are you the same one who called before?" she asked.

"Why yes."

"Didn't I tell you he left?"

"Yes."

"Well, don't ring here any more. I'm busy."

Horace Locke put down his telephone gently and leaned back in his chair and told himself to control his temper. Rebuffs like this always made him feel badly, made him want to go off somewhere

where there weren't any people, and he knew that this feeling was not right. It seemed to Horace Locke that people were changing. They all seemed rude and snappish, as if they were fighting their way into the subway after an exhausting day. He was appalled by their uniform rudeness. The waiters, the barbers, hotel clerks, Pullman porters, taxi drivers, redcaps, druggists, telephone operators, building guards—their characters all seemed in the process of chemical change. Fear and uncertainty were corroding them with selfishness and greed, and the corrosion showed in rudeness. "Maybe I'm silly," Horace Locke told himself aloud. "Maybe I'm just getting old, and it's me, not other people. Maybe I'm old and irritable. I must be getting old, or what would I be doing sitting here and talking to myself?"

He tried Matson's home once more, and he still wasn't there. Well, probably Matson wouldn't make his decision at once. It would take two or three days. He would see Matson in the morning.

He wondered whether it would do any good to try the Secretary's office, and decided against it. He had no right to know anything of this affair. It would be most presumptuous for him to take it to the Secretary. It might even endanger the chances of Nick's son. Anyway he wasn't sure the Secretary would see him. He had known the Secretary many years before, and from time to time had had business contacts with the Secretary, but he had not seen him, now, for four years. So he didn't dial the Secretary, although he had a hunch the Secretary would still be on the job. Horace Locke went home to his club.

6

That morning the Secretary had ridden for his usual hour in Rock Creek Park, breakfasted at seven, and arrived at the office at eight-thirty. The early morning broadcasts had warned him he'd have a busy day. Even Arthur Godfrey sounded lugubrious, and when there was no cheer in Godfrey then the world was in a sorry state.

It was, too.

The Russians had murdered an eighteen-year-old G.I. in Vienna. So said Headquarters of United States Forces Austria. Radio Moscow's version was different, but Moscow's version was always different. He would instruct Keyes to protest. The protest wouldn't do any good.

Stockholm was frightened. All night Stockholm had seen shooting stars that didn't come from Heaven.

Something foul was going on in the uranium mines of the Belgian Congo. Brussels blamed it on Soviet propaganda. But Brussels also suggested that if the Southern Senators could be persuaded to stop screaming their racism, the blacks in the Congo might go back to work.

The un-American Committee was sniping at one of his section chiefs whose wife's nephew had attended a Communist Front rally in San Francisco. The Committee wanted him fired at once, and the section chief was in the Secretary's outer office, hysterical and in tears, with an armload of affidavits saying he had always lived in Westchester County and voted straight Republican.

The President was in bed with Virus X.

Greece and Turkey needed more money.

So did China.

The Dominican Republic said Trujillo was en route to Washington, where he expected to be received by the President and presented with a four-motored flying yacht, and a cruiser, three destroyers, and a few tanks. He wanted to fight Venezuela.

There was bad news from Korea, Afghanistan, Damascus, Jerusalem, Prague, Indo-China, Trieste, and Rome.

The Secretary lunched with the Joint Chiefs of Staff and attended a three o'clock Cabinet meeting.

When he got back to his office memoranda and cables rose in a ten-inch pile from the center of his desk. They were all urgent, and all required immediate decisions and answers.

He cancelled his press conference.

He was presented with a scroll by the Daughters of the Spanish-American War.

He took two aspirins and a glass of bicarbonate of soda, and then dictated the speech he would make the following night at the Legion banquet.

A cable typed on red paper, labeling it extremely urgent and confidential, came in from the Counselor of a Central American Mission. It said the Minister had been on a three-week toot, and what should he do?

The Secretary telephoned his wife that he wouldn't be home for dinner.

He had chicken sandwiches and milk in his office, and talked by telephone to the President, the Ambassador in London, and his son, who was going to New York for the New Year's weekend and needed an extra hundred dollars.

France needed an extra hundred million.

No matter how fast he cerebrated, he couldn't seem to diminish the pile of papers on his desk, all tabbed red for urgent.

He became aware that one of his secretaries was reeling with fatigue, and sent her home.

The Department of State was quiet, now. It was past nine, and the business of government was slowing down. In all New State, only the lights in the code and cipher section and the Secretary's office still burned.

He was wearing down that pile. At ten o'clock a messenger brought four final cables, to be read and rejected or initialed.

The Secretary's hands and knees trembled with tiredness. His shoulders were broad and his courage limitless, but there was too much trouble in the world for one man.

The last cable was outgoing from Balkans to Budapest. It demanded the resignation of someone in the Budapest Mission named Baker. The Secretary lifted his glasses to his forehead and rubbed his eyes. It was too bad, he thought, too bad that some could not stand the strain, and must fall by the wayside. He initialed the cable. A secretary appeared and took it away. He must go home and get to bed, he thought. Tomorrow might be worse.

CHAPTER SEVENTEEN

1

The cable reached Budapest Tuesday morning, addressed BLAN-KENHORN FOR BAKER, but it was almost midnight before Jeff Baker sat down to type his answer. It had taken that long to make up his mind. Some decisions, even of life and death—such as whether to cross the street—are made in an instant. Others bear a clear sign saying "crossroads" and require thought and calculation.

The request for his resignation had hardly surprised him, but he was startled by the detail in which his sins were listed. The cable was like an indictment drawn up by a prosecuting attorney not quite sure of his case, who seeks to base an edifice of guilt upon many thin laths of accusation. It was not at all like a cable from the Secretary of State, and yet the Secretary's name was signed to it, and it could be assumed that such a cable would at least be seen by the Secretary, and initialed, before dispatching. But there was no way to be sure, for all cables from the Department bear the Secretary's name, whether they concern the drafting of a new treaty or the disposition of an old steamer trunk.

On this night candles lit his room. Whether there was a power failure, or the government was conserving electricity, or whether the lights were out in this sector of Budapest alone he did not know, and it was useless to inquire of Madame Angell or Sandor. He had placed candlesticks at each end of the long Italian desk, so that they framed his portable. The shadows shielded the imperfections of the furnishings, rounded the angular chairs. It was a Nineteenth Century room, and it became warm and mellow in Nineteenth Century lighting. It had been his home for almost four months. In that time his belongings had found their place here, like roots in hospitable soil. Now, whatever his decision, those roots would be torn up.

Before him was this implacable sheet of flimsy—a notice of eviction, certificate of failure, diploma of disgrace. Six other paraphrased copies of the cable would have been made in the code room, and distributed, so that by now everyone in the Legation would know. He suspected this was why through the whole day he had received no phone calls and no visitors. News of the cable would have seeped to the British and the French, and even the Hungarians, during the cocktail hour at the Park Club. The cable had come in BROWN, a code which the Germans had broken in 1941 but which was still used for matters classified as less than secret because it was economical, saving wordage by compressing standard departmental phrases into single symbols. So probably the Russians would read the cable too. It would puzzle them.

The paraphrase read:

"Most disturbing information has reached the Department concerning your conduct, which appears to border on treason, in the Budapest Mission. Specifically you are charged with the following violation of State Department regulations:

"1. Without authority engaging in diplomatic negotiations with an official of a foreign power.

"2. Endangering United States policy by indiscreet utterances to an official of a foreign power.

"3. Deliberately disobeying warnings not to associate with representatives of this power.

"4. Refusal to obey direct orders of superior.

"5. Conduct unbecoming of an officer of the Foreign Service.

"6. Purloining narcotic drugs from the Mission dispensary.

"Since all these charges have been substantiated the Department regrets requiring your immediate resignation. However, in view of your inexperience, and your previous record in the armed forces, the Department will permit you to resign without prejudice. In accordance with regulations governing such cases, passage will be furnished to your home station."

The last paragraph was the key, of course. It was an invitation to go quietly, without a fight. The rest of the cable was there simply to show him resistance was hopeless, as indeed it seemed to be.

All he had to do was write and sign a simple note of resignation and that would end it. It would sponge off the first thirty years of his life. No public stain would remain. He could go home and marry Susan. He could get a job and start over. If necessary, he could refer without shame to his short diplomatic career. It might even carry an aurora of distinction. He could say, "Oh, yes, I was Third Secretary in the Legation at Budapest. Had to give it up. Not enough money in it."

Yet he could not bring himself to write his resignation. All day he had known he would not write a resignation. He could go home and get a job, but never again for his government, for in the files would be this unchallenged cable. This was peculiarly important to him. He was a Washington boy and a government boy, and all his life a career in the Department had represented honor, respectability, and security.

And he couldn't let down Leonides.

Had he been a FSS or a FSR instead of a FSO he would have been deprived of choice. Those on the staff, and in the reserve, could be fired without formality. They could be labeled security risks and fired, and they could never discover by whom they were denounced, and only generally of what they were accused. But in his case it was different. He had been appointed by the President, and confirmed by the Senate, and it would take something approximating a court-martial to get rid of him.

He could use his hearing to tell his story. Perhaps he would be believed in Washington, even if unbelieved in Budapest.

There would be the unpleasant taint of a Departmental trial. It would undoubtedly leak to the press. To have a hundred people in Washington and Budapest know of these accusations was one thing. To have a hundred million people know was quite something else. If there was a Departmental trial, and he was not believed and fired from the Department, his name would be damaged beyond his own lifetime. So long as there were clippings in the steel morgues of newspapers, his name would be tainted. It would not be a good thing to pass on to a son.

Yet it was necessary that he fight. There was nothing else to do. The blank paper was already in his typewriter. While it seemed no more probable that the Secretary would ever see the letter than that God should note each sparrow fallen from Heaven, he typed it in the traditional form.

"To the Secretary of State,

"Sir—

"I have the honor to report receipt of your coded cable 49122692, classified confidential. Despite this cable I find I cannot resign from the Foreign Service of the United States. I will be happy to answer the charges contained in this cable at any time, according to your convenience."

He signed his full name at the bottom, boldly, Jefferson Wilson Baker.

He yawned, stretched, and broke open his pint of emergency rye. He poured three fingers of the whiskey into a water tumbler and drank it. Then he looked again at his reply to the cable. He would deliver it to the Admiral or Morgan Collingwood in the morning.

It looked right.

2

On that Tuesday morning Horace Locke had found a young woman outside his office door. He put his key in the lock and she said, "You're Mr. Locke, aren't you?"

"Yes, I'm Locke."

"My name's Susan Pickett. I wonder whether you could see me, Mr. Locke?"

"Certainly. Come in." Hardly anyone ever visited Horace Locke, except to peddle magazine subscriptions, or ask for donations to the Community Chest or Red Cross, or to get his name on petitions. People didn't seem to have much interest or pride in past diplomatic triumphs. They didn't care what happened to the original copies of old treaties. The trouble was, of course, that what had seemed triumphs in 1921, and 1925, and.1932 now were listed as disasters. This girl seemed tense, and agitated, and he wondered what she could want. Anyway, she was pretty. He didn't often see a girl so pretty in the dour and creaking pile of Old State.

He drew up the one chair he hoped was comfortable, and held its back for her in a courtly manner long out of fashion in government offices. "Now, Miss Pickett?" he inquired. She was extraordinarily vivacious. It would have been fun, having a daughter like this. Now that it was too late, he wished he'd produced children. A man was never really dead if he had children. Long ago he had loved a woman in London, but marriage had been impossible. It was unfortunate that he was a one-love man.

"Mr. Locke," she began, "I understand you're a friend of Jeff Baker's. He's mentioned you in his letters, and he's never mentioned anyone else in the Department, and so I felt you would be his friend and I could come to you."

"More precisely, I was his father's friend," Horace Locke said.

"Oh. Maybe I shouldn't have come to you. I don't suppose you want to get mixed up in this. But I don't think he has any other friends in the Department—and he needs a friend."

"Don't mistake me," said Horace Locke. "I'm very fond of Jeff Baker—very much interested in him. Have been all his life. Are you his friend too?"

She said, "I love him."

"Oh. I can only say that Jeff has very good taste."

"Thank you, Mr. Locke. He is also in very serious trouble."

Now his thin, sensitive hands were on the desk, and he was looking at her differently than he had before, and all his instincts were alert and wary. "How do you know that?" he demanded.

She took a cigarette from her bag and tapped it on her thumbnail, and he noticed that her nails were well shaped, but stubby from typing. He guessed she was deciding what to tell, or how much to tell, so he said, "You can tell me the whole thing, Susan Pickett. I'm on Jeff's side, and I think I know something of this too."

She put the cigarette back in her bag. "I work in the Department," she said. "Secretarial. I take the nine o'clock conference."

"This matter of Jeff's didn't come up at the conference, did it?"

"No. If it had, I couldn't talk about it."

"Of course not."

She went on, "I have a friend named Gertrude Kerns. She works in Balkans. We always have coffee together in the cafeteria after I've typed the agenda. This morning she told me Jeff was being recalled. He has been asked to resign. They sent a cable last night. She knows I know Jeff. She doesn't know how I feel about him."

"So quick," exclaimed Horace Locke. "So damnably quick!" Matson hadn't wasted an hour. Matson wanted Jeff Baker out of the Department. Locke didn't know why. He might never know. There could be so many reasons. In the internal workings of the Department there were always so many personal reasons. The Department was men, and therefore the Department possessed men's emotions, their frailities, hopes, ideals, and passions. Always hidden. Always the most secret of secrets.

Susan didn't seem to hear him. She resumed speaking, almost in a monotone. "I didn't know what to do. I told her I had a pain in my stomach and it might be appendicitis. I told her please to go to the Undersecretary's office and tell them I felt sick and couldn't take the conference. I went up to code and cipher and got a paraphrase of the cable. I suppose I'll get in trouble. I don't care. Here it is."

She had drawn a folded paper from her bag. Now she handed it across the desk.

Horace Locke read it, and read it again. "They didn't leave out anything, did they?" he murmured. He saw it was a carefully constructed cable, shrewd in semantics. It was strong enough to blast

Jeff out of Budapest, and out of the Department. It was not sufficiently specific, or important enough to the national welfare, to make further investigation necessary.

"What did you say?" Susan asked.

"Nothing. I'll handle this. I'll handle it and let you know. Now get this paraphrase back to code and cipher, and forget it."

"All right. I thank you so much, Mr. Locke. I feel better now."

He saw that she had something else to say.

"Mr. Locke, I almost didn't come here."

"I'm glad you did."

"I am too, now, but I almost didn't. I want Jeff home. I want him."

Horace Locke said, "I don't guarantee that he won't be home. I have very little influence. I can only do what I can. It may be too late already. Whatever happens in Washington, in the last analysis it will be his decision. Even with the six-hour time difference, he will already have this cable. It will have been decoded and paraphrased in the Budapest Legation, and he will have had time to answer. He may already have resigned."

"I don't think so," she said. "He'll think it over, and over, and over, if he has any chance at all. I don't know whether he can deny any of these charges. I can't believe that Jeff would endanger his country, or take dope, or disgrace the Department. I just can't believe it. If he did he'll have to quit, of course."

"I'm sure his behavior was correct," said Horace Locke. "I'm sure."

She raised her eyes to his. "You are sure, aren't you? You know something I don't know."

"Yes, I do." Naturally he couldn't tell her of the Russian business. Baker had entrusted him with important official information for official use. He could not use it for personal reassurance, and Susan Pickett's interest in this matter was personal.

"If he hasn't done these things Jeff won't quit," she said. "He mustn't quit. It would break his heart to quit. He might think he'd be the same if he resigned without prejudice. He might think he'd be the same out of the Department. But he wouldn't, really. He'd be a different Jeff. I've thought it through. I want him to stay there and do his job. I can wait. I've waited a long time for Jeff. I can wait two years more—two years and eight months."

Horace Locke said, "I'll do my best."

She rose, and he rose and opened the door for her. As she left he could not help putting his arm around her shoulder. She needed reassurance. She didn't have to sham her inner sickness.

3

Now the time had come for Horace Locke to act. There was no use appealing to Matson now. Matson had committed himself. Only the Secretary of State could save Jeff Baker.

He dialed 3071. A pleasant voice sang, "Office of the Secretary of State."

"This is Horace Locke, in the Department. I must speak with the Secretary."

"Is he expecting your call, Mr. Locke?"

"No. But it's very important."

"I'm sorry, Mr. Locke, but I don't seem to place you. What Division are you in?"

"I'm Adviser to the Diplomatic Monuments and Memorials Commission." He tried to make it sound important, but he knew it didn't.

"Well, may I suggest you send the Secretary a memo, Mr. Locke. You know he's terribly busy. He's never been busier."

"This is really urgent, and really important," Locke said.

The girl hesitated, and then said, "Well, in that case I suggest you dial one of the Secretary's executive assistants. Their branch is 2881."

"Very well," said Horace Locke.

4

He dialed 2881. He didn't know any of the assistants. They were all younger. But he knew their names. He asked for Mr. Partridge. He told Mr. Partridge he had to see the Secretary immediately, on a matter pressing and of vital importance.

"Couldn't you come over and talk to me?" Partridge asked. "You know how it is, Mr. Locke. The Secretary is snowed under."

"I'll have to see the Secretary himself," Locke insisted. "This is extremely serious, and extremely confidential."

"Couldn't you give me some idea what it's about? After all, that's all I do from seven in the morning until midnight—handle stuff that is serious and confidential."

"Hold on a moment while I think it over," Locke said. If he saw Partridge he'd have to start explaining from the very beginning. And when Partridge learned it concerned the cable asking for Baker's resignation, Partridge would say it was strictly an administrative matter, and should be taken up with the Undersecretary. Partridge would conclude it was just another case of an old hand in the Department interceding for a young man who was in trouble. It was routine. Partridge would consign it to the Undersecretary, if he was convinced it should go anywhere at all. "No, Mr. Partridge," Locke said, "I can't tell you. It must go to the Secretary, and to him alone."

"Well, I'm sorry that you feel that way, Mr. Locke. I can't do anything for you. I suggest that you dictate a memo."

Horace Locke put down the telephone. He chuckled. He couldn't dictate memos. He didn't even have a stenographer. He tried to think of a way to get to the Secretary. He was still thinking at lunch.

Early in the afternoon he looked out of the window. Across the street photographers were knotting at the entrance to the executive office of the White House. The President must be better. He saw a limousine swing through the White House grounds. It was a

Rolls-Royce, and that would mean the British Ambassador. He watched other limousines stop at the executive wing. More ambassadors.

He should have remembered that this conference was today, but he now was so far removed from the center of diplomacy and politics that a conference of this kind had become of no more personal concern than if he worked in the Department of the Interior, or Agriculture. He could see the Secretary's car at the West Executive Avenue entrance. He could make out the seal on the door, the same seal that was on the ceiling over his head.

He had to see the Secretary, if he was to help Baker.

There had been a time when he could have put on his hat and crossed the street and waited in the White House executive office until the Secretary came out of the conference. Those had been the happy, informal days when government had been personal and uncomplicated, when the Secretary of State was just another member of the Cabinet. In those days the Secretary could wander around Washington and attract only casual attention.

Now the United States Secretary of State was one of the most powerful men in the world. When he spoke the earth trembled. A sentence from his lips could stop a famine in India, start a riot in Berlin, uphold the Bank of England, or cast down a government. And when he moved he was surrounded by a phalanx of assistants and bodyguards and officials waiting to pounce upon one minute of unrationed time.

It was this matter of the Secretary's time that worried Horace Locke. Would it not be presumptuous, and even rude of him, to force himself upon the Secretary? Did he have the right to decide that a number of the Secretary's priceless minutes be devoted to this matter of Jeff Baker?

Was it not presumptuous of him to assume that the Secretary was not fully informed on this matter? Perhaps Matson had already consulted with the Secretary, and the Secretary knew the full story, and the cable represented his considered judgement. If this was the case, and he forced himself upon the Secretary, it would be most embarrassing. It would be so embarrassing that Horace Locke knew he would have to resign.

The conference across the street would last for perhaps another forty minutes. At the end of the conference the Secretary would return to his office. If he, Horace Locke, was seated in the Secretary's outer office when the Secretary came back to New State, then he'd have a chance to say something.

He must reach a decision. He tried not to think of Jeff Baker, personally, or Nicholas Baker. He tried to eliminate the importance of what was going to happen to Jeff Baker from his thought. This was the proper, the orderly way to do it. He concentrated on consideration of the importance of the letters Jeff had sent him—the letters that told of this movement inside the Russian forces.

If these facts were not known by the Secretary—and if they were true facts—how would they compare in priority and importance to all the other affairs the Secretary must consider this day? He projected himself into the position of the Secretary of State. Strangely, it was not difficult for him to do. He reached his decision. He didn't think that on this day anything could be more important than news of an anti-regime movement inside Russia.

Horace Locke put on his hat and coat and walked downstairs.

He walked through the door of the West Executive Avenue entrance. The guard nodded. He was an old guard who had always been at this entrance to Old State. "Nasty out, today, isn't it, Mr. Locke?" he said.

"Yes. It's foul."

"This Washington cold goes right through me. I'll never get used to it."

"None of us ever will," said Horace Locke.

"Now don't get a chill," the guard warned.

"Oh, don't worry, Gordon, I won't," Locke said. He went outside into the drizzle, and felt in his inside coat pocket to be sure he had Baker's letters. The Secretary's car was still there. Horace Locke caught a cab on The Avenue, and directed the driver to New State.

5

In New State he walked confidently to the Secretary's suite. Now that he had made up his mind, it would not be too difficult. In the outer office a receptionist asked his name, and he told her, and she asked whether he had an appointment. "No, but the Secretary will want to see me," he said.

She seemed puzzled by his answer. She said, "I'll send in your name, and you can wait." But she didn't seem to do anything.

That was all he wanted, a chance to wait. He took a chair in the anteroom where he could watch the door through which the Secretary must pass through his suite, and into his private office.

After he had been waiting for half an hour he sensed, by the activity, that the Secretary would soon be back. But yet another thirty minutes passed, and the Secretary did not come in. Other people came in, and were shown into the Secretary's office, and came out again.

Then Susan Pickett came in. She had a notebook and pencils in her hand. He saw her as soon as she walked in from the hall-way and he lifted his head suddenly so that she noticed him and came over to him. She said, "Oh, you've got an appointment. That's fine."

He rose, and winced. The chill drizzle had loaded his joints with aches and stiffness. "No, I haven't an appointment," he whispered. "I'm just waiting for him to come back."

"Oh, he's back!" the girl said. "He's been back, Mr. Locke. He comes up on his private elevator on the other side of the building and goes directly into the inner office. He doesn't use this entrance."

Horace Locke realized suddenly how he had lost touch with what went on inside the Department. Everyone in the Department would know that the Secretary used a private elevator—everyone except himself. This was only the second time he had been in New State, and the first time he had been in the Secretary's group of offices. He could feel his confidence ebbing. He said, "I suppose it was foolish of me, waiting for him here."

"Golly, Mr. Locke, you could wait here all day and you'd never see him," Susan said. He could see that she too was shaken, and worried. He knew that she had depended on him, that she had faith in his ability to help Jeff Baker, and now that faith was gone. It was gone simply because he had not known the mechanics of the Secretary's entrance.

"I'm going in to see him in a minute," Susan said. "I have to see him every day at this time. He dictates part of tomorrow's agenda. I told everybody I felt better and was able to work. I don't know why. I had to. I guess I can't stand not knowing what's going on. Would it do any good if I told him you were here?"

Horace Locke considered this. "I'm afraid not," he said.

She said, "What would happen if you went in with me?" Her eyes, which had been so dull, now suddenly were alight.

"What do you mean?"

"I could take you in with me, just like I'd been sent out to get you. I go in and out so much nobody notices."

Horace Locke knew he was going to perform what for him was a desperate act. In his whole life he had never entered an office, a drawing room, or any gathering where by any chance he might be unwelcome. He said, "I will go in with you."

She caught her breath. "I don't suppose the world will come to an end if we do," she said. She smiled, and Horace Locke admired her. He had not known many women who were unorthodox and daring, but those he remembered were the most charming women he had known.

So together they walked into the Secretary's office. They walked past the receptionist, and the uniformed guard at the double doors, and through the secretarial office inside, and into the Secretary's presence. Everyone could see that Susan Pickett was escorting a friend of the Secretary into his office, and nobody thought it unusual.

6

The Secretary was alone. His shoulders were bowed over his desk and his glasses had slipped down the bridge of his nose. His eyes, as always, were chained to the pile of red-tabbed papers before him. He looked up over his spectacles, started to speak to Susan, and saw Horace Locke. He did not seem disturbed, but he did seem puzzled.

"Good afternoon, Mr. Secretary," Horace Locke said. He was at ease again. His confidence had returned now. He could be rattled by picayune indignities, because he was not accustomed to them, and hopelessly entangled in the fresh crops of red tape that grew each new year in the Department, but when it came to a matter of discussion with a man on his own intellectual level, then he was at ease.

"Well, hello Locke—Horace," the Secretary said. "Good to see you. Haven't seen each other in some time, have we?"

"No, we haven't," said Horace Locke.

"How've you been?"

"Fine, thank you, Mr. Secretary." He knew what would be passing through the Secretary's head. The Secretary would be thinking he must have some appointment with Locke, and yet he would be quite certain he didn't, and he wouldn't want to be rude, and so he would wait and find out, from the conversation, what it was all about.

Horace Locke plunged. "Mr. Secretary, I don't have any appointment, but I had to see you. I had to see you at once. First I want to apologize for the intrusion, but after we've talked I'm sure you'll agree it was necessary."

The Secretary took off his glasses and laid them on the desk. "Well, what is it, Horace? I assume it must be of surpassing importance. You know how unusual this is."

"It is an affair of state, Mr. Secretary." The words rolled out rounder and bigger in this office than if said anywhere else. For them both it had a special meaning. An affair of state was a matter of the national safety.

Now Susan thought she had to say something. For the first time since she had been employed in the Secretary's office she felt like an eavesdropper. This affair of state was not for her impersonal. "Mr. Secretary," she asked in a small voice, "do you want me to come back later?"

"No, Mrs. Pickett, I want you to stay and make notes. All right, Horace, go ahead."

Horace Locke brought out Jeff's letters. "Mr. Secretary," he said, "I have received two letters safe hand from Budapest. They were sent to me out of channel by a Third Secretary who because of my long association with his family trusted me implicitly. It was the opinion of this Third Secretary, in which I concur, that the matter was of a nature so secret that the information could not pass through ordinary channels. The letters concern this Third Secretary's liaison with a Russian officer who claims to be a leader of a revolutionary group which intends to fight, and if possible overthrow, the present Soviet regime."

Horace Locke paused. It was best to present it factually and without involving personalities. If the Secretary already knew of this thing, and had discarded it as impossible or a fabrication, then the Secretary would tell him. He would apologize, then, and he would go home, and he would resign from the Department.

But he could see in the Secretary's face that this was fresh intelligence. "Sit down, Horace," the Secretary said, "and let me see those letters."

Horace Locke sat down. He knew now that he had his chance. He decided it would be best to read the letters, because he knew that the Secretary's eyes were always tired from too much reading, and he would grasp it more quickly, and perhaps more completely, if the letters were read. "I think we can save time if I read them," Locke said.

"Yes, do. Go ahead," the Secretary agreed. He turned to Susan. "You'll take all this, please, Mrs. Pickett. Girl, why are you shaking?"

"Oh, I didn't know I was shaking," Susan said.

"You weren't at the nine o'clock conference today, were you? Wasn't there another girl there?"

"Yes, sir. I didn't feel well. I'm all right now."

"Are you sure you're all right? If you're not feeling well, Mrs. Pickett, I can buzz for another girl."

"Oh, I'm absolutely all right!" Susan insisted.

The Secretary frowned. A young girl could be as peculiar and puzzling and impenetrable as Molotov. "All right, go ahead, Horace."

Ten minutes later the Secretary touched a key on his interphone and said, "No more appointments until I let you know."

7

When it was all finished the Secretary said, "I suppose, Horace, that you know I signed a cable last night asking that boy to resign?"

"Yes, Mr. Secretary. That's why it was so urgent that I bring the matter to your attention." Horace Locke hoped the Secretary wouldn't ask how he knew Jeff Baker was being recalled because if the Secretary did ask he wasn't going to tell him. But the Secretary would understand that his Department did not operate on a basis purely official. The Secretary would remind himself, as Horace Locke did so often, that the Department was not buildings and files and code machines and typewriters. The Department was people.

The Secretary must have thought of this, because he said, "I think you were perfectly correct, Horace." He tapped a pen on his desk, as if rapping out points in his reasoning. "There is a very weak point in Baker's story. There is no corroboration. There is no corroboration from anywhere in the world. Perhaps Baker himself can furnish that corroboration. We will see. He will have a hearing. I will talk to him."

"Thank you, Mr. Secretary," Horace Locke said. He glanced at Susan Pickett. She was containing herself beautifully now. She was a lady, in the sense that a man was a gentleman. She was a diplomat.

The Secretary rose and held out his hand. "Thank you, Horace. I'll take care of this now. I'm going to check with our people in Vienna, and with the British in Klagenfurt, and of course with Budapest. And I'm bringing Baker home."

As Horace Locke left the office he heard the Secretary speak into the interphone. "Have Mr. Matson up here at once."

CHAPTER EIGHTEEN

1

JEFF SLEPT LATE Wednesday morning, and when he awoke he smoked a cigarette in bed and considered what he must do next. He decided he must present his answer to the cable to Morgan Collingwood. That was correct protocol. Collingwood would take it in to the Admiral, and the Admiral would snort at it, and then order it transmitted to Washington.

After that it would be Washington's move. His refusal to resign would go to the Balkan desk. Undoubtedly Matson would send another cable, ordering him home to face a Departmental trial. They probably wouldn't bother to bring him home by air. They'd furnish the most inconvenient transportation available—jeep to Vienna, trains to Genoa, and then an Army transport or freighter to Newport News. It would take weeks.

When he got back to Washington—he didn't like to think of it. He showered and dressed automatically while his mind retraced all the arguments of the day before, and reached the same conclusion. He had nothing else to do.

Madame Angell brought his hot water, and he was drinking his black coffee when the phone rang. It was Quincy Todd. "So you're finally there," Todd said. "I tried to get you all last night. What's the matter with your phone?"

"I don't know," Jeff said. "I didn't have lights last night either, so I guess wires were down somewhere. What'd you want?"

"Oh, I just wanted to offer liquid courage and consolation. Now it may be different. You just got another cable. My little mouse told me."

"I'll be right down," Jeff said.

2

Jeff folded his reply to the cable into an envelope, and put it in his pocket with the cable itself. Then he walked to the Legation, and went to the message center. Quincy Todd was waiting there, and with him was Marge Collins, from cryptography. She looked pleased. Quincy said, "I think she's got good news for you, Jeff, but she won't tell me."

She had an envelope in her hand. "I'll give you this cable," she said, "but first you have to give me back the paraphrase you got yesterday."

"Why?" he asked. "It's mine, isn't it?"

"Not any more. I've got orders to destroy it. You'll see."

Jeff brought the sheet of flimsy out of his coat pocket and handed it to her, and she gave him the envelope.

"Well, hurry up and open it," Quincy Todd said.

Jeff opened the envelope. It was addressed as before. It read:

DEPARTMENT'S 49122692 CLASSIFIED CONFIDENTIAL IS TO BE DISREGARDED AND ORIGINAL AND ALL COPIES AND PARAPHRASES REMOVED FROM FILES AND DESTROYED. BAKER IS TO RETURN TO WASHINGTON ON FIRST PLANE AVAILABLE AND REPORT IMMEDIATELY TO THE SECRETARY OF STATE.

Quincy Todd, who unashamedly had been reading over his shoulder, slammed him on the back and said, "Saved! You must have a cousin in Congress. When I heard about the one yesterday I thought they'd hang you."

"They may hang me yet," Jeff said. He musn't let his hopes run away with his common sense. He guessed that Horace Locke must have done something. Horace Locke must have reached the Secretary, or this cable wouldn't be ordering him to report to the Secretary. So the Secretary must know of his letters to Locke. The Secretary must know of Leonides. Whatever happened now, that vicious cable was destroyed. It did not necessarily mean the charges had been withdrawn, but at least they were held in abeyance. Back in Washington somebody had given him a fighting chance. "That means tomorrow's plane, doesn't it?" he said.

"Yes, tomorrow's plane," Quincy Todd said. "You'd better stick around the Legation, because the Admiral will be wanting to talk to you."

"You think so?"

Todd smiled. "I certainly do."

3

The Admiral had him at his table at lunch. The Admiral was affable and pleasant and very nearly apologetic. Jeff felt that the Admiral must believe he had powerful friends in Washington.

Actually the Admiral was congratulating himself on passing the buck to the Department. Something was going on back in Washington that he didn't understand, and it was best that he stay out of it. Whatever happened, the Navy would be pleased that he had not involved himself in a State Department affair. He was concerned with policy, not administration, and this had become an administrative matter.

4

Jeff saw Keller that evening. "When you see the Secretary," Fred cautioned him, "simply present the facts as you know them. Don't be frightened. The Secretary's very decent, very human."

"I wonder if he remembers me?" Jeff said. "I wonder if he remembers when I took my orals?"

"He never forgets anyone," Keller said. "His memory is phenomenal. He sops up knowledge, and facts, and he never forgets any of it. In a matter of this kind he'll consider only the cold facts.

But at least you know you're going to get a square shake. That's the important thing."

That night Jeff went to the Arizona with Keller and Todd, and they watched Rikki Telredy dance. She smiled at them from the stage, but when the show was over she didn't go to their table. She had drinks with some Russian colonels, and chatted at a table occupied by Polish diplomats, and finally left with a Hungarian drama critic. Keller said Rikki was a smart girl—very smart. Keller said to Jeff, "She'll still be here when you come back."

"Do you really think I'll be coming back?" Jeff asked. He knew that he wanted to come back. He didn't want to be a liquor salesman, or a school teacher, or a peddler of used automobiles, or even be rich. He wanted to be in the Foreign Service.

"I think you'll be coming back," Keller said. "I think you'll be coming back, and that I'll be leaving, because I think our job is finished here. I think there will be more productive work for us."

"I wish you guys wouldn't talk in riddles," Quincy Todd said. "But one day I'll have my revenge. One day I'll stop being nursemaid to this Legation. One day I'll have some other job. And I don't care what it is I'm going to be mysterious about it. I'll be so mysterious that nobody will know what I'm doing. Everybody will think it's real important, and so I'll get to be a Class Three, or maybe even a Two."

5

Thursday morning Quincy Todd helped him pack. When they were finished Todd asked Jeff about the maps that covered an enormous footage of wall. They were beautiful maps. They were Army Air Force aeronautical charts of the Mediterranean and the Adriatic, of The Straits and the Baltic, of inner Europe and the Danube. They had been part of Jeff's existence ever since Charley Born had presented them to him in Bari. It had been better than receiving a medal. Jeff said, "I think I'll leave them here for a while."

"I like your confidence," Quincy said.

"Oh, I'm not so confident," Jeff said. "I'm just tired of taking 'em down and putting 'em up. And if things turn out bad I won't want them anyway."

"I'll take care of them," Quincy promised, "one way or another." Jeff left on the evening plane.

6

When Jeff arrived in Washington he called the Secretary's office from the airport. The girl said, "Oh, Mr. Baker. I've a message for you. The Secretary left instructions that if you came in in the morning he'd see you at eleven. Can you make it?"

Jeff looked at his watch. He had thirty minutes. "I can make it," he said.

He checked his bags and went to the washroom and washed his face and combed his hair. He was glad he'd had the foresight to shave on the plane, but there was nothing he could do about his suit. When you slept in one position across an ocean then your suit simply announced that it had been slept in.

He got in a cab and said "New State" and looked again at his watch. He'd be on time.

He wondered if he'd run into Susan in the Department. He wondered if she had heard anything. He wondered if she knew anything at all of what had happened. He kept thinking of what he should tell the Secretary first, and discovered that he lacked any plan of what to say.

He reached New State and walked to the elevators, and his elevator was crowded and stopped at every floor. Everyone in the elevator looked so neat and freshly cleaned. He felt they must be noticing his suit, and the crushed collar of his shirt, and the wrinkled tie. They'd never guess he was thirty minutes off a plane from Budapest. But then, who knew where these other people had come from? Perhaps Saigon or B.A. or Hong Kong or the Mayflower Hotel. In Washington you never knew.

He got off at the fifth floor and gave his name to the receptionist, and he could tell he was expected, for she said, "Just a moment, Mr. Baker." She lifted her phone and said, "Mr. Baker is here," and another girl came out and said, "The Secretary will see you now, Mr. Baker." It was happening too fast. He wasn't getting a chance to think.

He followed the girl through the secretarial office, and there were four other girls sitting there typing, and one of them was Susan. Her back was turned towards him and he wanted to yell at her, but of course he didn't dare.

7

The Secretary got up when he came in and extended his hand, and said, "I'm glad to see you again, Baker," and he sounded as if he really was glad to see him. "Just sit down," the Secretary said. He told the girl, "No calls until I let you know."

The girl left, and he was alone with the Secretary.

There was a cable file at the edge of the desk, and now the Secretary drew it to him. "Good trip?" he asked.

"Yes, sir," Jeff said. "I slept all the way across."

"I never seem to have time to sleep on a plane," the Secretary said. "Every trip I make I tell myself I'm going to take a rest, and sleep all the way, but it never turns out like that. There are always papers, always more papers."

The Secretary glanced at the top papers in the file. "Now, Baker," he said, "to save time I'll tell you what I've done, and then when I'm finished you can add anything you want, and I'll have some questions to ask you.

"In the first place I've talked to Matson and Quigley and Locke, and they've told me all they know of this matter. I want to apologize to you for one thing, Baker. I wouldn't have initialed the cable requesting your resignation had I known at the time what I know now. I'm not blaming Mr. Matson for this. It is nobody's fault but my own. However, that doesn't mean that I may not request your resignation at the end of this interview. I'm just telling you that I initialed the cable without having complete information."

"I see, sir," Jeff said.

"After learning all I could in Washington I cabled our Embassy in Moscow, our occupation headquarters in Vienna, and the British in Klagenfurt. I requested any information that would corroborate your story." The Secretary took three priority cable forms from the file. Those must be the replies, Jeff thought, and he knew that they were critical for him.

"Briefly," the Secretary went on, "Moscow has never heard of any organized revolutionary movement in the Red Army or the Soviet diplomatic corps. Neither has Vienna. I am taking into account the probability that they might be the last to hear. But the important reply came from the British Zone in Austria. They are certain that nobody answering the description of Leonides Lasenko has crossed into their zone. They know nothing of any underground transmitters operating in the Hochschwab. They do have a good many Russian deserters who have taken refuge in their zone, but then, so have we."

"Oh, that's too bad," Jeff said. He wasn't thinking of himself. He was thinking of Leonides. He tried to follow, in his mind, the route that Leonides and Marina, the gypsy girl, had taken out of Budapest towards the sanctuary in the Hochschwab. Perhaps the gypsies moved slowly. Perhaps they were very careful. Leonides said the gypsies alone knew how to run a border. He hoped Leonides was right.

"I do have one small fact to back your story," the Secretary said. "It is a fact that the Russian Naval Attaché, Yassovsky, was recalled to Moscow and has since disappeared. But that happens to a lot of Russians. So you can understand, Baker, the position I am in. If your story about Major Lasenko and his underground was provable, then I would naturally believe your story about the penetration of Atlantis Project—which incidentally was quite a blow to us—and about everything else."

"I understand, sir," Jeff said. He wished his mind was sharper.

His mind seemed numb, as if it had surrendered under the impact of the cables from Moscow, Vienna, and Klagenfurt. His mind had given up.

The Secretary lifted his head so that Jeff could see how grave and serious were the eyes behind the spectacles. He said, "I hope your story is true, Baker. It would be a great thing for us—for all of us, and I include the Russians—if it is true. If there are people within the Soviet Union who are willing to risk their lives for peace, then I would be confident of peace. I have not abandoned hope in any case, but such a thing would hearten me greatly. Is it true, Baker?"

"It is, sir."

"You are sure of this Major Lasenko?"

"I am, sir."

"Can you show me any proof—any small proof?"

Jeff shook his head. "This proof doesn't exist, sir. I can only give you my word and my judgment."

"And your judgment is immature," the Secretary said.

"I don't think it's so immature," Jeff said. "I think men my age grew up awfully fast."

The Secretary leaned back in his chair, and examined this statement. "In most cases that's true," he said. "But I'm not sure in your case. You see, Baker, your reaction to that explosion indicates that you might be a psycho. Now understand that I am sympathetic with men who suffered battle fatigue, but I must take this into account."

"I know it, Mr. Secretary," Jeff said. He hoped the Secretary would notice how calm he was. He added, "I'm not certain, but I don't believe I could ever go to pieces again."

"I hope not, but as you say, you're not certain. And we have to be certain of our men, Baker. Particularly in a question like this —which I believe is a major question—we have to be certain."

Jeff knew that the cards had fallen against him. He had not been fully prepared for the worst, the worst was happening, and yet he found he could maintain his nerve, his calm, and his courage. He felt inwardly pleased with himself that this was possible. He said, "Mr. Secretary, I suppose you will want my resignation."

"I think that would be best for us," the Secretary said. "I was not going to demand your resignation, but since you yourself suggest it I think it would be best. If you remained, I could not under the circumstances entrust you with responsibilities fitting your ability. You would not like that."

"No, I wouldn't like that. But before I give you my resignation, Mr. Secretary, there is something I must submit. Please, Mr. Secretary, do not allow the Atlantis Project to continue. Because if you do, Mr. Secretary, it will cost lives. Some of our friends in Budapest will surely die."

The Secretary rose. "I'm going to accept your suggestion, Baker," he said, "but I'm also going to accept your resignation. Good luck, Baker."

"Goodbye, Mr. Secretary."

As he walked out of the Secretary's office he was aware that the traffic of the State Department had congested in the outer offices while he had been inside. He realized that this matter which for him meant his whole life and his whole world was only twenty minutes out of one day for the Secretary of State.

8

In the outer office Susan was still at her desk, and now she was watching for him. He tried to smile at her, and she tried to smile back. She said, across the room, "I'm off at five."

He said, "I'll see you at five."

He didn't think that anybody noticed. He hoped not. He didn't want to embarrass her. He realized that henceforth his association with her would embarrass her in the Department. From now on, he was an outsider, and branded unreliable.

He knew something else, too. He knew that she knew. She could tell by his face. He didn't have a poker face, or a diplomatic face.

9

He went back to the airport and got his bags and dumped them in Stud Beecham's apartment. He could tell by the neatness that Stud was off somewhere on a field trip, and the maid had finally caught up with the disorder. He was glad Stud was away. He would have to explain to a great many people, and in every case it would be difficult, even with Stud.

He bathed, and sent out a suit to be pressed, and fashioned a peanut butter and jelly sandwich and washed it down with milk, and then he sat down at Stud's desk and wrote his resignation.

"To the Secretary of State

"Sir:

"Pursuant to our conversation of even date I have the honor to inform you that I am resigning from the Foreign Service of the United States."

It was an archaic way of saying I quit, true, and yet the words seemed to possess their own majesty.

And once again he signed his full name, Jefferson Wilson Baker. He mailed the resignation in the letter box at Dupont Circle.

CHAPTER NINETEEN

1

HE WAS WAITING at the Virginia Avenue entrance of New State when she came out. When he saw her his eyes became camera-like in their precision. She was sharp, and everyone else pouring down the steps of New State at the quitting hour was out of focus.

She came directly to him, her steps never hesitating, and she put her arms around his neck and they kissed right there at the corner of Twenty-first Street and Virginia Avenue, Northwest. In front of God and everybody.

People stopped to stare. There was something of a jam at the entrance to New State. Washington is not like Paris, or New York. In Washington it is not good form to display affection in public. In Washington love is almost a bad word.

2

That evening he took her down to the waterfront for lobster. She had suggested that they eat at her apartment, but he didn't want to do that. He was afraid that if he went to her apartment his resolution would dissolve, and they would spend little time eating. He had made his decision, it had been difficult, and it would only make it harder to tell her if they were alone in her apartment.

There was an hour spent in explanation of what he had done, and what she had done, and what both had left undone. And then there was the critical moment when she asked:

"Jeff, what about us? Where do we go from here?"

"Let's go to the Footlight Club," he evaded. He knew he had to end it, and yet he wanted all of this last evening.

"You know that's not what I mean."

"I know."

"What happens to us now, Jeff—you and me?"

Now the time had come. Now he had to tell her. "I'm afraid this is our last time together, Susan," he said.

"Jeff!"

She seemed startled and shocked as if he had struck her in the face, and yet he could not believe that it was this much of a surprise to her. She must sense, she must know that a man who had just resigned, by request, was not the same man who was beginning his career in The Department. "That's the way it has to be, Susan dear."

"But why? Why, Jeff?"

"Lots of reasons." It was terribly difficult to put them into words. Could he say that he would be a bitter man, and a bad husband who envied his wife's work? Could he explain that he couldn't bear to live in Washington any more? Could he tell why he would want to avert his head every time he passed the Department of State? For one career alone he had been prepared, and now that career was gone as finally as if he had passed the age of retirement. And she was to have been part of that career.

She leaned across the table and took his hand in both her hands, and held tight to his hand. "You're not thinking straight, Jeff," she said.

"Yes I am thinking straight."

"No you're not." She was trying to speak lightly and with confidence. "You're out of the Department now and we can get married. I want to marry you. I want to be with you every night, Jeff."

He tried to pull his hand away but she clung to him. "It wouldn't work that way, Susan. You marry me and you know what'd happen?"

"We'd live happily ever after."

"No we wouldn't, Susan dear. You'd find yourself transferred to being stenographer on the Costa Rica desk. They wouldn't let you take the nine o'clock conference any more. They'd put you in a cubbyhole for life. They don't want women in sensitive jobs whose husbands have been kicked out of the Department with a mark on them."

"You haven't any mark, Jeff."

"Yes I have. Nobody will say so, and nobody will speak of it, but I have a mark."

The grip on his hand relaxed, and he drew it away. "My darling," she said, "my Jeff. I don't care if I have to work on the Costa Rica desk, or even if they put me in the International Boundary Commission, or the Hemp and Flax Policy Board."

He shook his head, and she thought how much older he looked. He had grown up, attained maturity and mature judgment. "You think you wouldn't care," he said, "but you would. Just as I am going to care. There will be no moment when I will not wish I was back in the Department. I'll get a job all right, and I'll have enough money for myself, and outwardly there won't be any blemish on me. But inside I'll never feel right."

"Oh, Jeff."

He knew she was beginning to understand, as Rikki had understood. He was poison. "Can you imagine how it would be," he went on, "if you still had a job in the Department and we still lived in Washington and we invited our friends in the Department to a cocktail party, or dinner? They'd clam up. They'd be afraid to talk in front of me. I'm an outcast, Susan."

"I can quit. We can go away, Jeff," she said.

"No, Susan."

"You don't have to be married to me to live with me," she said.

"That won't help. That'd be worse. That isn't the way we were supposed to live, Susan."

She saw she was defeated. She lowered her head so he could not see the defeat in her eyes. "Pay the check," she said quietly, "and take me home."

As they went out of the door she said, "Jeff, you forgot your hat."

He put his hand on the top of his head, awkwardly, as if he expected a hat to grow there. "I guess I didn't have it on tonight," he said. "I must have left it somewhere."

CHAPTER TWENTY

1

THE CENTURY PASSED its halfway mark, and raced onward towards
its destiny.

One night late in January, at eleven o'clock Central European
Time and five in the afternoon Eastern Standard Time, a new short-
wave radio station went on the air in Europe. It called itself RFR—
for Radio Free Russia—and it pirated a wave length in the eleven
megacycle band, right next to Radio Moscow, so that everyone who
customarily listened to Moscow heard it.

It caused quite a sensation, because it was the first Russian resistance radio.

2

Madame Angell was among the first to hear it in Budapest.

She didn't remember when she had been so excited, and yet there
was no one to tell except Sandor, the building superintendent and
elevator operator, who naturally wouldn't believe her.

She put on her tattered and stained wrapper and rushed out into
the hallway, not that she expected to find anyone there, but simply
because she felt she must do something.

The room that had been occupied by Mr. Baker was still vacant.
Mr. Todd had paid the rent for January, as if he expected Mr. Baker
to come back. She entered this vacant room. She hadn't made a
thorough inspection of the room since Mr. Baker left, and now was
as good a time as any. Mr. Baker had always been so attentive

when she brought him the news. She had liked Mr. Baker. And who could tell, the American might have forgotten some candy, or a package of sugar?

It was peculiar that he hadn't bothered to take down his maps. She examined the maps carefully, and she recognized that they were very good maps. How wonderful it would be if she herself had those maps! How much more the international broadcasts would mean with maps such as these.

Yet she dared not take them down, for fear Mr. Todd might come and see they were missing.

She looked in the bureau drawers. Sure enough, there was half a chocolate bar under a newspaper. She took a bite, and put the remaining fragment in the pocket of her wrapper. She wished either Mr. Baker would come back, or Mr. Todd would get her another American. She missed her sweets.

She looked in the closet. There was a shape in the top of the closet. She reached up and took a hat off the top shelf. It was Mr. Baker's black homburg. She was aware that it was the only hat Mr. Baker had and she wondered how he could be so careless as to forget it.

She scurried out of the room and back into her own apartment, taking the hat with her. It was, anyone could see, an expensive American hat, a diplomat's hat. It would bring a fancy price on the Black Bourse. One didn't see hats like this in Budapest, except on the heads of foreign diplomats. It would, she estimated, bring three hundred forints. That was a considerable sum of money.

Yet she hesitated to sell it. She had a premonition that Mr. Baker was coming back, and if she kept his hat for him, he would reward her with sweets, and that was better than money.

Madame Angell put the hat into her own closet, and listened again to this fascinating new station, that was Russian and yet was not Russian.

3

Others were listening.

In the American Legation on the Szabadzag-tér a bi-lingual monitor was taking it off the air. He soon knew it was important enough to be recorded, and switched on the recording machine.

In Klagenfurt the monitors of the British Political Warfare Executive were listening. The signal of RFR was very strong in Klagenfurt, and the chief monitor ordered that other stations in the British Zone of Austria tune it in, and obtain a triangulation, for he suspected that the transmitter was very close.

In addition he had a watch order for such a station. London had wanted to know whether such a station existed. London had said Washington was curious. He had replied that no such station had ever been on the air in his area. Up to now, he had been right. Washington must have known something.

In the morning he would draft a synopsis of these broadcasts and telegraph them to London, although he suspected that the transmitter was sufficiently powerful to be heard both in London and across the Atlantic.

It was heard in London. A complete text was recorded, quickly transcribed, and sent to Whitehall, with a copy to Washington. This was an unusual matter.

It was even heard in Washington. Out on the Maryland capes the monitors of Central Intelligence Agency, dialing for Radio Moscow, had picked up this RFR instead. They missed the first few minutes of the broadcast, but they kept themselves eagerly tuned to the rest. And they recorded it, and prepared to send a special bulletin to the War, Navy, Air and State Departments so they'd have it in the morning.

The CIA cabled its people abroad for additional information.

4

Radio Moscow was the first to react to the new transmitter. At two in the morning, in a Hindu broadcast to India, Moscow said:

"The desperate Anglo-American political warfare offensive has just tried an infamous trick. Using a British station in the British Zone of Austria they now pretend to be the mouthpiece of a Russian counter-revolutionary movement.

"There is no counter-revolutionary movement against the Union of Socialist Soviet Republics. No such station as RFR actually exists. It is most contemptible. At no time since Lenin overthrew the Czarist regime has there ever been such complete accord and tranquility within the Soviet state."

When they heard Moscow's denial the British in London and Klagenfurt, and the Americans in Budapest and Washington knew that RFR was genuine. It was the goods. They got their propaganda planners out of bed to tell them the news, and lay plans to capitalize on this crack within the Soviet ranks.

5

Admiral Blankenhorn heard of it at breakfast. When his Filipino mess boy brought breakfast to the Admiral's bedroom he also brought a summary of the night's news, and the monitoring report, the mimeographed paper still damp, from the Legation.

On this day there was a special box drawn on top of the monitoring report, headed "BULLETIN."

It read:

"A new short wave station with a very strong signal came on the air last night with news and propaganda especially directed to Russian troops in the occupied areas. Its call letters are RFR—for Radio Free Russia. It also calls itself the station of the Second Russian Revolution.

"This new station claims to represent a group of Soviet military men and government people. It says that an underground battle against the present regime has been going on.

"A portion of the broadcast was devoted to a memorial to those men, who, this station claims, have already died for the Second Russian Revolution. It mentioned twenty or more names, but of special interest to this post were the names of Yassovsky, former Naval Attaché, and a Major Leonides Lasenko, who had been stationed in

Budapest, according to the broadcast. According to the broadcast Yassovsky was murdered after torture at a Black Sea naval base, and Lasenko was shot to death while trying to cross the border into the British Zone of Austria. Also named as a hero was an unidentified gypsy girl who supposedly gave her life trying to lead Lasenko to safety . . ."

The Admiral didn't read any further. A good commander expected the unexpected. On occasion the Admiral hadn't been a good commander. There were ships in Iron Bottom Bay to prove that. But he was learning.

The Admiral thought it over very carefully as he had his two poached eggs on toast, frozen orange juice, and small cup of coffee. And when he went down to the Legation he drafted a cable to the Secretary of State:

"I have always had greatest confidence in Jefferson W. Baker and for this reason felt that his story, improbable as it may have seemed at the time, be brought to your personal attention.

"In view of today's developments I feel that Budapest is the logical place in which to initiate liaison with the Russian group fighting against the present Soviet regime. I also feel that Baker, working under Keller's direction, would be the logical man to undertake such liaison. Naturally operations of the other project which must be unnamed have been discontinued ever since I talked to Baker."

This was what was known, in military parlance, as seizing the initiative. The Admiral didn't want to be returned to Navy yet. If he was returned to Navy now they'd put him in command of an inactive fleet. They'd give him a battleship as a flagship all right, but the chances were that it would be an old battleship. It might even have been used at Bikini, and therefore be so radioactive that neither he nor anyone else could safely board it. It would be much better, for the time being, to remain in Budapest.

6

Jeff Baker read the news in *The Post*. He had gone around the corner to the little breakfast shop on Connecticut Avenue, and he'd bought a *Post* on the way so he could go through the help wanted ads. He didn't really think he'd get a decent job out of the ads, but whenever he read them they gave him ideas. It wasn't tough to get a job—*a* job—but it was hard finding a job he thought he'd like.

He sat down on a stool in the breakfast shop and ordered a pineapple juice and ham and egg sandwich, and first black coffee. He would drink this first coffee, and then he'd read and eat, and then he'd have another coffee, as was his custom. He opened *The Post* and looked at the front page headlines. Headlines are so impersonal. It takes a long time for you to understand that a headline can be personal. Like this one-column headline on the first page:

"FREE RUSSIA RADIO
TAKES AIR; PLEDGES
DEMOCRATIC ACTION"

He read it three times before he realized it might be personally interesting.

Then he raced through the banks, and the lead, and came to the paragraph about Leonides being killed, and he couldn't eat any more.

The waitress said, "Whattsa matter, bad egg?"

He said, "Oh, no. The egg's all right." He wanted to get out of there. He wanted to be by himself. He left a dollar on the counter, which was more than his usual payment and tip, and left. He went back to the apartment on Riggs Court. He lay full length on the bed, face down with his toes hanging over the end, and cried. In the course of a lifetime a man has so few real friends that when he loses one it is as if he himself had died a little.

Jeff's mind distorted the first impact of the news, the way minds will when emotion elbows out cold logic. His first thought was that with Leonides dead he'd never be able to prove what he had told. Then he began to understand that the broadcast itself was proof.

He had a tendency to feel elated. He had a bloated "I told you so" feeling. He tried to fight down this feeling, but he felt he must talk to someone. Stud had now left for the office. It was not yet ten o'clock so Susan would still be in her conference. He hadn't seen Susan. Now he wanted to see her.

There was Horace Locke. He dialed the State Department, and asked for Locke's extension, and Locke answered. He said, "Hello, this is Jeff Baker. Mr. Locke, did you see the story about the Russian broadcast—I mean about RFR like I told you?"

"I saw it," Horace Locke said calmly. "I was just going to call you."

"Well, what do you think about it, Mr. Locke?"

"I think this is an excellent time for you to contain yourself. You were right. But it is not enough that you be right. You must accept your rightness gracefully and diplomatically. You've won a victory, Jeff, but you mustn't gloat."

"I don't quite get it," Jeff said.

"Think it over," said Horace Locke, "and I think you'll get it. It's quite simple. You've got to be a diplomat. You can be tough now. You're on top. But if you're smart you'll be generous."

"Yes, sir," Jeff said. He thought it over, and he understood what Horace Locke meant.

7

Gerald Matson heard of the broadcast. The news of it went through every Division of the Department, even into the Visa Division. Matson didn't quite know why he was in Visa, instead of Chief of Balkans.

He had taken a backward step. Quigley, the security man, had talked to him, and talked to Anya, and even talked to Iggy. Everything had been pleasant, and conducted in what the Department called a "good atmosphere," but Matson knew he was through, finito, kaput.

8

The Secretary of State learned of the broadcast, and of Moscow's reaction, at the nine o'clock conference. Usually the Secretary plucked his early morning news out of Art Godfrey's broadcast. But on this morning he overslept and missed Godfrey.

The news was on the top of the Secretary's nine o'clock conference file. Usually the monitoring reports were on the bottom, for they were considered of less importance than the spot news, and the cables from London, Berlin, Rome, Paris, and Moscow. But on this day the girl who arranged his file—Mrs. Pickett—had somehow managed the file so that the monitoring reports met his eye first.

The Secretary looked at this thing, and digested it. All its potentialities were instantly clear to him. He knew that what some of his advisers had said could not happen, had happened nevertheless. He sought a parallel in history, and found it easily. People had said the Japanese would never surrender, that the Japanese were monolithic and would fight fanatically to the last man. But Zacharias and Mashbir had contended otherwise. They'd said the Japanese were human beings, and being human had no love of death. The Russians too were human.

The Secretary's thought changed from politics to people. He said, "Where's Jeff Baker?"

Everybody was silent. Nobody knew.

"What happened to Baker?" the Secretary demanded. "Where is he?"

Nobody said anything except the girl who took the nine o'clock conference and all she said was, "I know where he is, Mr. Secretary."

"I'd like to see him," the Secretary said, "after the conference."

Everybody at the conference—the Undersecretary, and the Assistant Secretaries, and the Chiefs of Division, and the Special Planners —looked at Susan Pickett. An unexpected thing had happened: It was as if a chair had spoken.

"I think I'll be able to find him," Susan Pickett said.

The Secretary said, "Thanks, Mrs. Pickett." His eyes were hurting again. He frowned and took off his glasses and laid them across his file. Sometimes he wondered whether he knew everything that went on inside The Department of State.

About the Author

PAT FRANK (1908–1964) is the author of the classic postapocalyptic novel *Alas, Babylon*, as well as the nuclear satire *Mr. Adam*. Before becoming an author, Frank worked as a journalist and also as a propagandist for the government. He is one of the first science fiction writers to deal with the consequences of atomic warfare.

ALSO BY PAT FRANK

ALAS, BABYLON
A Novel

Available in Paperback and E-book

When a nuclear holocaust ravages the United States, a thousand years of civilization are stripped away overnight. But for one small town in Florida, miraculously spared, the struggle is just beginning.

MR. ADAM
A Novel

Available in Paperback and E-book

One of literature's first responses to the atomic bomb, *Mr. Adam* is equally a biting satire and an ominous warning to society— that will resonate deeply with readers today as it did when it was first published in 1946.

HOLD BACK THE NIGHT

Available in Paperback and E-book

The riveting story of a Marine captain, his soldiers, and their arduous, difficult retreat from Changjin Reservoir to Hungnam during the Korean War.

FORBIDDEN AREA

Available in Paperback and E-book

A classic of science fiction and an eerie cold-war thriller that is a cautionary tale of the dangers of nuclear power.